MASTERED

THE BLOODSTORM
BOOK 2

VAUGHAN W. SMITH

FAIR FOLIO

Her will and power are mastered.

ISBN: 978-1-922569-02-8

For Ana

1

AN ANCIENT LAND

M aya stepped out, the bright lights and sensation of motion taking her by surprise. Buildings were so bright that the night sky looked like day, and a sea of people swept over the concrete.

"This is Atlantis then? I'm impressed. So modern," she said.

Anders chuckled. "This is it. I'd like to wow you with my local knowledge, but this is my first time too." Anders stepped out further, surveying the area ahead of them. The road was not far away, a continuous stream of vehicles coming and going.

This place even smells busy. I can't put my finger on it.

A sudden blur whizzed past, and Maya stepped back quickly. As fast as it had appeared, it was gone.

"What was that?" Maya looked at Anders with concern.

"Speedster. They shouldn't be doing that so close to the airport, but I suppose it still happens." Anders shrugged.

"I saw nothing like that in New York."

"Well, things are under tight control there. It's the Life-Death HQ. Here, things are more relaxed." Anders continued toward the road, glancing over the vehicles. "We should get in a taxi."

"Fine by me." Maya sped up to close the distance, her shoulder bag banging against her as she went. Before she could reach Anders, a man stepped in front of her. He was average height but wearing a black uniform and a black hat. He was holding up a sign.

"Maya Mills is it?" the man said, breathless. Maya nodded slowly.

"Yes, who's asking?"

"I'm your driver. We've been expecting you." The man bowed and gestured for her to follow. Maya glanced over at Anders.

"Worth a shot," he said. Maya followed along with caution.

Not quite sure about this, but we shall see.

The man led them across the road to a black limousine parked nearby.

"Please enter," he said, opening the door. Maya paused before getting in.

"You know my name. But what's yours?"

"A thousand pardons, my name is Fong. Pleased to make your acquaintance." Fong bowed again and Maya slung her bag into the vehicle, following close behind. Anders walked around and entered from the other side. Within moments they were speeding off into the night.

"Where are we heading, Fong?" Maya asked.

"It's a hotel, that's all I know," he replied. Moments later, a black divider rose blocking sight of him.

"Not much of a conversationalist, is he? Maybe you can play tour guide then," Maya said with a laugh.

"Coming up." Anders concentrated and then began again. Only this time his voice was louder and more excited than Maya had ever heard him before.

"We find ourselves on the mystical island of Atlantis. The hidden jewel of the Atlantic Ocean. This modern marvel is a gift to us from the Master Sage."

"A gift from the Master Sage? How?"

"Taming the chaotic power of the BloodStorm, the Master Sage used his divine skill to raise Atlantis from the depths of the ocean. Thus began a new era for the once disgraced nation with countless funds poured into its restoration and redevelopment." Anders was puffed up like he was going to burst, quickly releasing his breath.

"You can talk normally now. Why was it sunk in the first place? Did the Master Sage clarify that?"

"Not in a satisfactory way," Anders said, staring out of the car at the city whizzing by. "He just echoed the old story of Atlantis being sunk by pride and greed. They were on the wrong side of a battle over the future of bloodlines."

"That sounds pretty interesting. What was the issue?" Maya leaned in closer.

"It does sound interesting. Pity that nobody ever explained it. Only, the bloodlines did end up being sealed away. It probably happened at the same time." Anders focused instead on Maya, watching the light pass over Maya's face as they left a giant shopping center behind. "How are you feeling?"

"Totally fine. Just becoming more accustomed to my new situation." Maya reflexively closed her fist and opened it again. She had been practicing as much as possible, but she sorely needed training. Her progression in her new power didn't feel as natural as LifeDeath had been.

Was it good instruction? Or was I more practiced since I had been using it unconsciously?

"This is the best place for you. Kora and I agreed."

"This doesn't feel like the right place, though. The masters are all here?" Maya said, doubt tingeing her voice.

"Not here exactly. We're in the International Quarter." Anders pointed out of the window at all the high-rise buildings. "The masters are all in the Ancient Grounds. There's a lot of secrecy surrounding them. But this is where you begin. There are schools here that can get you started and prepare you before you take that step to continue your training." Anders gave her a reassuring smile. Before she could answer, the car suddenly stopped. Maya lurched forward, bracing herself on the chair in front.

"What's going on, Fong?" Maya raised her voice.

"Unscheduled stop. You may need to exit the vehicle," Fong said. Maya looked at Anders.

"We better investigate. C'mon." Anders left, and Maya opened her door, stepping out cautiously and looking around. They were in an abandoned parking lot, in the middle of nowhere.

"This is a little too convenient. Suddenly we're isolated," Maya said.

"Agreed. Keep your eyes and ears open." Anders removed a stun wand and held it ready. Maya prepared her internal energy as she had practiced. A man stepped out of the shadows and sauntered over. He was tall, dressed in a suit, with short black hair and sunglasses.

"This is the great Maya, then. In the flesh." The man spoke slowly and in a mocking tone.

"You've heard of me? How flattering." Maya kept a close eye on him.

"You think you can waltz over here and wow us like those LifeDeath simpletons? You're dreaming." The man stopped and regarded them both.

"I'm here to educate myself, nothing more."

"Oh, of course, just education. You're not here to plunder our secrets at all." The man glared at them and was suddenly in front of Maya.

I didn't even see him move.

Maya blinked, and then she was flying backward, crashing into a concrete wall. The impact knocked the wind out of her. The man calmly approached.

"What are you?" Maya said, gasping for air.

"One of those precious Chakra masters that you are looking for. I'm here to tell you not to waste your time. You are not worthy." The Chakra Master stopped a few paces away and stared at her.

"You're giving me a lot of ideas. Since we're having a lesson, how about explaining what's so different about you? I could increase my speed and strength with the LifeDeath bloodline." Maya injected just the right amount of disdain into her voice. The Chakra Master's mouth twitched.

"I know you're trying to bait me, but since you're so ignorant I'll provide some instruction. It's a matter of precision. Those oafs blindly train their muscles to do more, to push the physical limits." The Master started walking away. "But we harness the true energy of the body. We don't push limits, we transcend them. It's a completely different matter altogether." He stopped over near the car and snapped his fingers. Two more shapes stepped out of the shadows.

"I've spent enough time on you. These two will continue your lesson." The Chakra master kept walking and was soon out of sight.

"Not much for chitchat, but all the same loves the sound of his own voice," Maya said as she dragged herself up.

"I should be able to help with these," Anders said as he crept closer. Maya nodded.

"Good, I don't want to hog all the fun." Maya watched the new entrants closely. They were both men and dressed in business attire. Their speed, however, spoke to their true nature. Maya barely dodged back, avoiding a palm strike. Anders was ready, though, and landed a hit with the shock wand. Maya let loose with a right hook, connecting with the attacker but instantly feeling pain.

"It's like hitting iron," she said, shaking her hand. The man somehow laughed through the shock attack.

"I'll give you something to laugh about," Anders said as he stepped behind the man. The sound of the Bloodcuffs snapping shut was incredibly satisfying and seemed to take all the bravado out of the first attacker. The second one backed away, eyeing them from a distance.

"Hang out over here, won't you?" Anders shoved the cuffed man closer to the wall, and he landed awkwardly.

"Nice one with the cuffs. You have more, don't you?" Maya whispered. Anders nodded.

"Just one more. Enough for this guy, but I feel he's going to be more careful than his friend." Anders bent down, examining the ground.

"I'm not sure the best way to tackle these guys. They're basically much better versions of my current self," Maya said, sighing.

"You have me. I've taken down my fair share of these tough guys. Mastering one's body and energy doesn't always mean mastering one's mind and emotions. At least not at this level." Anders stood up again. "You going to have a nap back there?" he called out. The man instantly appeared behind Anders and readied a strike. Maya reached out and grabbed the man's arm before his attack could land.

"Try to hold him," Anders said.

"Sure." Maya moved in closer. The man looked confused and started struggling against her, trying to get away, but he seemed rooted to the spot. Maya stepped around the man and tried to restrain him further. He pivoted and started unleashing an impressive flurry of blows with one hand. All Maya could do was take the hits and try to keep on her feet.

Anders fired something at the man, and it quickly wrapped around him. It looked like a black cord. Within seconds it glowed and sizzled, and then the man dropped to the ground. He continued to struggle a bit, before relaxing completely.

"That did the trick. What was it?" Maya said, carefully stepping around the enemy.

"I laid down a gravity snare and then hit him with an electrified tranquilizing rope." Anders grinned at her and looked down at the man.

"Feeling a little loose?" Anders said. The man struggled to say something but gave up after a few tries.

"Most of them don't know how to deal with these tricks. They do figure it out eventually, but it's often too late." Anders dropped to his knees and unwrapped the cord. The man stayed limp, but he looked seriously angry. Anders collected something else off the floor and stashed it.

"We shouldn't hang around too long." Anders looked up at a sound. It was their ride speeding off.

"We should have expected that," Maya said.

"I did, here's our replacement ride," Anders said, gesturing ahead. There was a black car pulling in.

"Look at who's not just a pretty face?" Maya said, chuckling.

"I am a professional. I came prepared." Anders walked over to the cuffed man, had a few words with him, and then injected something into the man's neck. He fell unconscious. Anders removed the cuffs and put them away, walking back to Maya.

"I suggest we get in our ride as soon as possible." Anders strode over to the vehicle, opening one of the back doors. Maya had a last glance at their attackers and quickly joined him. The car sped away, the entire scene quickly disappearing behind them.

"Welcome to Atlantis," Anders said with a grin.

"That was some welcome. I need to up my game, and quickly."

"There are ways to help with that. For now, let's appreciate the little things." Anders patted his pocket, and Maya gave him a curious look.

"Do I want to know what's in there?" she said.

"I'll show you later. Enjoy the scenery." Anders winked and then gazed out the window. Maya did the same, trying to get a feel for where they were.

Soon enough they were back in the midst of the city. There were people everywhere, lights, and movement.

Looks like a fun place, it's totally buzzing.

Then the nightlife faded away, and they ended up in a quieter area again. The car slowed and then stopped.

"Is this us?" Maya asked. She looked up and saw a sign. It said, 'Modest Motel'. The building in front of her was a featureless grey block.

"Only the best for my VIP." Anders got out and Maya joined him. She immediately cursed under her breath.

"My bag. It's in the other car."

"You didn't bring anything that critical, did you?" Anders asked.

"Just clothes. So, no. And I'm wearing the jacket. That's critical." Maya winked at him.

"Of course. Well, we can replace any of that stuff. Let's check in and order some food." Anders strode through the car park to the reception area.

"What did you take from those men back there?" Maya asked.

"Oh, just a token." Anders pulled out two phones from his pockets.

"Nice. Might take them a while to get home," Maya said with a laugh.

"If the driver doesn't circle back for them. At any rate, I'm sure Kora can do something with these. I'll give her access once we're all settled in." Anders held the door open and Maya walked in. The reception area was tiny, but very well furnished with a luxurious wooden desk and grand paintings.

Maybe there's more to this place than it appears. Not so modest?

2

DEREK AND COMPANY

Anders returned, waving key cards.

"Let's go check out the room. Don't worry, it's a suite." Anders tossed her a key card and Maya pocketed it.

"I'm surprised they have rooms that big in this place," Maya said, looking around. The motel didn't look big at all.

"You'll see." Anders walked over to the end of the hall and pressed a button.re

"Is this an elevator?"

"Sure is." Anders winked and offered no more information. A few moments later there was a 'ding' and doors opened nearby.

Looks like a normal elevator.

Anders ushered her in and swiped the key card. He then pressed level five. The elevator doors closed, and it sped off.

"We're going down?" Maya gasped.

"This place isn't much to look at, but it's quite expansive. Hopefully, the rooms live up to their reputation." Anders grinned at her.

"I'm not sure how I'll feel about being underground." Maya

sighed, trying to keep an open mind. The elevator slowed, and then the doors opened. They stepped out into a luxuriously decorated hallway with lots of mahogany trim along the dark navy walls and a beige carpet.

"This way," Anders said, leading them down the hallway. He stopped at the end and unlocked a corner room.

"Ladies first," Anders said, holding the door. Maya stepped inside, her footsteps echoing off the marble floor. The room was built in a lavish European style with marble, antique furniture, and stylish recliner chairs.

"Wow, just wow." Maya walked through, taking it all in. There was a separate study, decked out like a hacker's dream, and both bedrooms had king-sized beds.

"It certainly impresses. This was a good tip." Anders wandered around the apartment, checking out the rooms.

"I'm not sure how I will fare being underground, though. There's no natural light," Maya said.

"They say sunrise is a wonder all of its own."

"What is this place?"

"It's a secret. Designed for discerning clientele and doesn't have an obvious footprint at the street level. I heard about it on the bounty hunter grapevine."

"Thanks, I appreciate you doing the research." Maya settled down on one of the special chairs and relaxed back into it.

"I take my assistant duties seriously," Anders said. He eased himself into the next chair. "These things are dangerous. How are you supposed to get up again?"

"I know. We should have offered these chairs to those goons tonight," Maya said with a laugh. She sat up straighter and looked directly at Anders. "Speaking of which, we need to get to work on that as soon as possible. My training, that is."

"Don't worry, I have a contact. We're heading over there tomorrow. Beyond that, no promises. But it's a start."

"Good. I can't afford to lose any time."

"I know. Trust me, I know. But tonight, we are safe. Just rest, and we can get started tomorrow."

"I'm going to hold you to that." Maya leaned back into the chair and wondered if she could fall asleep right there.

The next morning, Anders was waiting for her in the lounge area with two coffees.

"I should stop being so surprised," Maya said, settling in a comfy chair and picking up her coffee.

"I'm an early riser. At least I put it to good use, right?" Anders chuckled and picked up a remote from the coffee table. "I've been incredibly patient. Aren't you curious about the windows?" Anders pointed to the blackout blinds with the remote.

"I hadn't really thought about it. But now that you mention it...yes." Maya stared at the windows expectantly. Anders pressed a button on the remote and the blackout blind ascended. It revealed a thinner blind behind it. However, Maya could see light behind it.

"Interesting. How about the next one?" Maya asked. She could see a natural-looking luminescent glow behind the current blind.

"Here we go." Anders pressed another button, and as the next blind rose, golden light filled the room. The blind slowly retracted, but the light remained the same. Bright, but nothing else.

"Hmm, I suppose there's nothing to see because we are underground," Maya said. She put down her coffee and approached the window carefully. "Is it natural light?"

"So they say. There's a network of light shafts, mirrors, and all. No view, but actual sunlight. What do you think?"

"I think it's great. An excellent compromise." Maya returned to her coffee, drinking it quickly. Anders brought her a crois-sant and sat across, munching his own.

"Thanks, I think you missed your calling. You make an excellent assistant," Maya said with a beaming smile.

"I'll keep that in mind. In case the whole bounty hunter thing falls through." Anders grinned and took another bite of his croissant.

"If you don't mind, I'm rather keen to see this contact." Maya finished her coffee and stood quickly.

"I don't mind. Let's head out." Anders shoved the rest of the croissant into his mouth and strode over to the front door, the food bulging one of his cheeks. Maya stifled a laugh.

I don't think he's used to eating in front of others.

The trip back up to the lobby was uneventful, and there was a black car waiting for them in the parking lot.

"Don't worry, I'm driving today." Anders unlocked the car with his phone and walked over to the driver's seat. Maya opened the back door and pretended to get in.

"Oh, so that's how it is, is it?" Anders shook his head and put on a disappointed expression. Maya laughed, closed the door, and headed for the front.

"Just playing. Maybe when I'm a bit richer and more famous."

"So next week then?" Anders winked and pulled the car out.

The sun was dazzling, and the streets looked relatively empty.

"Why so quiet?" Maya asked.

"It's still early. Anyone who's out is already at work or school or whatever else. You'll see the hordes at lunchtime."

"Should be fun. Who's this contact?"

"Name's Derek. He's a bounty hunter here in Atlantis, a Chakra bloodline. He can get you started and help explain the lay of the land here and give inside information on the clan."

"Sounds useful. But he's not a teacher?"

"No, but he's in the system. He's got a Mastery Mark and can explain the entire process." Anders stopped at the traffic lights and glanced over at her. "Trust me, he's who we need right now." Anders gave her a reassuring smile.

"I'll be the judge of that." Maya grinned. "But seriously, thanks. It's been nice to just be a passenger for a little while. Everything has been so exhausting."

"Happy to help. And believe me, once this gets going I'll be the passenger, I bet. Enjoy it while it lasts."

"Words to live by." Maya returned to staring out the window. Within half an hour Anders pulled into a parking spot. They were outside a modest office block.

"Reminds me of your office building," Maya said.

"Sure does. Great minds think alike, I suppose." Anders turned off the car and stepped out. Maya followed suit, and they entered the reception area.

Nobody was around, but Anders didn't seem troubled by that at all. He strode past the desk and straight to the lifts. He called the lift and waited.

"Is he on level thirteen too?" Maya asked with a laugh.

"No, level eighteen. But I don't think they are so concerned with thirteen over here, anyway. I doubt it's at a discount."

"You know, we can probably improve your office when we're back in New York. I have money for that, right?" Maya said, winking. Anders groaned.

"Yes, you're loaded. I will take you up on that at some stage, but I honestly doubt we will spend much time in New York." Anders noticed the lift open and stepped inside, holding it open. He pressed the lift number and leaned back against the wall. The elevator zoomed up at a rapid pace and within seconds slowed down again.

"Impressive," Maya muttered as they left the elevator. They were in a run-of-the-mill corporate office space with a series of glass-paneled offices. The one outlier was a wooden door at the end. Maya could read the name on it easily.

"Derek and Company," she said.

"I'm not sure what company he keeps, ask him," Anders said with a wry smile. They walked down the hall and entered the office. It was a similar setup to what Maya remembered from Anders' place with a tiny reception desk and a few chairs. Behind the entry was another door, and it was open.

"Come through, I sent my receptionist home today," a voice called out.

"It's Anders," he called back as he walked ahead. Maya followed close, getting a glimpse of the room beyond. It was very neatly organized. Shelves held various books and odds and ends, and an enormous desk housed a computer monitor and some stationery. Derek was leaning back in a leather chair, his feet on the desk. He looked at ease, wearing a similar suit to the men who had attacked them the night before.

"Suits are all the rage here?" Anders said.

"Mostly. It helps to adopt a uniform. Helps you blend in." Derek stood and offered his hand. Anders extended his and they shook hands.

"Nice to meet you in person, Anders. And is this the lovely Maya?" Derek looked over at her, smiling.

"That would be correct, not that I'm often introduced that way," Maya said with a laugh. Derek gave her a broad grin.

"I find that highly surprising. But please, take a seat and we can have a chat." Derek gestured to the seats and returned to his own, sitting properly this time.

"I'm always happy to help a fellow hunter. To recap, Maya, needs an introduction and some training?" Derek said.

"That's about the size of it. Care to elaborate, Maya?" Anders said, looking at her.

"I need to attain the Mastery Mark. As soon as possible." Maya smiled but noticed a puzzled look on Derek's features.

"Hmm, that's an odd request. For several reasons. But for starters, which mark are you after?" Derek asked. Anders shrugged and let Maya answer.

"The one that shows you have mastered the Chakra bloodline?" Maya said.

"It's the sixth one, I've never seen the seventh one. Although I suppose the old masters would have it."

"Sixth one?" Maya blurted out. Derek chuckled.

"Oh, you have much to learn. There are seven Chakras, well six regular ones and a special one. For each one you master, you earn the mark."

"I see. I thought it was just one, but I can see that it's more involved than that. How long does it often take to achieve all six?" Maya said, a lot quieter this time.

"Several years, provided you are enrolled in a good school. And if you optimize your timing to gain access to the Hopeful's Path."

"Hopeful's Path? I've never heard of that," Anders chimed in. Derek glanced at him, and then at Maya.

"You two are a barrel of laughs. It's the sacred pilgrimage a candidate makes before meeting the masters. There are three trials that you must pass." Derek sighed, shaking his head.

"I'm very keen to learn all I can. I'm amazing at absorbing information from books or other references," Maya added hopefully.

"Precious little is written down. You're going to have to learn this the old-fashioned way." Derek stood and started pacing around the room. He stopped and assessed Maya.

"Do you have any marks?" he asked.

"Chakra Mastery Marks? No," she said. Derek shook his finger at her.

"No, no. Anders mentioned you're different. I'm guessing you have another Mastery already?" Derek looked her straight in the eyes and Maya realized there was no hiding it.

"Well, yes. I suppose I should level with you." Maya pulled up her sleeve and held out her hand and arm. Derek came in closer and took her hand in his, examining it.

"LifeDeath, how interesting." Derek straightened again, scratching his chin. "I'm not an expert on MultiBloods, but I know you can use your other power passively. The additional resilience and regeneration will help you speed up things."

"How exactly?" Maya asked.

"You'll heal faster than a normal person. People say almost twice as fast."

"That sounds amazing." Maya grinned with delight. Derek sighed.

"By now you're accustomed to rapid healing. In comparison it will seem painfully slow." Derek started pacing. "You'll also keep your toughness, and any increased muscle mass." Standing by the window, Derek paused and stared out. Silence reigned, and Maya waited for him to talk again. After a minute, he turned and addressed them.

"I can help you. I'll get you started on your training and pull a few strings to get you into a school. It's going to be tricky, but let's see what we can do. Oh, and you're going to have to hide that mark. If they see it, they'll refuse to teach you."

"Because of the LifeDeath mark?"

"Bingo. It's a brightly lit neon sign advertising that you have multiple bloodlines. And they're frowned upon by the Master Sage. The Chakra masters won't want to draw any unwanted attention to themselves by training you."

"I see, thanks for the tip." Maya carefully pulled her sleeve down again.

"Just for my sake, how many bloodlines do you have?" Derek said. He spoke casually, but his eyes were intense.

"All of them," Maya said, matching his gaze.

3

FIRM FOUNDATION

"This is wild, this is absolutely wild," Derek said as he led them into the training area. It looked like a derelict old gym.

"Think of it like a holiday from the daily grind. That's what I do," Anders said with a laugh. Maya ignored them both and glanced around at their surroundings.

"This place seems a bit abandoned," Maya said.

"By design. We don't want too many people hanging about." Derek directed them to a set of old wooden double doors, and they pushed through. After a dark hallway, they emerged into another room. This one was more modern and well maintained. A square, raised platform made of wooden planks was the centerpiece with various pieces of training equipment around the walls.

"Now, this is better," Maya said, nodding along.

"Of course. Grab a uniform and change." Derek pointed out a rack of outfits and a slim door on the far wall. Maya strode over and examined the outfits. They were a simple loose-fitting tunic and pants, unisex, and in white. She grabbed some and headed into the change room.

It was a simple affair, some wooden racks for sitting on and hooks to hang clothes. She changed quickly and returned to discover Derek had changed clothes into a matching outfit.

"Good, we can begin." Derek walked into the middle of the training area and motioned for Maya to join him. She walked over with as much confidence as she could show.

I really wonder how this is going to go.

Derek waited until she was an arm's length away, and then he held up a hand.

"The first Chakra you need to master is referred to as the Root and is associated with earth. It's about strength and resilience. Luckily for you, it should be easier to master because of your prior experience." Derek paused, waiting for Maya to respond.

"Great. I assume we need to do them in order?"

"Yes. We're going to try to hack the process a bit, but we can't ignore that. The Chakras need to be mastered from the bottom up. You will literally ascend in your mastery and power."

"So, I need a firm foundation. Hence the Root," Maya added.

"Exactly. Tense your stomach muscles, please." Derek watched Maya, then in a flash, he extended his arm and hit her in the stomach with his palm. Maya was knocked over easily, tumbling to the floor.

"That was surprising," she said, dusting herself off and getting up.

"That was the idea," Derek said drily. He waited for her to get back into position.

"Did anything feel different?" he said. Maya shook her head.

"No, I just felt like I got hit."

"That's fine. The Chakra point is at the base of your spine. I will not hit you there, but you need to focus on it. Rest your attention there, and really dive into it. Close your eyes and take a deep breath." Derek closed his eyes and Maya did the same. She thought over what he said and tried focusing inwards. She also remembered the notes that Anders had passed her previously, on how to focus her energy.

"Place your awareness there and imagine the space around the base of your spine," Derek said in a slow drone.

I can do this. Just focus.

"As you connect your focus, imagine that you have a center of energy collecting there. Allow the energy to be, and to collect all on its own. It doesn't need you to interfere." Derek stopped talking, and Maya follow his directions, allowing her focus to dwell.

"I can sense you are doing it. Allow this energy to infuse you gently to reinforce your body. It's your rock, your support. This power is your strength and protection." As Derek talked, his voice sounded like it was coming closer, but also seemed far away.

Maya dove deeper, slowing her breathing, and allowing the feeling to spread. It started with a slight tingling, then a feeling of energy. Like the rush of adrenaline or emotion she associated with a stressful or terrible situation. But it was different.

It's not forced, it's not emotive. It's just...there.

Maya let the energy wash over her, and just as she felt a sense of accomplishment and peace, a large object slammed into her. She crashed to the floor and opened her eyes. Disoriented, she looked up at Derek.

"What was that?"

"Did it feel different?" he said. Maya pushed away her annoyance for a moment and thought about the impact.

"I didn't feel any pain, it was just the surprise of being knocked over. Was that really necessary?"

"Of course. Unless you want to spend years on this, which is always an option." Derek grinned at her, and Maya sighed.

"I asked for this." She looked over at Anders, who was sitting still on the ground, his eyes closed. "What are you doing?"

"I'm practicing too. Why not?" he said.

"But you have no bloodlines," Maya said, confused. She stood up again.

"True, but also these are not entirely new concepts. People have been tapping into this for thousands of years."

"But didn't they have dormant bloodlines? Isn't that why it worked?" Maya asked.

"In this area, there's still a lot of unknowns. How much is the domain of the bloodline, and how much is inherent in the body? He may as well practice," Derek said with an approving tone.

Well, that's embarrassing.

"Sorry, I didn't mean to say you can't try," Maya said. Anders chuckled.

"It's fine, I understood what you were getting at. It was more trying to further your understanding." Anders smiled at her. "Can you believe that was her first reaction?" Anders said to Derek, smirking at Maya.

"It is a little surprising. Somebody doesn't want to share," Derek replied with a grin. After a few moments, he took on a more serious expression. "We need to keep going. I'll start us off again."

Maya stepped closer and closed her eyes, ready to start again.

It's going to be harder to concentrate knowing that he could hit me at any point.

~

Maya opened her eyes and analyzed the situation. She had withstood a blow without moving. She was still completely centered and stable.

"Huh? Now that's something, isn't it?" she said with delight. Derek nodded.

"Well done. The practice is paying off."

"I feel like I did well too," Anders said from the sidelines. He opened his eyes and looked refreshed.

"It must be nice doing all the relaxation and mediation without the extra work," Maya said pointedly to Anders.

"Oh, it is. Much more relaxing than traipsing all over New York trying to respond to bloodline violators," Anders said with a grin.

"Let's break for lunch. We'll get back to it after, and I'll use some actual force," Derek said.

"What do you mean, actual force?" Maya said as they walked out of the room.

"I'm hitting you with maybe one-tenth of my usual strength. We have a little way to go," Derek said. Anders laughed, and Maya gave him a little punch on the shoulder.

"Oi, cut that out," she said.

"Just enjoying myself. Don't let that detract from your achievement." Anders gave her a genuine smile, and she let her annoyance drop.

He does want me to succeed, that much is certain.

Back out in the entry room, Derek dragged out a rickety, old, wooden table and chairs.

"Make yourselves comfortable, I'll be back in a minute." Derek darted off to the front door. Maya selected a chair and eased down into it. It only creaked a little.

"They look safe enough, if not as comfortable as I'd like," Anders said.

"I'm getting a sense of just how far I need to go," Maya said.

"And?" Anders said, leaning back in his chair precariously.

"It just feels like it's a vast mountain to climb. That's all. I feel like LifeDeath was much easier."

"It probably was easier." Anders adjusted his chair, so he didn't topple back completely. "Also, you're more aware of what needs to happen now. And there's no shortcuts. There might be faster ways up that mountain, but you can't skip anything. You had what, twenty years of passive practice with LifeDeath?" Anders said.

"You're right. I can't really compare the two."

"So, don't. Yes, you have an expectation to do things faster, but let's see it for what it is. Don't try to prejudge too much." Anders turned to look at Derek as he entered. His chair rocked past the point of no return, but Derek swiftly tapped it forward with a foot, not breaking his stride.

"You're going to want to sit up for this," Derek said. He dumped a few bags of steaming hot food on the table. Anders dove in, unpacking the food despite the obvious heat.

"Dumplings! Oh, you shouldn't have," Anders said. He started inspecting and divvying out the boxes. "These are the vegetarian ones," he said to Maya, pointing out a few boxes.

"Dumplings in Atlantis. I never thought I'd be doing this," Maya said.

"Lots of Asian influences here, which is fun." Derek cut the sentence short so he could stuff a dumpling into his mouth.

"Where's the sauces?" Maya said, roving her eyes over the feast.

"Here," Derek said in a muffled voice, his mouth still full. He offered her another bag. It was full of tiny containers with different sauces. There was sweet chili, soy sauce, vinegar, and other blends.

"Derek, you make the cut," Maya said, before shoving a dumpling into her mouth.

"That's high praise. I hope you recorded that," Anders quipped before eating.

"I'll try to get it next time. And I'll remember that you love dumplings," Derek said with a chuckle.

Derek told them more of the city while they ate, and a few stories of famous bounties he had taken down.

"I can see now why you took this line of work. You're well suited to it," Maya said. She expected the compliment to go down well, but Derek looked withdrawn. He focused on his food. Maya looked over at Anders, and he shrugged.

"I am, but it's not by choice, sadly. It was the path of failure that led me here," Derek breathed. The energy and warmth that she had associated with him had dissipated instantly.

"What happened?" Maya said.

"It's a long story. Perhaps I'll tell it another time." Derek started looking for other dumplings to eat.

"Is it related to the Mastery Marks? The Chakra tests?" Maya said. Derek looked up.

"Yes. I failed to achieve Mastery over one Chakra."

"How many did you get?" Maya asked without thinking and instantly regretted it. A very quick look of frustration passed over Derek's face, but he hid it well.

"You can never ask that. Only those who are your teachers or elders can request that information. It's like a social taboo. I'm not sure how else to explain it." Derek spoke calmly and patiently.

I feel like a fool. Of course, I should have thought before asking.

"I'm sorry, I didn't stop to think. I didn't mean to offend you," Maya said.

"I understand. It's a logical question for you to ask since you're entirely committed to speeding up your path to mastery. Now, when you get out there with others, never ask how many Mastery Marks a Chakra bloodline has, or ever ask to see them. That's private. Just this time, I will show you." Derek pulled up his sleeve and showed Maya his arm. Just below his shoulder she saw a series of tattoos. They were arranged in a circle. Five symbols with a space at the top that would have closed the circle.

"I see. Thank you for sharing that with me. Just one last question, if you don't mind?" she said.

"Tread carefully," Anders said with a laugh, but his eyes looked concerned.

"Just about the Mastery Marks. Mine are somewhere else compared to yours. Can they be anywhere?"

"That is an acceptable question. They do differ between people, however, there are limited places. There's a known set of locations. I've heard that for people that are MultiBloods, the marks will cluster around the same area."

"That's why you said I would need to hide my LifeDeath Mastery Mark?" Maya said.

"Precisely. Your teachers and elders will ask to see your marks, and they are in their right to do so. I'll help advise you on what things you can do to conceal yours." Derek stood and pushed his food away.

"Enough chatter, we need to train again. Are you ready?"

"I am. Let's see how far I can go." Maya got up and followed Derek back to the training room.

4

INTERVIEW PREPARATION

Derek clapped her on the shoulder. Maya appreciated the fact that she had changed, and her leather jacket provided some padding. It had been a long and tough afternoon.

"You've done well. I think we've done enough for your interview tomorrow," he said with a smile.

"Interview?" Maya asked, confused.

"You want to join a school, correct? You can't just enroll online." Derek laughed and glanced over at Anders.

"He's right, you know. I've been researching."

"And you didn't mention it because..." Maya started.

"I wanted you to focus on the job in front of us. And you've done well. We can discuss the interview tonight now that you've done as much training as possible."

"I appreciate it, but maybe next time just fill me in on the whole plan?" Maya said. She was too exhausted to get that upset.

It's not a big deal, and you wanted things to happen fast. This is fast.

"How's she going? Really?" Anders asked as they walked back through the main room.

"I'm not a teacher, so it's hard to judge. But Maya's willingness to focus, and her general strength and resilience are making her progress faster." Derek gave her another slap on the back.

"Thanks for the vote of confidence. What's the general plan?" Maya said.

"I'm hoping that we can do enough to get a breakthrough before you start at the school. It may be an entry requirement to have some Mastery Marks already. We will find out tomorrow."

"I guess we will. Can it happen that fast?" Maya asked. She watched Derek's face carefully to gauge his response. He had a hopeful expression.

"There's no reason why not, there are no artificial limits. It is the first mark, some find it easier, and some find it harder. It's up to you." Derek shrugged and pushed through the main doors to the outside. Maya followed them out, surprised by how dark it was.

"I really trained a lot today, didn't I?" she said.

"You really did. Hopefully, it compounds. This is uncharted territory for me, so I'm as interested as you to see what happens." Derek stopped outside and glanced over at Anders. "I think you two owe me dinner."

"It's only fair. What do you recommend?" Anders said.

"Something authentic. Come on, I'll drive you there." Derek strode across the road to a sleek silver car.

"Nice wheels," Anders said, circling around the vehicle.

"They get me from 'A' to 'B'," Derek said with a grin and unlocked the doors. Anders sat up front and Maya sat in the back.

"Driver, take us to the finest food in Atlantis," Maya called out from the back.

"Yes ma'am," Derek said, looking into the rearview mirror and saluting. He stepped on the accelerator sharply, and the car lurched forward. They sped through the streets, Derek driving like they were being chased.

"Is this really necessary?" Maya said as they lurched around another corner.

"Yes," Derek said. He took his eyes off the road to grin at Maya in the rearview mirror.

"Just keep your eyes on the road!" Maya cried out, as Derek narrowly missed another car.

"I've noticed more drivers and less autopilot here," Anders said. Derek nodded.

"Yeah, those that want cars want to drive them. The others hail a ride or use the metro. Makes for some exciting trips," Derek said, as he swerved between cars.

"Aren't there like police? Road rules?" Maya said nervously. Derek laughed.

"Police are too busy dealing with bloodlines. Cars are the least of their problems." Derek slammed on the brakes, and they came to a sudden stop.

"We're here. Bring your taste buds, as this is going to be something else." Derek parked and left the car immediately. Maya carefully extracted herself and looked around properly. They were in front of a rather derelict-looking complex.

"I didn't expect to find so many, well-loved buildings here in Atlantis," Maya said.

"You mean falling apart? The truly ancient places are rare and protected. Everything else was thrown together rather quickly," Derek said.

"And not maintained I take it?" Anders said, pointing out a rather large crack in the wall.

"Bingo. The International Quarter is not exactly a priority."

"Is this going to be another 'broken on the outside, opulent on the inside' type of deal?" Maya said, hope tingeing her voice.

"Oh no, it's falling apart on the outside and inside. But you won't care. Come on." Derek led them through the main doors. There were people everywhere inside, going in all different directions. What drew Maya's attention, however, was the multitude of food stalls. Rows and rows of stalls. Clusters of four to six stalls sandwiched together with spaces between for tables and chairs and access to other aisles of food.

"Wow, this is something else," Maya said.

"I had no idea. And it's all good?" Anders said.

"Most of it. Do you want to wander around or want me to order?" Derek said.

"Is that honestly even a question?" Maya said laughing. "Go and find stuff, please."

"My pleasure. Grab a table, won't you?" Derek disappeared off into the crowd. Anders and Maya set to finding a table big enough for the three of them.

After a solid five minutes of wandering and stalking tables, they finally nabbed one. Not long after they sat down, Derek appeared with a tray loaded with food.

"Here I present the best of the best." Derek put down the tray and started pointing out food. "Stinky tofu, that's for you Maya. We also have various food on a stick options. My favorite is the deep-fried pig intestines!" Derek grabbed one of those for himself.

"What else is over here?" Maya asked, after handpicking some stinky tofu.

"Three treasures, eggettes, and some bowl pudding." Derek rattled off the list and then sunk his teeth into his food.

"Something for everyone," Anders said with a laugh. After getting past the smell, Maya loved the tofu. And there were enough other things to try, too.

"Hands off my pudding!" she declared to Anders, as he tried to grab the last one.

"Good times, good times," Derek said, leaning back and patting his stomach.

"You did well," Maya said, a little surprised at the meal. It had hit the spot. "Anything you can tell me about tomorrow?"

"The school is called Floating Lotus. I can't say what the interview will involve, but they will probably assess your form and perhaps even test you."

"Not a lot to work with," Anders chimed in.

"Sorry, but the schools are pretty secretive. I have heard that this one is more open to foreigners, which gives you a chance."

"I'll do my best to make a good impression. And I'll try to find out more of what they are looking for. Will they decide tomorrow?"

"Unlikely. But you'll know where you stand, and if it's worth continuing through their process." Derek turned to Anders. "Did you order those things I recommended?"

"I did. And a few things for ourselves. We should head back soon, so we have time to get organized."

"I recommend it. I'll also forward you the address." Derek moved his chair back and stood up, stretching.

"You're not coming?" Maya said.

"I shouldn't, there's too much risk that I'll influence proceedings. You can go with Anders."

"You can't ditch me just yet, it would seem," Anders said with a chuckle.

"So, it seems." Maya stood and felt the same urge to stretch. *It must be from all that food.*

They headed back outside, and Derek drove them back to their car.

"Good luck. Call me when you're done, and we can debrief," Derek called out as he sped off.

"He's a good guy. I can't believe he took out an entire day to help."

"Don't worry, we paid him handsomely," Anders said. "But

you're right, he is a good guy." Anders turned on the car and
pulled out from the curb.

Anders left the car outside their hotel with a plain-clothed valet
and headed straight to the reception desk. After a few words, he
nodded and made for the lifts. Maya followed close behind.

"Everything we need is in our suite," Anders explained.

"What's with all the mystery?" Maya said. Anders grinned.

"Just having a bit of fun, nothing major." He called the lift
and selected their floor. The same speedy lift whisked them
away, and they were at their door within moments.

"Here we go," Anders said, opening the door. On the coffee
table was a neat pile of boxes.

"I think we should start with this," Anders said. He handed
Maya the plain black box. She opened it and saw a strange kit
inside.

"It's a Mastery Mark cover kit," he said. Anders came closer
and pointed out a few elements. "These match your skin color
and mask the mark completely."

"They won't use the sensors?" Maya asked. Anders shook
his head.

"Not over here, luckily. There are solutions to that,
however, I think your blood is probably fine. Since your Life-
Death isn't active right now. Not that I'd want to test it, mind
you." Anders gave her a nervous chuckle.

"Right. I can handle this. What else is there?"

"Mostly just gadgets for me. But one of them will interest
you." Anders walked over and opened one box. He removed a
fancy-looking tablet computer.

"Bring your phone over to this sensor," he said. Maya
walked over and waved her phone as required.

"Great. This tablet has a lot more function than your phone, and it's hooked up to the LifeDeath network. You can start querying people now. A gift, from Kora." Anders looked pleased with himself too.

"Amazing. I'm going to put it through its paces tomorrow."

"Great. It's here for whenever." Anders gave Maya a concerned look. "You look like you're about to keel over."

"I think you're right. The day has taken its toll."

"No problem. Go rest, we have a big day ahead of us tomorrow."

"I think I will," Maya said.

And I can't shake the feeling that this interview is going to go very poorly.

The hired car came to a stop, and it shook Maya out of her thoughts.

"Is this the right place?" Maya said, confused.

"This is the address you requested," the driver said. He pointed to his GPS to demonstrate.

"Thanks," Anders said and left the car. "C'mon." Maya. reluctantly stepped out and walked closer to Anders.

"This looks like another office block." She pointed at the revolving door and lobby before them.

"You don't get to interview at the school, they hold it else-where. They'd rather not have rejected students hanging around."

"Not like any school I've ever heard of," Maya said.

"Great way to think of it," Anders said with a smile as he walked through the revolving doors. A security guard stepped forward to greet them immediately.

"State your business, please," the guard said. He was taller than Anders and had a slim build.

He seems more dangerous than he looks.

"We have an interview on level five," Anders said. The guard nodded.

"Use the second lift." The guard looked over at Maya. "Good luck."

"Thanks," Maya said, caught a little off-guard.

"He's a Chakra bloodline, isn't he?" she whispered to Anders as they walked away.

"I used to have a machine to verify that sort of thing," Anders said with a chuckle. "But yes, I believe so."

"You didn't replace your machine?" she said, surprised. Anders grinned.

"Oh, I did. Just didn't bring it on this trip. Didn't see the need and thought you might find a reason to break it again."

"I thought as much." Maya sighed. She spotted the lift the guard mentioned and stepped forward to press the call button. The doors opened immediately, and there was an attendant in the lift.

"Floor, please," the attendant said. His tone was polite, but he had no expression on his face.

"Five," Anders said. The attendant nodded and pressed the button once Maya was inside. As the lift ascended, he looked at Maya.

"Good luck," he said.

"Thank you," Maya said, a little less surprised this time. Once the doors opened, the attendant held the 'Open Door' button and waited patiently for them to leave. They emerged into a plain white corridor. To the left was a dead end, and to the right was a plain wooden door.

"This way," Anders said, making a start. Maya took a slow and deep breath before hurrying off to follow him.

You can do this. Just be calm.

5

SNAP ASSESSMENT

Anders paused outside the door.

"You should open it," he said, standing aside.

"Wish me luck," Maya said.

"Good luck. Break a leg," Anders said with a chuckle.

"Hilarious," Maya said, smiling despite her disapproval. She turned the brass handle and pushed open the door. Inside was an almost empty room with only wooden boards covering the floor, walls, and ceiling. A woman sat in the middle of the room, cross-legged and with closed eyes. Her black hair was tied up, and she was wearing a simple tunic, like the ones Derek had used.

"I am Song, your third interviewer. Please, come and sit next to me. Your companion can wait outside," Song said. Maya gave Anders a brief wave and made her way into the center of the room. As she sat, she heard the door close behind them.

"Good, we are alone. When did you activate your bloodline?" Song asked.

"A few weeks ago."

"On purpose, or accidental?" Song asked quickly. Her eyes were still closed.

"Neither. Someone else initiated it," Maya said. There was no reply. After a few moments of silence, Song spoke again.

"Who performed the activation?"

"I don't know his name. I've heard he was probably the ambassador. This was in New York," Maya said carefully.

I feel that I shouldn't lie to her, but I should try to keep some things back. I don't want to be turned away by admitting I have multiple bloodlines, either.

"How strange. There is more to this story." Song spoke slowly, then was silent. Maya almost said something. The pull of the silence was so strong. But she resisted and waited.

"Perhaps the conclusion of that story will be told at another time. Close your eyes and prepare your mind." Song spoke differently, her voice taking on a more melodic tone. Maya closed her eyes and tried to clear her mind. She practiced the exercises to access her Chakra. Suddenly a dense fog surrounded her, and she was whisked away.

Maya stood, sensing she was somewhere else. It was a quiet plain, the tall grass swaying slowly in a gentle breeze. Song walked toward her in a flowing and fine robe.

"I will take the measure of you. Show me your power," Song said. Her voice had that same strange quality. Maya knew exactly what to do. She held out her hand and a ball of pure white energy amassed there. Occasionally arcs of blue or gold crackled through it. The ball grew larger, and the light grew more intense. Song walked closer, examining it.

"Very interesting." Song looked straight through Maya, her eyes glowing. "You have opened none of your Chakras, though you have amassed power. What is holding you back?"

"I need more training. I've had very little instruction."

"I don't want your assessment. I have made my own already." Song turned and started walking away. The mist rose again, and a dark cloud swallowed Maya up.

She opened her eyes, gasping. They were seated again, back in the wooden room.

We never left. Of course, we didn't. But what happened? It was so much like that time they activated my power. What is that?

Song opened her eyes.

"You have not been forthcoming. One does not amass that much power without a reason. Or without instruction. There is an answer to this riddle, but you hold it back."

"I can't help what I am. I need help and guidance to open my Chakras."

"I am not satisfied with your answer. If you want to enter our school, you must present yourself and undergo a test. But don't bother until you have surpassed the Water gate." Song stood gracefully and directed Maya to the door. Maya stood and walked away. Song escorted her the whole way. As Maya reached for the door, Song spoke again.

"Call in your friend," she said. Maya opened the door.

"Anders, come in for a moment." Maya saw that Anders was very close and after a few steps he joined them in the room.

"Your leg, what happened to it?" Song asked.

"It's a long story. Happened years ago. An unfortunate incident with a vampire, would you believe?"

"It can't heal," Song said.

"Trust me, I know all about that. I've had a few people look at it, they say nothing can be done." Anders sighed, looking reluctant to discuss the topic much more.

"It's not hopeless, but it's not a normal injury. There's damage to the internal energy of your leg. I can see that plain as day."

"You're the first person who's been able to state that with any confidence. Have I been talking to the wrong people?" Anders had a glint of hope in his eye.

"I won't give you false hope. Those of the Chakra bloodline cannot heal you, it is not our power. We can only diagnose and explain the problem. If you were one of us, you could correct it yourself." Song paused, looking Anders straight in the eyes with an intense gaze. "You need someone else to heal it. Such a person would be rare."

"I understand. Thank you for your advice." Anders gave her a quick bow, which Song returned. She then turned and started walking away. Anders opened the door and held it open for Maya. The two walked together back to the lift.

"We need to talk about that. But first, how did you go?" he said.

"Not that well. She wasn't comfortable with my level of power, and my lack of progress in opening Chakras. She said it suggested something of a problem, one which I was hiding."

"Wow, she's good. Where did things end up?" Anders said, looking concerned.

"I need to do another test. I need to present at the school. And I should have surpassed the Water Chakra. I don't know how far that is." Maya shrugged. Anders called the lift and looked back at her.

"Sounds promising though, you have something to work toward. Let me call Derek when we get downstairs and organize a get-together. We need a proper debrief and to pick his brain."

"Sounds good to me." Maya stepped into the lift and retreated into her thoughts.

Derek was pacing outside when they arrived. He looked up sharply as they approached him in the parking lot.

"Anders told me nothing. What happened?" Derek asked.

"Can we at least get inside?" Anders said. Derek hurriedly opened the door and waved them inside. Maya strode over to the rough table they had eaten at the last time and sat down.

"She asked me a few questions about how long since they activated me, and who did it."

"Standard. You answered honestly?" Derek asked, focusing his entire attention on her.

"I did. She did some sort of test, where she assessed my power. I have a lot."

"This I know. What else?" Derek was quite insistent and asked her immediately.

"She did some sort of weird mind thing as well, and she said my Chakras were not open. And that it was surprising that I had this much power without opening any." Maya watched Derek for a reaction, but he gave nothing away.

"As expected. She pressed you for an explanation, didn't she?" Derek asked. Maya nodded.

"Obviously, the answer is too risky, so I said I was untrained. She didn't find it acceptable."

"I see." Derek looked quite concerned. His attention seemed to be elsewhere, but he snapped back and looked at her with that same intensity. "Where did you leave things?"

"It could have been worse. She told me to present myself for a proper test and to make sure I have surpassed the Water Chakra. How bad is that?" Maya cringed, waiting for Derek's assessment.

"Hmm. She's thrown the gauntlet. You'd need to open the first two Chakras and discover the location of the school."

"You don't know where it is?" Anders blurted out.

"Of course not. I didn't study there," Derek said like it was common knowledge.

"Alright, well I'm working on the first one, surely getting the second one isn't the end of the world. And she didn't mention a time limit," Maya said, trying to sound hopeful.

"She didn't need to. They all run on the same schedule. You have a week before the testing ends," Derek said. He didn't look comfortable at all.

"I assume this is a big ask then?" Anders said, regarding them both.

"It is. She really doesn't trust you," Derek said with a chuckle. Then he burst out laughing.

"What's so funny?" Maya said.

"Oh, it's just the situation we are in. This is the only school in Atlantis I could line up, and you basically need to move a mountain to even get a look in." Derek threw his hands up. "You have to just laugh."

"I can work on the research for the school. You get her over the line, Chakra-wise," Anders said, pointing at Derek.

"I have a job, you know," Derek said. "And I'm not a Master. I can only do so much."

"Be creative. She's a quick study, she's got power, and can recover quickly. You could even say she's the perfect student." Anders grinned at Derek. "What can you say to that?"

"I got myself into this. Talk about crazy challenges. Alright, I'm in." Derek threw his hands up in defeat.

"There's another thing of interest. Maybe you can give some context," Maya said. Derek gave her a curious look.

"He doesn't need to concern himself," Anders said. Maya waved him away with her hand.

"She said that the injury to Anders' leg is not a normal one. There is damage to the internal energy of his leg. A Chakra bloodline cannot heal it, but the person who could, would be a rare person." Maya sat back and let the words sit. Derek appeared to be deep in thought.

"I don't have the sight. I cannot confirm what she said. Yet, it rings true. I can think of only one scenario that fits."

"Which is?" Anders said.

"Someone who has mastered both the LifeDeath and Chakra bloodlines. If one has the sight, and ability to manipulate Chakra, and yet the mastery over Life Force and the healing that comes with LifeDeath, then the impossible may just be possible." Derek spoke slowly and didn't sound too sure of himself. But he did nod at the end, slowly. "That could work. And I don't know anyone like that."

"I can make inquiries. Leave it with me," Anders said.

"We don't know one. But we can make one," Maya blurted out. Anders and Derek looked at her immediately. "Once I master the Chakra bloodline, I will have access to both. Wouldn't I be the perfect person?"

"In theory, yes. I don't know enough about what needs to be done," Derek said.

"Don't put that kind of pressure on yourself. If you can help, great. But there's other things to worry about first. This leg doesn't hold me back anyway," Anders said.

He can't lie to me. I can see how much he wants it. That pain in his eyes, he can't hide it like he thinks.

"It's on my list now. I promise you, one day I'll fix that leg. Mark my words," Maya announced. Anders nodded and looked away. Before he did, she noticed what looked like the glimmer of a tear.

"These sure are interesting times. You weren't wrong when you said you had something interesting for me," Derek said with a sigh, shaking his head.

"I asked around before I contacted you. You were ready for a break from the normal, Derek," Anders said with a chuckle. Derek nodded.

"I can't deny it."

"You're in my circle now, Derek. And it's pretty safe to say your life will never be the same." Maya paused for a moment before adding, "I seem to have that effect on people." She grinned at Derek and winked at Anders.

"She's right. Look at me, I followed her to Atlantis."

"I need to break out the scotch. Come on, let's go plan some insanity." Derek stood up and left.

"You think your leg can handle all this excitement?" Maya said to Anders.

"Perhaps not. Maybe we should invest in a walker. Or a ride-on scooter," Anders said, returning her grin.

"Just say the word." Maya winked at him and headed for the door.

6

PRECARIOUSLY PERCHED

Maya stepped into the building with trepidation. Derek had kept the entire thing secret. He had just harped on about how amazing his idea was, and that it would revolutionize the training.

"Looks like an aircraft hangar?" Maya said. She stepped inside the vast space, her footsteps echoing loudly.

"Even better," Derek said with a grin. He immediately searched the area and then grabbed his phone to make a call.

"Did he at least clue you in?" Maya said to Anders.

"No, he said you'd get it out of me. I was happy to be spared that," Anders said with a smirk.

"I see. Surely you know where we are, though?" Maya said slyly. Anders chuckled and shook his head.

"Nope, not falling for that. Let's just wait for the big reveal." Anders nudged her shoulder and pointed out Derek returning.

"The last piece is almost here. It ties the whole thing together. Let's open the side door, so they can bring it in." Derek led them over to a nearby area and pressed a large red button. Giant roller doors in the facility's side rose, and a truck started reversing in.

Once it was fully inside the facility, two men hopped out of the cab and sauntered over to the back.

"This has got to be the strangest thing we've delivered this year," the first one said. "Who's Derek?"

"That would be me."

"Read and sign, please," the man said, thrusting a tablet in front of Derek. Once Derek finished, the man called out, "Open her up, let's get this thing out of here." His partner opened the back of the truck and then operated a mechanical lift at the back. Together they hopped inside the truck and pushed something onto the lift. The leader jumped down and operated the lift while his partner steadied the object. It was covered in a brown wrap and hard to identify.

"Looks pretty strange," Maya said.

"Oh, you'll love it," Derek said. Once it was safely off the lift, the two men started packing up.

"Take care, I'm not even going to ask what it is," the leader said.

"No worries, thanks for getting it here so fast." Derek waved and watched the two men pack up and drive away.

"Can we look now?" Maya asked. Derek strode over to the strange object and inspected the brown wrap. He unfastened it.

"Prepare yourselves for pure genius." Derek ripped the cover off in a single motion, unveiling a strange earthen sculpture. It had a wide but short base with a single thin pillar in the middle. At the top was a small square.

"I don't get it?" Maya said, looking over at Anders. He shrugged.

"Is it to inspire something?" Anders said.

"You'll see. Just help me get it safely over there," Derek said, pointing to a corner of the cavernous area. It was the only feature of a note, a dome-shaped area that looked a bit like a tunnel.

"This better be worth it," Maya said with a sigh.

⁓

With the help of a few trolleys and a lot of sweat, they safely maneuvered the sculpture over to the right place.

"Fits perfectly. Ah, I love it when a plan comes together." Derek stood back, admiring his handiwork. The sculpture's top sat comfortably about two meters below the height of the tunnel.

"One initial test, then we can get started. Stand back here, please." Derek led them out of the tunnel and over to a control panel nearby. He pressed a few buttons and then a giant turbine rose out of the ground. A few seconds later, it started. An enormous gust of wind thundered down the tunnel. The statue remained solid.

"Perfect," Derek said, powering down the device.

"It's a wind tunnel then?" Anders said.

"Exactly. This is our ticket to fast-tracking Maya's training."

"This, I have to hear," Maya said, her hands on her hips. Derek grinned back at her, his excitement spilling out.

"The Earth or Root Chakra is about strength, resilience, and a stable foundation. It's about connection to the earth, it's about anchoring yourself."

"That I can understand," Maya said. "I'm waiting for the next bit."

"You're going to sit up on that chair, carved from the earth and connected to it. By sitting there and performing the appropriate meditation, you can cement your connection to the earth and help unlock the energy of the Root Chakra. You must master it, to avoid being blown away."

"I'm going to sit up there, cross-legged, and meditate? Inside a wind tunnel?"

"Precisely. Don't you think it's a brilliant plan?" Derek said to Anders. He scratched his chin before replying.

"Well, it is inventive. We may need a cushion behind the

chair, for the inevitable tumble," Anders said. Derek shook his head.

"No, it's better this way. Maya can work harder to prevent that, or she can try to shield herself from the damage. It's a win-win." Derek grinned even more. He looked at them both.

"It's worth a try, I have a pretty crazy deadline."

"You've gone through worse, already. Why not try?"

"I'm pretty sure I'm going to regret this." Maya sighed and started off toward the sculpture.

As she approached, she noticed tiny grooves cut into the central pillar.

"Hand and foot holds, nice touch." Maya stepped onto the base and climbed. The structure was more stable than she expected, but she could tell it was ever so slightly flexing and moving from the weight of her climbing. As she rose, she felt a bit exposed. And as she reached the top, after awkwardly clambering onto the chair, she felt like she was perched on a cliff side.

"It's really not comfortable up here," Maya said. She carefully rearranged herself, so she was sitting cross-legged. It didn't really help.

"Looking good. I'm going to talk you through the meditation. Here's some music to help." Derek pressed a few buttons and a speaker nearby started playing gentle and relaxing tones. Derek's voice started coming over the top. Maya closed her eyes and concentrated on his voice.

Within minutes, she was forgetting about her precarious perch and was more focused on her body, and her seated position. She was becoming more aware of her connection to the earth, the root, and foundation of her energy. As she became more and more comfortable, she noticed a slight breeze.

It's happening. Don't freak out.

Maya tried to tune out the wind and focus on her energy.

On the meditation. She anchored herself to Derek's voice. It worked; her focus shifted away from the minor breeze.

See, you can do this. Ignore what's outside, focus on the inside.

Maya continued deeper into the meditation. She soon became oblivious to the wind. So much so, that she didn't notice as it slowly ramped up in intensity.

Suddenly Maya felt her body being pulled in different directions. Her modest earthen chair was rocking and swaying. It instantly reminded her of the position she was in, and how easy it would be to topple off.

Struggling against the wind, Maya lost her focus.

C'mon. Hold on.

In an instant, it all fell away. Maya opened her eyes just in time to see the world spinning around her. All she could do was try to cushion herself from the fall. And in moments, she felt a crashing thud and then the roar of the wind died away.

"Ow," Maya said and then groaned. She had landed on her right side, and it throbbed. Footsteps rushed over and Derek was there first. He quickly knelt by her and examined her body.

"How are you going? Anything broken?" he said, concern in his voice.

"I don't think so?" Maya said, sitting up slowly and feeling around. Nothing seemed to be broken, just bruised. Anders was there soon, checking on her.

"What happened?" he said to Maya but was also looking over at Derek.

"If I had to hazard a guess, she focused too much on the meditation and lost track of the wind. By the time she realized and tried to adjust, it all fell apart. Am I right?" Derek said. Maya nodded.

"How'd you know?"

"It's what I would have done. Plus, it neatly explained your behavior."

"You couldn't warn her against that?" Anders said, not bothering to censor the annoyed tone.

"It's the best way to learn. I don't think I could have explained it appropriately otherwise." Derek watched Maya, waiting for her to say something.

"I think he's right. I had to feel it. I overdid it, ignoring my surroundings. That will not work." Maya stood and stretched. "I'm fine. It was a bit jarring is all."

"As long as you're alright," Anders said. Maya nodded.

"It was the right thing. Thanks, Derek, let's see how far we can get," Maya said. Derek pumped his fist in the air.

"It's going to work. Let's go back again, and again." Derek ran back over to the controls.

You can do this. It's just persistence. Keep getting back up.

It was a grueling day. Multiple times Anders suggested breaks in different ways. Maya always said no, and Derek was all too happy to keep on.

"She's the best judge, she's built for this," Derek said, for probably the twentieth time. Anders threw his hands up, exasperated.

"Surely it's diminishing returns now," he said.

"Look, she's not toppling off immediately, and we've really cranked up the intensity. It's working. Let it continue to work," Derek said. Their voices were becoming hard to hear. Derek had started the machine, and from up on her perch it suddenly became very noisy.

"Derek," Maya called out. Somehow it cut through the noise enough that he switched off the machine.

"See, I'm paying attention. What is it, Maya?" Derek said, hurrying closer. Anders was close behind.

"I think Anders has a point, I'm tiring," she said.

"See?" Anders said, triumphant.

"Just put it on the max and let's get this done," Maya said. Derek laughed and Anders looked speechless.

"You got it. Let's smash through the wall," Derek said as he jogged back to the controls. Anders rushed back as well, shaking his head in disapproval.

I appreciate you looking out for me, but we need to make this happen. We don't have the time to be careful on this.

Maya took a deep breath and closed her eyes again. The preparation was becoming second nature, almost automatic. She centered herself, focusing her energy on the first Chakra point and the connection with the chair and earth beneath her. She really anchored herself to it, becoming one with the energy, and immersing herself in it.

The wind picked up as before. She devoted part of herself to monitoring it, like a watcher. And another part of herself strengthened and reinforced her connection with the earth to buffer against the increasing wind. The effort was tiring, too tiring. It exhausted her.

It's been such a long day. I can't keep up this effort forever.

But Maya couldn't let herself fall. She refused to.

Just be better. Just make it happen.

In an instant, her thoughts changed. Everything became still and silent. The roar of the wind was far away now. It was just a nuisance. Rather than focusing on her Chakra, her position, the intensity of the wind, and trying to coordinate it all, she just let it be.

I am in the wind and on the earth. I'm balanced and where I need to be.

With that decision made, the effort to maintain it was minimal. She simply existed in the way required. As the wind increased, so did her connection to the ground, and her resistance to being knocked down. The two attributes and opposing forces moved in unison, hand in hand. Eventually, they stopped moving and reached an equilibrium.

Maya enjoyed the stillness. In perfect balance, it felt like she was seated on a wooden floor, in a silent and windless room. Much like the one she had experienced when meeting Song. Maya relished the stillness for a while. But then, she knew it was time. Time to move on.

"We're done here," Maya said and opened her eyes.

7

A WARNING SHOT

Too he wind was still swirling around. Maya almost felt alarmed, but she held on to the feeling of stability she had been cultivating.

They can't hear me over all the noise.

She calmly removed her legs from under her, swiveled, and found some holds to insert her feet into. Carefully she climbed down from her perch like there was no wind at all. Once she reached the bottom, she gave herself a nod of approval and walked forward into the wind.

She could see Derek and Anders standing at the far end, staring at her. She couldn't make out much of anything. But she saw Anders reach over for something, and Derek stopping him.

It's fine, I'll go to them.

Maya walked forward through the raging storm, feeling no resistance. The wind whipped around her but didn't push her back. With each step, she felt her connection to the earth. The strength it lent her. Mountains did not move for the wind. Why should she?

She calmly continued, and once she was right in front of them, Derek finally shut off the machinery.

"Excellent. I think we're done here," Derek said with a massive grin. Maya smiled back.

"I said the same thing, only you couldn't hear me."

"That was something else. How'd you do it?" Anders said. Maya shrugged.

"It was as easy as breathing. Wouldn't you agree, Derek?" Maya winked, and he burst into laughter.

"Nice. I don't want us to get ahead of ourselves, but I'd say you mastered this one." Derek gave Maya a questioning look.

"It feels that way. Let's see how the evidence stacks up." Maya rolled up her sleeve and examined her arm. She noticed a tiny tattoo of a rock with a vine or root growing on it.

"And there it is," Maya said, showing off her arm.

"Nicely done. Masterful display." Derek bowed to her overly elaborately. Maya laughed, delighted.

"I don't know what to say. It's fantastic, I'm shocked," Anders said.

"Surely it's not that much of a surprise?" Maya said.

"No, it's just the way you made it look effortless. I haven't seen it before."

"Chakra done right is like this," Derek said, pointing at Maya. "You need more education on this."

"That's fair. We really don't get enough of the Chakra bloodline causing trouble in New York. Funny hearing me say that out loud," Anders said with a chuckle.

"Would you mind terribly if we continued this somewhere I can eat?" Maya said.

"Of course, let's go celebrate." Derek motioned to the exit and started heading off.

Maya was soon eating her fill of a smorgasbord of street food. They were in the same center as the previous evening, only Derek had bought twice as much. And she was devouring it all.

"Being this awesome is hungry work," Maya said before grabbing another dumpling.

"No complaints here. You did very well today. Though you had an excellent teacher," Derek said.

"I think you may have mentioned that a few times," Anders said dryly.

"Let him enjoy this. It was a brilliant move. Now we can focus on the next Chakra I need to master," Maya said. Anders gave her a slight nod while grabbing a skewer of mystery meat.

"Yes, of course. The next Chakra." Derek paused and took a swig of an unidentified black drink. He wiped his mouth and then continued, "Water, the establishment of the self. Think clarity of thought, loss of fear, and being able to overcome desire." Derek leaned in closer. "Mostly sexual desire."

"OK," Maya said, unconsciously looking over at Anders. Then examining her food.

Idiot. Could you be more obvious?

"Could you explain a bit more about what to work on with this one? Sounds a bit nebulous," Maya said, not moving her gaze away from the dumplings she was eating.

"Hmm, let me continue with the water concept. It's like you're swimming in murky water. There are dark shapes nearby, and they distract you. You see them as either enemies or possibly even objects of desire. It's the whole idea of being lost in your own mess if that makes sense." Derek paused speaking, and Maya assumed he was fetching more food. She looked up again.

"So, we're going to metaphorically clean the water?" she said slowly.

"Yes, when the water is clear, you can see and think with clarity. You see things for what they are. You move past the base instincts of fear and desire to go for what really matters." Derek gave her a kind smile and grabbed a pudding for himself.

"And you've done that. I guess you must have," Maya said, thinking out loud. Derek nodded.

"Yes. Now look, I'm not a monk. I have my lapses; I live in the real world. But I've done the work, I've moved past the blockage. It's transformational." Derek ate his pudding with earnest.

It kind of makes sense, but I just don't see this in him. Not really.

"It doesn't sound like a fighting thing at all," Maya said. Derek pointed at her excitedly.

"Yes! See, everyone thinks the Chakra bloodline is about making yourself into some sort of living weapon. That's not the idea at all. Yes, it's a by-product of the process, and is a useful way of maximizing the utility of the bloodline. But it's not the purpose." Derek was about to continue when he paused. A look of concern suddenly came over him. He whipped out his left hand and caught something out of the air.

"What the?" Maya said, astonished. She hadn't even noticed anything was there, but Derek was now holding a metal dart with a blue and brown tassel hanging off it.

"Where'd that come from?" Anders said, searching the surrounding area.

"Far side of the room, it was an excellent shot." Derek brought the dart closer, examining it. "It's not poisoned. It's the very definition of a warning shot."

"For me?" Maya said, looking over at where Derek had caught the dart and its likely target.

"Definitely. Somebody wants you to know they're watching." Derek deftly pocketed the dart and continued eating his pudding.

"Can you tell who?" Anders pressed. Derek waved him off.

"No idea. It's a very generic item, chosen for this purpose. It could be anyone. Representatives of the school Maya interviewed with, a rival school, someone on the street who doesn't approve of Maya. Maybe even colleagues of those delightful fellows who accosted you the night you arrived." Derek kept eating, scooping out the last few remnants of his pudding.

"I'd forgotten about them," Maya said with a sigh.

"I hadn't. Do we need to worry about this?" Anders said. Derek shook his head.

"Not yet. They're not trying to hurt anyone. Of course, that could change." Derek fished out the dart and tossed it to Anders. He held it up close, feeling the weight, and testing the point.

"It's not heavy enough or sharp enough to do any actual damage. You should hold on to it." Anders carefully handed the dart to Maya. She turned it over once, taking it in, and then pocketed it.

"Can we at least investigate where we think it came from before we leave?" Maya said.

"Sure, at least let me finish another pudding?" Derek was about to start on another.

"Save some for me," Maya said with a laugh.

After dessert, they cleared away the table, and Derek pointed them in the right direction. They walked carefully in as straight a line as possible, weaving through the tables until they reached something significant. Their search ended in a wall.

"There's a notice here," Derek said. He tore it off and started reading it. "Throwing Darts for sale. Only one owner, alumni of the International Chakra School. Greystone Hills." Derek handed the note to Anders.

"That's pretty clear cut. It's from the school, right?" Maya said hesitantly.

"Yes, that's the right school. It seems to be a lead. Whether it's from the school itself, or someone else, I don't know. What's your gut feeling, Anders?" Derek said. Anders smiled.

"You feel it too, don't you?" he said.

"Feel what?" Maya asked, looking from one to the other.

"My gut says don't trust it. Not completely," Anders said with conviction. Derek nodded along.

"We've been in too many dodgy situations and traps. Found too many misleading clues and red herrings. You get a feel for it." Derek chuckled.

"So, what do we do?" Maya said, confused.

"We do what we were doing anyway," Derek said.

"And we focus our search in the Greystone Hills," Anders said, finishing the thought. "Either the school is there, or what they want us to look for."

"I can handle that. So, speaking of which? Have you dreamt up a new crazy training method yet?" Maya said to Derek.

"It's not fully formed, but the ideas are there. Let me work on it, and I'll call you in the morning." Derek was about to head off when he stopped. "Do you want an escort back?"

"I think we're fine. Maya?" Anders asked.

"We're fine for now. Get to work," Maya said, pretending to cuff Derek on the back of the head. He pretended to get whacked and darted away.

"Yes, boss!" Derek laughed and disappeared into the crowd.

"He's quite the character. And yet, he's still super skilled. He makes you forget," Maya said.

"Oh yes, I think he downplays his abilities. I'm definitely intrigued to see what he comes up with for your next training."

"Do we need to make any additional preparations?" Maya asked as they caught the lift down to the ground floor.

"I think it's time we organized our own transportation. I don't want to be relying on others any longer," Anders said. Maya stepped back and laughed.

"You've been waiting for an opportunity to score some wheels, haven't you?" she said. Anders feigned innocence.

"What me? Never. But for your safety, I feel like I need to drive you around."

"Fine. Knock yourself out," Maya said with a chuckle.
I bet he's already planned out what he's going to get.

The next morning Anders rushed through a light breakfast and dragged Maya outside. Once they reached the lobby of their accommodation, he suddenly stopped and turned to Maya.

"Now, I want you to close your eyes and I'll take you outside," Anders said.

"Am I going to regret giving you access to my fortune?" Maya said in a joking tone.

"No, I don't believe so. Now hold my arm and keep those eyes closed." Maya reached out and felt Anders' arm and clung to it like she needed support.

"Oh, you kind soul," she said, making her voice sound older. Anders chuckled.

"Mind the step," he said. Maya purposefully didn't adjust for it and stumbled. Anders caught her in his arms, holding her for a few moments before easing her back up.

"Did you do that on purpose?" he breathed.

"What step?" Maya said, moving her head from side to side, pretending to look for something.

"Come this way," Anders said, gently guiding her through the car park. Soon enough he stopped and spoke up.

"Now, before you open your eyes, I got a tremendous deal..." Anders began.

It's more fun if I look now.

"Oh, she's beautiful," Maya said, taking in the sleek red sports car. It had only two doors and made her think of a spy's car.

"Do I own this?" she said to Anders.

"Yes, technically," he said.

"Good enough for me. You going to take us for a spin?" Maya said.

"Of course. We have somewhere to be as well. Derek has something to test out."

"Let's not keep him waiting then." Maya smiled and then jumped into the passenger seat.

This should be interesting.

8

FOG OF CONFUSION

Anders sped through the streets at a ridiculous speed, rivaling Derek.

To his credit, he's being very precise with his control.

Maya tried to relax and enjoy the ride. The sensation of speed was wonderful, but it was hard relaxing when they were constantly close to disaster.

The car came to a gliding stop, and Anders finally released the wheel.

"That was amazing. What did you think?" Anders said.

Hair-raising and not in a good way. But a lovely car.

"Pretty fun. Makes me want to take it for a drive myself," Maya said with a smile. Anders grinned back.

"I suppose we can schedule something. Let's go see what Derek has cooked up." Anders exited the vehicle and waited for Maya before locking the car.

They were parked outside a business park. There were multiple factory units inside, each aligned in a row like boxes.

"Derek is meeting us at the last one, number fourteen," Anders explained.

"He seemed pretty excited last night, I'm really curious about what he's set up," Maya said.

"I think he's exploring his creativity in ways he never imagined," Anders said with a chuckle.

"That's for sure." Maya spotted the unit and pointed it out. They altered their path through the units to take a more direct route.

Anders tried the glass door, and it opened the first time. They walked through a completely empty opening space and continued into the factory proper. As Anders pushed the doors open, smoke gushed out.

"This is interesting," he said as they stepped inside. The whole space was filled with an acrid smoke.

"It's not a fire. It smells like it's from a smoke machine," Maya said.

"Can't say I've smelled that before," Anders said.

"Really? You've never been at a school play?" Maya said, then stopped herself. "Hang on, maybe you haven't."

"Correct. School as you know it ended twenty years ago. What we got back, didn't have plays. For those who could attend," Anders said.

"I'm sorry. Let's find Derek," Maya said, eager to move on.

Way to put your foot in it. At least you didn't suggest that maybe his brother had done a school play.

They walked through the dimly lit space, seeing nothing else except the smoke. A dark shape started moving toward them. It was coming faster and faster. Maya instinctively stood in front of Anders, readying her stance to engage the enemy. As it emerged from the shadowy smoke, Maya was about to strike when she noticed something odd.

"It's a cutout of a person," Maya said, confused. The shape stopped right in front of them. Now that it was motionless, it was easy to see.

"I wonder what it's attached to?" Anders said, moving

closer. "Oh, and thanks for the rescue."

"Well, you're like my squire, right? They were the knight's assistants. When danger comes knocking, it's my job as a knight to step up and do my job," Maya said with a cheeky grin.

"Oh, you're my knight in shining armor. Classy," he said with a chuckle. But his heart wasn't really in it.

He looks a bit hurt. Maybe I overdid it a bit. Don't remind him you saved him from that Degeneration Field.

"Just having some fun. You've saved me before already," Maya said.

"And I'm saving you, now. From yourself," Derek said from the shadows. He was laughing and slapped the enemy cutout on the back.

"I see you've met my good friend, here," Derek said.

"Oh, we have. You're lucky the knight here didn't vanquish it already," Anders said.

"I have others. It's part of the training today." Derek threw his arm in a sweeping motion to take in the rest of the factory. But there was nothing to see except smoke.

"There's more tucked back there?" Anders said.

"Yes, lots more. I don't want to ruin the surprise. But the premise is simple. We're going to do a meditation and create some challenging scenarios to help you reinforce the learning required to open the next Chakra." Derek was grinning from ear to ear.

"How do I help?" Anders said.

"Oh, you've already helped," Derek said with a wink.

"I'm not sure I like the sound of that," Anders said. Derek laughed.

"Don't worry. But I have a more important job for you. While I'm running this, I could use your help running down that lead we discussed." Derek's face took on a more serious tone.

"Yeah, I'm on it. Good luck, Maya," Anders said and waved

to them both.

"Thanks, good luck to you too. And bring the car back in one piece?" Maya said. Anders grinned back.

"No promises, but I'll see what this squire can do." Anders winked and disappeared into the smoke.

"We each play our part. Follow me into the center," Derek said and headed off. Maya swiftly followed close behind, knowing that she'd quickly lose him in the smoke.

"I'll be sitting near you to begin with, but then I must go run the training. But I've rigged up speakers around the place to keep my voice close to you."

"Pretty elaborate setup. How'd you have time to do this?"

"I didn't sleep last night. Plus, I have some good contacts."

"But, I mean, you can't possibly build all this. That enemy cutout moved fast and straight, for example."

"Oh, that was easy. I repurposed a shooting range target mechanism. Anyway, I need to stop myself there. I'll chatter the entire day away, talking about the cool things we put in here. Let's sit down and get started." Derek sat cross-legged, and Maya sat opposite him. The concrete floor was cold, but after the initial shock she could ignore it.

"I'm going to take you through the meditation. There's not much for you to remember. The key thing is to focus on is a sense of clarity and purpose, and yourself. And of course, channel that through the Chakra point as well."

"And that is?"

"Higher than last time. It's centered around your...reproductive organs," Derek said delicately.

"Really?"

"Yes. Don't worry, this isn't some strange, perverted ritual. It's an energy center and you need to learn how to harness it correctly. This center can also be blocked with the feeling of guilt, if that makes sense," Derek explained.

"Hmm, yes, I can see how that works."

Guilt, regret, and sexy times. They too often go hand in hand. Now I know why.

"Some of this is just going to make more sense as an experience. My advice for now, is to focus on acknowledging your feelings, and yourself. And to see things for what they are, not what your impulses and desires may suggest they are." Derek closed his eyes and started chanting. Maya closed hers as well.

Here we go.

Derek's voice droned on, the words soon becoming lost. Maya felt her focus turning inwards, toward the energy center he had mentioned. Initially, she felt something, potentially the wrong thing. But stopped herself from judging.

Just stay present in this.

Maya continued in that state, focusing on her presence, and trying to connect. After what felt like a while, Derek's voice broke the trance.

"You can open your eyes but keep the state going."

Maya opened her eyes. The smoke was even thicker now. She may as well have had her eyes closed.

I can't see a thing. I guess that's the idea.

She felt a rush of wind and noticed a dark shape fly past her. Her initial instinct was fear, and her adrenaline kicked in. Maya became instantly alert, pulling her out of the meditation. She sighed and tried to calm her mind again. It was a struggle, but things settled again.

"Open your eyes," Derek said from somewhere. Maya opened her eyes again. This time she saw nothing, she just heard the whooshing sounds that showed that objects were flying nearby. She felt the breeze of something passing very close, and she instinctively turned to look. Because she moved, the dark object almost smashed her in the face, and Maya's heart rate doubled instantly.

This isn't working so well.

"Try again," Derek said. He resumed the guided meditation,

and Maya closed her eyes, attempting to reset. She relaxed, and the recent events faded away. She felt whole and focused once more.

What's that smell?

She picked up something different in the air. Maybe it had been there for a while, but she hadn't noticed previously. No matter how much she tried, she couldn't really put her finger on it.

Nothing is happening, so it must be nothing.

Within a few minutes, the smell either went away, or she stopped noticing.

I'm glad he's giving me a break. Now I can handle whatever the next thing is.

Maya heard what sounded like footsteps. Without raising her alarm, she carefully listened for where they might be coming from.

Hard to pinpoint but getting closer.

"Maya, I came back for you," Anders said. His voice sounded so smooth and exciting. "I couldn't stay away."

Maya heard the voice behind her. She could feel a hot breath on the back of her neck. A wave of heat rushed through her body.

What's going on?

Maya turned, against her better judgment, to look at him. The urge was too powerful. Once she could see behind her, there was nothing there.

"Try again," Derek said. And then the realization hit home.

It's another test. And I failed. This is impossible. I can't control this!

"Focus and try again. If you're trying to ascend the mountain faster, it's going to be more difficult," Derek said, like he could sense her frustration.

"I made a mistake. He is a monk," Maya whispered to herself.

"I heard that," Derek said, before continuing the meditation.

Anders sped through the streets, enjoying the freedom of just driving. Unfortunately, the journey just didn't last long enough. With a sigh, he parked the car and stepped out.

Last stop.

The lead had been a merry scavenger hunt through the Greystone Hills. Whoever had set it up had meant for them to succeed, provided they had the right determination. Luckily, Anders could have solved these clues in his sleep.

Now, what do we have here?

Anders scanned the area, taking it in. He stood before what seemed like a deserted alley. A single piece of rogue packaging blew along the street, rustling on the ground.

After looking up and down the walls, examining the map on his phone, and listening out for any signs of life, Anders finally decided it was safe to walk down.

Don't get surprised. Always be prepared.

Anders continued to repeat the mantra. He noticed nothing suspicious about the alley, and it looked like a dead end.

It will be awkward if I get trapped in here.

Anders turned, looking for any signs of a trap. A few people walked past the alley entrance, but none lurked. He bent down to inspect his shoe, placing a device on the ground at the same time. As he stood up again, he noticed a tall man standing in front of him.

That was curiously fast.

The man was wearing casual pants and a button-up shirt and looked around the same age as Anders.

"You are not the one which seeks training," the man said. Anders nodded.

"We're multitasking. She's trying to be more worthy, and I'm following the breadcrumbs."

"This is not usually the way," the man said, his gaze fixed on Anders.

"She's not your usual person, either."

"I hope for her sake that you are not." The man stepped forward, imposing his presence on Anders.

"I'm not looking for trouble, just following the trail," Anders said.

"You need to overcome trouble to find which you seek," the man said. The glimmer of a smile was in the man's eyes as he cracked his neck.

"So be it." Anders took another step back. He clicked a button in his pocket, activating the device on the ground.

Bzzt

The man stepped on it and looked down in surprise.

"Parlor tricks," he said. He tried to move forward but was stopped. His foot stuck.

"Not just tricks," Anders said. He withdrew a stun wand and jammed it into the man's leg. The shock looked like it did nothing.

"Now that is a toy," he said with a chuckle. Anders nodded and repeated the action, using the second charge. The man's leg locked up completely, and a look of surprise went over his face.

"Still a toy?" Anders said. The man reached out a hand, and Anders expected the motion, fishing out another device in the same motion. The man grabbed Anders and hauled him off his feet, but Anders could still use the device.

"What's your next trinket?" the man said, holding Anders up by his shirt.

"Just your run-of-the-mill Bloodline Sensor," Anders said. The man raised one eyebrow.

"What's the point of that?" he said.

"Oh, well, I know they're not so popular around here. But

they have this handy ability of showing whether you have other bloodlines that aren't activated. Now let me see here," Anders said, glancing at the device.

The man snatched it immediately, holding it in both his hands and studying it. Anders used that opportunity to pull out his Bloodcuffs and slap them on the man. By holding the bloodline sensor, he had unwittingly placed his wrists close together and right in front of Anders.

The man grew livid instantly and hurled the device to the ground. Anders dove to catch it, narrowly saving the device.

"Someone needs to invent a more rugged version of this," he muttered. In moments, the man dropped into a seated position on the floor.

"I see you've tricked me. Not an honorable move," the man said.

"You have a name?" Anders countered.

"Sam."

"Well, Sam, I don't have the same power as you. I need to improvise." Anders stepped back and examined the device.

"Well, well, well. I see now why the bluff worked so well." Anders glanced over at Sam. He looked slightly annoyed, but Anders could tell there was more to it.

"I'll say it. You've got the Haste bloodline as well. But you knew that, didn't you?" Anders said with a grin. Sam glared at the ground.

"I'm not here to cause you any trouble. How about we just complete this transaction and go our separate ways?" Anders pocketed the device and waited to see Sam's reaction.

"Fine. I'll agree that you fulfilled the challenge. Bring the note attached to the back of the alley and I'll give you the code for deciphering it." Sam sounded defeated.

"Perk up, your day is about to get a lot better," Anders said. He rushed over to grab the note.

Still got it. Even though it was a lot of luck.

9

THE FINAL WAVE

Maya lay back on the ground, groaning.

I'm never going to get past this.

The last few days were slow progress. She felt like she was getting a better handle on things and going deeper into the meditation. But as Derek kept explaining, it was going to be slow gains until big breakthroughs.

Anders walked over, for real this time. It was strange seeing him now.

Is the trial messing with my emotions, or is it surfacing them?

"You look done for the day," Anders said with a smile.

"Totally and completely. There's always tomorrow," Maya said.

"There's only tomorrow," Derek said, walking over. Maya sat up suddenly.

"What do you mean?"

"You need the breakthrough tomorrow, otherwise we're out of luck. You can't sit the exam at the temple any later than two days from now." Derek looked over at Anders.

"I told you, I got the location. I'm confident."

"Even though all the online research and maps show nothing?" Derek said.

"Yes! You yourself said it, they pride themselves on secrecy. And you also said we can't verify in person until the day of the trial," Anders said, frustrated.

"As long as you're sure. We don't have any room for error." Derek gazed at Maya with concern. "I have another idea. If you don't mind, I'll skip dinner with you tonight and prepare."

"Anything that can improve our chances, I don't see how I'm going to get there otherwise." Maya glanced over at Anders.

"No problems here. If it truly is the last day tomorrow, then now's the time to try. There won't be another chance." Anders extended a hand and helped Maya up.

She felt a jolt of energy flow through as their hands touched.

Now is not the time for that.

"Rest well, Maya, I'll call you tomorrow," Derek said as he walked away.

"Thanks, and good luck," Maya called out after him. Once he was gone, she turned to Anders.

"He's really going all out. Is this too much disruption for his business?"

"Don't worry, we're funding it all. And giving him a consulting fee. It's all above board." Anders turned and started searching for the way out.

"It's this way, let's go," Maya said. She grabbed his hand and guided him through the smoke. She was a bit rough, hoping to avoid any uncomfortable moments. Once they reached the edge of the space, Anders freed his hand.

"Wow, you really can find your way through this," he said.

"I'm glad I achieved something these last few days." Maya sighed.

"It seemed pretty intense. And a bit out of left field. I stumbled upon...me?" Anders said. Maya felt herself turning red.

"Well, apparently Derek had some technical wizardry at his

disposal." Maya suddenly stopped talking and stared at Anders. "You didn't record those lines yourself, did you?"

"Haha, no," Anders said with a laugh. "I promise. Why'd he pick me?"

"Who knows? I guess he needed someone we both knew?" Maya turned and shoved open the doors, stepping into the relatively fresh air of the entry area. Anders was a bit slower at coming out.

"Let's go grab some dinner. I'll surprise you," Anders said.

"Great, thank you. I really don't have the energy to think right now," Maya said. She followed him out to the car like she was on autopilot.

I could sleep right here.

As Maya finished her morning coffee, she noticed Anders reaching for his phone.

"It's Derek," he said, stepping away from the table. For the first time, they had tried the hotel restaurant. The fake natural light and surroundings made it feel like it was dawn. Nobody else was dining with them. The server had mentioned that most of the guests preferred their privacy.

Suits me. I can have my privacy out here instead. It really is beautiful; I keep forgetting that I'm underground.

Anders walked back and leaned over, gulping down the rest of his coffee.

"He's ready, the sooner we get you there, the better." Anders grabbed his things and quickly stood up again.

"I'm ready." Maya rose from the table and quickly glanced over to see if she had left anything. By the time she looked up, Anders was already moving.

"You sure aren't mucking around. Where are we going?" she asked.

"I can't tell you. I don't even really understand it myself." Anders spoke quickly without turning around. He punched the lift button and tapped his foot impatiently.

"Is it that bad?" Maya said.

"There's a time limit. We can't use it all day, so every second counts." Anders stepped into the lift and soon it was speeding them up to the street level.

"It's a good excuse for you to set some land speed records in the car," Maya joked. But Anders looked somewhere else.

I'll leave him to it.

The car trip was as exhilarating and terrifying as Maya expected. Anders drove very well, only he pushed every single rule there was and narrowly avoided multiple incidents. Finally, he parked, and the tension drained out of him. He relaxed back into the seat.

"We're here," Anders said with a smile.

"I can see that. Just not sure where here actually is." Maya stepped out of the car and looked up.

"A water park?" she said, scrunching up her forehead.

"Not just any park, it's something else. Let's get you inside." Anders led the way, walking confidently through the entry gate and through a special side passage. They strode down a plain hallway, down some stairs, and then through a few sets of doors into a different facility.

"Wow," Maya said as soon as they stepped inside. They were inside a cavernous space with what looked like a giant swimming pool inside.

"It seems more like a beach?" Maya said, thinking out loud.

"It's a man-made beach with realistic waves," Anders said. He pointed out something at the far end of the room. "There's Derek."

"He'll have some answers," Maya said, and together they headed over immediately. Derek watched their approach and checked his phone nervously multiple times.

"Good, you're here. We don't have any time to spare. Are you ready?" Derek said to Maya. He looked like he hadn't slept, and his right eye twitched a few times.

"Ready for what?" Maya said.

"Your training. I've secured a mechanical wave pool and done some adjustments. But the clock is ticking. There's a window we have, before I have to stop and let them return it back to normal in time for tomorrow's sessions," Derek said.

"How long have we got?" Anders said.

"Just over six hours," Derek answered Anders and turned directly to Maya. "Basic principles are the same, I think you've got the foundation. And you have the power reserve. The whole idea is to kick it up a notch. You're going to stand in the middle." Derek pointed to a spot in the middle of the wave pool area.

"Sure. I'll head down. Shouldn't I change?" she said. Derek shook his head.

"No. Your clothes will be fine, but it's imperative you make no adjustments to your clothing during the trial."

"No worries. I'll see you down there." Maya started off, but Derek grabbed her arm.

"Wait and watch." Derek pulled out a remote control and hit a few buttons. The water drained away, and Maya could now see the fake sand underneath. The water came back, but it was different. Following the initial surge was a wave. Then a bigger one. Then a wave that almost reached the top of the enclosure.

"That has to be four meters high!" Maya said with a gasp.

"Yes, it is. Do you understand now?" Derek said.

"Yeah, I understand that you'll drown me," Maya said.

"You won't drown. Probably. Trust me," Derek said. He softened the intense stare slightly and attempted a smile.

"I'll try."

"Do or do not. There is no try," Anders said with a grin. Maya looked back at him sharply.

"Have you watched Star Wars?" she asked. He nodded.

"Yes, actually. My older brother was into science fiction, and I hunted down some old movies. I figured you'd get the reference."

"They were a bit of a guilty pleasure. Not exactly what my father wanted me studying," Maya said with a chuckle. "Thanks for reminding me a bit of home."

"Anytime." Anders flashed her a big grin. She waved to them both and started off toward the stairs.

This is crazy. So crazy that it might just work.

Maya took care on the way down and waded through the water once she reached the bottom.

This is going to ruin everything.

"I'm starting it up!" Derek yelled out from above. Maya nodded and peered into the distance.

There's the first wave.

It didn't look too big but was noticeable even from this distance.

What am I supposed to do? I'll just get accustomed to the first few before trying anything else.

The wave rippled toward her. Maya jumped enough to crest the wave and not have it crash over her. She continued that for the next few as well.

I can't train like this!

The next wave was even bigger. She tried to rise through the water but failed. The top of the wave crashed over her. Coughing and spluttering, Maya resurfaced after narrowly avoiding being completely dumped into the sand below.

That was a failure.

Looking ahead, she saw an even bigger wave.

I must try going under them.

Maya let the wave approach and waited for the right moment. As it curled and crashed, she dove under the water and passed through it. With great relief she emerged from the water and saw the wave continuing past her to the back of the area.

That went better. But this isn't a surfing lesson. How do I open the Chakra? There's no special chair this time.

The thought of the chair took her mind back to the previous training, where she had the breakthrough. The challenge had forced her to connect with the earth and meditate with the right balance of inner focus and external sensitivity.

I need to somehow tie that in with all the training we did in the smoky warehouse.

She spotted the next set of waves and gasped. Two gigantic waves, right after each other.

I don't think I can easily dodge these. If I dive and come up, I may come up smack into the middle of the next wave. Maybe there's another way.

Maya closed her eyes and centered herself. She focused on the meditation she had used to open the first Chakra. Just before the waves hit, she latched on to the power, feeling its strength bolster her resilience.

Break over me, waves.

Maya stood resolute, aware of the water, but strong in her connection to the earth, her stability, and foundations. The water crashed over her. The first wave smashed down hard, and then the second. There was a moment of panic, but she let it pass. She was confident in her own strength and resilience. The water subsided, and she opened her eyes. She had withstood the waves.

Yes. Now we're talking. Now to move past the next Chakra.

It was fine to show the first breakthrough. Now she needed to achieve the second one. Another wave crashed over her, and Maya held steady.

I can do this.

She felt more centered and calmer. Looking up, Maya noticed the waves coming closer together. Much closer together. Something was different this time. They were joining and merging into much bigger waves. But it wasn't one giant wave. It was an entire sequence, as far as Maya could see.

Oh no. I can't do this.

There was nowhere to run, nowhere to duck away to. The first one hit, the power and ferocity much more than Maya expected. Even with her increased resilience, it knocked the wind out of her, and she gasped for air too early, swallowing a bit of water. Panic set in just as the next one crashed over her.

I can't do it.

Coughing and spluttering, Maya slowly opened one eye.

There's at least two more. They're monstrous.

Her legs trembled and threatened to fall over. The next wave crashed, and Maya fell. She was dumped and dragged along the bottom of the pool. A world of thrashing blackness pulled her in every direction. All the while, she knew that while she may drag herself up from this one, there was one or more waiting to crash over her again.

Can I stand again? It's too much. Maybe you deserve this. You shouldn't have survived for this long. Look at this world you created. Look at Eric, he had to die for you.

Her heart sank, and she lay back, defeated. The guilt. The pain. The strain of the last few days. It was too much for one person. Too much to grasp. And she let go. She let go of the fear of the water, the fear that Anders would never see her as something more. The fear that she had alienated him forever because of the fate of his brother.

Isn't my body mostly water? Let it come. What more can be done to me?

A new energy rose within her. She pulled herself up through the water, standing tall and firm. Her strength returned, and the water lost its dark and foreboding nature. She could look through it, like it was glass.

You're not here to attack me or ruin me. You're part of me.

10

THE DRAGON'S BACK

Maya wrapped her towel tighter. The air was cooling fast, and she felt a chill run down her legs.

"Nice work out there. I was thinking my plan wouldn't work," Derek said. He let go of the grin and gave her a respectful nod.

"Thanks. I thought it was all over, myself. But I guess you knew that would happen."

"There was a good chance you'd come through. But no guarantees. Of course, I wouldn't have let anything permanent happen to you." Derek's expression was more serious.

"I know," Maya said. She glanced over at Anders. He still seemed in shock.

"I think it's customary to say congratulations," Derek said, nudging Anders playfully in the shoulder. He seemed to get roused out of wherever his mind was.

"Congratulations, Maya. It was an amazing feat out there. I'm sorry, I was really worried for you out there. It was terrible to watch," Anders said. Derek slapped him on the back.

"Don't worry, my friend, it means you're human. It's a good thing."

"Thank you," Maya said, giving him a warm smile.

He cares about me.

"I'll call them in to fix all this stuff. How about you go get changed and we can go eat," Derek said. He was already pulling out his phone and examining it.

"Absolutely. Give me a few minutes," Maya said. She gave them an exhausted smile and rushed over to the changing area.

They all met back outside the building. Maya felt a lot more comfortable in some dry clothes, and Anders was carrying her bag of wet clothes.

He seems more relaxed now. That's good.

"Celebration time. What are you keen for?" Derek said. He looked relieved as well.

"To be honest, dessert. Lots and lots of dessert," Maya said with a laugh.

"We have you so covered. Let's start with pineapple bread and egg tarts and go from there." Derek looked quite excited by the idea.

"I'm in. Lead the way," Anders said with a grin.

"Thanks. I think I've earned it." Maya rolled down her sleeve and flashed her arm. Derek nodded and Anders leaned it to inspect it.

"And there's the fresh addition. A tiny water droplet. Nice one," Anders said with a smile.

"Let's get to eating, then?" Maya looked at them both, and Anders started heading to the car.

"Better not keep the lady waiting," Anders said with a chuckle and opened the car door for her.

"Follow me, yeah?" Derek said as he stepped into his car.

"I'm sure it will be harder than it sounds," Maya said with a grin. Anders winked at her.

"We'll manage."

Derek sped away, and Anders leapt to the challenge. The two cars screamed through the streets, dodging between vehicles, and careening around corners. They wove through the city, finally, they stopped in a quiet neighborhood at the city limits. Derek parked and stepped out of the vehicle, and they followed suit.

"What is this place?" Maya said.

"It's a bakery. But it's amazing. Trust me," Derek said with a massive grin.

"You've done well so far, I'm ready to be wowed." Maya quickened her steps to catch up to him.

The meal was as good as promised. There were a few savory treats to mix things up, but true to form it was dessert after dessert. At the end, Derek leaned back in his white plastic chair and closed his eyes.

"Good call, Maya. That was so satisfying." Derek looked ready to fall asleep.

"I honestly can't say I've had a meal like that. Thanks for the suggestion." Anders grinned, but he also looked quite lethargic.

"Happy to be the one to give you all the excuse. Now that you're about to enter a food coma, any last words of wisdom, Derek?" Maya said. He laughed deeply and opened his eyes.

"You know just the right time to ask. You're ready. Just arrive tomorrow and follow their instructions." Derek paused, then added, "during the daylight, obviously."

"I'm on it, don't worry," Anders said, giving Derek a thumbs up.

"Good. Now I can rest properly and wait for the good news." Derek settled into the chair like he was trying to sleep.

"That looks like a plan. I need to go crash," Maya said.

"That can be arranged. Let's go." Anders stood with a little difficulty and extended Maya a hand.

"Enjoyed those sweets a little much?" Maya joked, ignoring the feeling of their hands touching. Anders chuckled.

"I sure did. Let's get you that beauty sleep." Anders smiled.

"Are you saying I need it?" Maya said, a dangerous look on her face.

"No, no. It's just a saying?" Anders said nervously. Maya laughed.

"Just joking around, I couldn't help myself. C'mon."

The next morning, Maya awoke to a note on the coffee table. She picked it up and read it out loud.

"Breakfast is awaiting you downstairs." Maya put the note down.

I better not keep breakfast waiting.

Maya gave a tiny chuckle at her poor joke and readied herself quickly. She purposefully focused on that, and not what she had to do today. She found breakfast, and Anders, downstairs as promised.

"Good morning. I'm glad you caught the sunrise," Anders said. He pointed to the simulated light behind them.

"Good morning. It was so thoughtful of them to keep it going so long," Maya said as she sat down.

"I think you're pretty much on time, anyway. How are you feeling about today?" Anders said.

"Not thinking about it. Well, until we get there." Maya started eyeing the spread on the table. She grabbed a croissant and started buttering it.

"Right. Well, enough about that. Coffee is still hot." Anders demonstrated by taking a small sip from his steaming cup.

"Great." Maya took a tentative sip and then continued preparing her breakfast.

"Is there anything you need to do before we go?" Anders said, eyeing her carefully while he drank his coffee.

"No, I don't think so. After we're ready, we can head out." Maya spoke slowly with a calm voice.

I just need to keep this energy going. If I can keep it together, things will go smoothly.

"Right, well that's settled." Anders looked a little awkward but buried his face in his coffee cup.

"I'm sorry, I'm not the best company right now. My entire focus is being composed for the test," Maya said, flashing him a tiny smile. Anders nodded and returned the smile.

Breakfast carried on in the same fashion, and Anders seemed incredibly relieved when they left for the car. He even drove like a normal person which was a bit jarring.

Maybe I should just ask him to drive like he normally does?

But Maya appreciated the effort he had made, so she let her mind wander as the city unfolded before her.

It became apparent that there were heading east, and eventually, Maya spotted large swatches of greenery.

"Are we almost there?" she said.

"Yes. Very close now." Anders made a turn, and they continued down another road, this one even closer to what looked like a heavily forested mountain ridge. She could see some buildings coming up, and Anders turned into a windy driveway and continued up. A large gate rose before them with a checkpoint and a guard sitting inside. Anders stopped the car outside and opened the window.

"Hi..." Anders began, but the guard waved him on without even looking. The gates slowly swung inwards.

"Thanks," Anders said. He slowly drove up the driveway, following a sign to park the car in a marked bay off the side. An overweight man was waiting nearby patiently. He approached the car.

"The applicant must ascend the Dragon's Back. You, sir, can wait here." The man bowed and then waited.

"I suppose this is it," Anders said, turning to Maya. "Good

luck. See you on the other side." Anders gave her a confident smile and Maya returned it.

"Thanks," she said and left the car. As she walked around to meet the man, he started walking ahead. They continued past the cluster of buildings until they reached the beginning of a path.

"This is the trail. Complete your ascent and undertake your evaluation." The man bowed again and started back.

"Thank you," Maya said, watching him leave. She turned and gazed up at the ridge ahead.

Here we go.

Maya walked, relishing the break from the city. But within a minute the path stopped, and she was confronted with a thick wood.

It can't be easy, can it?

Maya left the path, picking a way through the dense trees. At each dead end, she had to pick a way and push on. The ascent began rapidly, and soon enough she had to pause and catch her breath.

Funny how I can still tire easily when I push myself hard in a way I haven't trained.

Maya recovered quickly and pushed onward. While she wasn't making efficient progress, she was confident she was going in a consistent direction.

Finally, she saw something beyond the next trees. Maya rushed over, eager for something to break up the rather tricky hike.

It's a path. A real path.

There was a proper clearing and a well-traveled dirt path. Maya ran over, realizing just how in the open she was.

Left, or right?

Maya looked in both directions and headed right. It was much easier walking along the trail, and she was getting an amazing view of the ocean. The ground undulated up and down, and it reminded her of the name.

Dragon's back indeed.

Just as Maya was getting into the walk and enjoying the scenery, she noticed a figure standing in the distance. Curious, she kept approaching.

I recognize her.

The woman standing there was Song, wearing the same outfit as before.

"The applicant approaches, please sit." Song gestured at the ground and sat cross-legged. Maya approached and sat opposite her.

"Are you ready for your test?" she said, looking Maya in the eyes.

"Yes. What do you need?"

"First, I will see you." Song closed her eyes and started chanting. Maya closed her eyes too, readying herself. The words washed over her, and she found herself transported somewhere else.

Maya was seated on a grassy hill with Song close by, the same distance as they had started. Song stood, and a mist rose around her, hanging over both of them. Song seemed to somehow grow taller and towered above her.

"I can see you have opened the first two Chakras. Quite an achievement for a week," Song said.

"Thank you," Maya said simply.

"No, it is not a compliment. I am not congratulating you. This is not the way things are done." Song sounded quite disapproving, and she stressed her words.

"You said it was unusual that I had that much power but had opened no Chakras. Now that I have, you disapprove. Why?" Maya didn't like where this was going.

"I gave you an impossible task, to see how you would respond. To truly see you. And I can see you now. I can see that you'll do whatever it takes to move forward, no matter the method or cost."

"It shows that I'm determined. I faked nothing." Maya pushed her anger down. It would not help her.

"You enlisted the Dishonored one to help you. That was a mistake." Song shook her head and walked away.

"What are you talking about?"

"He thought like you. To find new ways to surpass the trials. He was not as," Song paused, scrunching up her expression is distaste, "successful as you have been. I see that he has refined his methods."

"Who? Derek?"

"That's his name. There's a reason he's a bounty hunter, and nothing else. He has no honor." Song wheeled around quickly and advanced on Maya.

"How about that test?" Maya said, challenging Song with her stare.

"There's no test required. I know all that I need to know."

"I demand a test. It's my right," Maya said, rising to her feet. A sly smile crept onto Song's face.

"Had you passed the criteria I had specified, I would have no choice but to test you. And you likely would have passed. But in this, you have failed too."

"I found the school. I surpassed the Water Chakra. That was the requirement."

"No, you mastered the Water Chakra. Had you surpassed it, you would have mastered the Fire Chakra." Song paused, giving Maya a moment to consider her words.

"An even more impossible task? You set me up!" Maya's anger flared up, and she didn't care.

"You trained under the Dishonored one. You cheated your way through the first two Chakras and did not meet the bar which I set. And you even sent your lackey to get the location of the school." Song stopped talking, looking triumphant. "I will not accept you, and the masters will not accept you."

"You can't stop me. There are other places to learn."

"No school in the International District will take you now. And then there's no path to complete your training. Go now and learn the lesson of humility." Song snapped her fingers, and they were back to their seated positions. Maya stood up swiftly.

"You may think you've achieved something here, but you haven't. I'll find a way." Maya gave Song a final defiant stare and marched back the way she had come.

This is a disaster. Everything I've been preparing for, all in ruins.

11

TRUE ATLANTIS

Maya ran down the ridge, tripping and bumping into trees on the way down. It didn't bother her. The same thoughts kept cycling through her mind.

How dare she? Who gives her the right?

After that experience, she had to move. She had to be in motion. When she did finally reach the tiny path near the school, she stopped and drew in some deep breaths.

I don't want them to see me running.

After composing herself, Maya meandered carefully down the path. She saw Anders standing and leaning against the car. He looked up and noticed her, a smile on his face. He quickly hid it and waited with a concerned look on his face.

"Is everything alright?" he whispered when she was closer.

"Let's go, I'll explain on the way," Maya said. They both entered the car, and Anders started driving immediately. After they were clear of the school and back on a major road, Maya finally spoke.

"It was a trap. They had no intention of allowing me in. The test was a sham, it was too difficult to pass with a method they considered proper. And I didn't even meet the grade. They wanted me to surpass the Water Chakra by opening the Fire Chakra. And not to mention Derek. They called him the Dishonored one and said he had no honor which is why he is a mere bounty hunter. And they said the masters won't accept me. No school here in the International District will accept me. And good luck completing my training that way." Maya stopped and drew in a deep breath. Anders was silent for about a minute.

"That's a lot to take in, I'm so sorry. We'll figure something out."

"It sounds pretty hopeless." Maya sighed. "You're right, I know. We'll figure something out. But, for now, it just seems so far away." Maya stared out the window as they drove.

"We'll meet Derek at the old training area and brief him. He will have some good ideas," Anders said. Maya nodded and said nothing more. She needed time to think everything over.

Derek looked solemn as Maya completed her tale. He leaned back in the rickety chair and scratched his chin.

"I am deeply sorry that my help has hindered your chances," he said at last.

"But without your help, I wouldn't have made it as far as I did," Maya said.

"I really thought I could keep my involvement quiet, to avoid this situation." Derek stared off into the distance.

"What happened? Why are you so dishonored?" Maya asked. She noticed a look of pain cross Derek's face.

"I don't want to open those wounds. Not right now. But essentially, I failed on the Path of the Hopeful. They gave me another chance, and I tried to find a different way. A non-standard way. It didn't go down well, they're quite traditional in that way." Derek looked awkward as he spoke and didn't offer another word.

"I see. Is that for the sixth Chakra?"

"Yes. That test is conducted in the Lost Lands, in a secret location hidden in the mountains."

"Song said I can't get there, now. Since the school won't take me. Why is that?" Maya said.

"To protect the masters and also the secrets of the final trial, all foreigners of the Chakra bloodline are only permitted to cross over into the Lost Lands if they have an official pass from a registered school. None of the schools in the International Quarter will do that for you," Derek said, shaking his head.

"There must be another way," Maya said, looking at Derek. He seemed conflicted.

"Can I just interrupt for a moment," Anders said. Once he had their attention, he continued, "I just want to play this out a little. You've achieved notoriety, a considerable fortune through your tournament win, and the freedom you wanted. Can't you just, I don't know, step back a bit. Enjoy life?" Anders said.

"I thought you supported me in this?" Maya said.

"I do. But the question needs to be asked. What's driving you this hard? There's no danger lurking here. We're not wanted, and nobody has tried anything since that first night. Can't you just work your way through the rest of the Chakras in time, on your own? Or with Derek?" Anders looked at both, trying to gauge their reactions. Derek spoke first.

"In theory, you could eventually get them all. But it would take a very long time. As you've discovered, they are harder and harder to attain as you progress. And I'm not confident you can achieve the sixth one alone. Or, at least, without a significant amount of time. Maybe years?"

"I can see what you're getting at." Maya sighed and then continued, "It's hard to explain. I have this feeling, deep inside, that I can't just rest. I must keep moving forward. There's too much at stake."

"The Master Sage?" Anders said. Derek raised an eyebrow.

"Yes. I'm still so vulnerable now. I can't sit by and try to live a different life. I need to master these powers. I'll spend my life looking over my shoulder otherwise."

"What's going on with the Master Sage?" Derek said evenly. His expression, however, was much more intense.

"He's got a grudge against Maya. Or is it more of an obsession?"

"More of an obsession. It's a long story. Maybe we can trade painful stories one day," Maya said to Derek, smiling and trying to make light of it. "Oh, and don't forget your leg, Anders. I will fix it."

"That's not really the chief concern here. Anyway, I just wanted to understand better. So, I can help you plan the best approach," Anders said. He gave her a hopeful smile. She reached out and held his hand, feeling the warmth. It was encouraging.

"Well, if you're dead set on this. There is another way. Another shot at legitimacy," Derek said, looking up at them.

"What is it?" Maya said.

"If the International Quarter is off limits, we can try somewhere else. True Atlantis." Derek's eyes darted from Maya to Anders. Maya laughed.

"True Atlantis?"

"Yes, True Atlantis. It's where the locals live. They have a different system of schools, probably even better. And they send students to complete their training in the Lost Lands as well."

"Won't we run into the same problem as now?" Anders said. Derek gave him a sly grin.

"Being a foreigner isn't a deal breaker. As for being black-listed in the International Quarter, let's just say there's a certain amount of rivalry between the different locales. Enough to jam the lines of communication on this. What do you think?" Derek said.

"If it's a way forward, I'm game. Maybe we'll have more luck there. Anders?" Maya said, looking at him.

"I've never been, and I've heard they have a good gadget game. I'll go along."

"True Atlantis. Having a good gadget game. It's unbelievable," Maya said, shaking her head.

"It's a new world," Anders said with a shrug.

"I have a request," Derek said, leaning in.

"Of course. What is it?" Maya asked.

"When you get your shot to go to the Lost Lands, I want in. If there's a way."

"Sure. Do you think you'll get another chance?" Maya said.

"I've heard it said that the masters never reject a candidate who is on the Path. If I can find my way there, I can try again." Derek's eyes had an intensity and fervor that Maya hadn't seen yet.

This means so much to him. I must find a way.

"I'll get you there. Even if I have to smuggle you in my suitcase," Maya said with a chuckle. That broke the tension, and Derek laughed a little.

"But maybe that's plan 'C'?" he said.

"Fine. Does that mean you need to come with us?" Maya said.

"Most likely. I'll make a few inquiries." Derek's eyes were gleaming.

"I think that means you're now officially on the team," Anders said with a grin.

"It would seem that way."

"Does anybody in True Atlantis have a grudge against you?" Anders said.

"I don't think so. I grew up in the International Quarter and used their school system. The same lack of communication that will help you, should assist me as well." Derek smiled as he spoke.

"Let Derek and I tee things up. We'll organize it all," Anders said.

"Good. I'm going to figure out how I feel about seeing the real Atlantis," Maya said.

Maya stepped out of the train station into the chill night air.

"Here are we, True Atlantis," she said. Anders nodded and signaled to someone waiting on the curb. A black car pulled up.

"Perfectly on time. As I mentioned before, we need to drive from here to where the school is. They are expecting us, right?" Anders said to Derek.

"They are. I can't guarantee much more than that. I had to be rather circumspect in my inquiries. For obvious reasons." Derek seemed embarrassed and looked away.

"Don't worry, that's all behind us. Here's to the future." Maya strode over to the car. As she neared, the driver opened the rear door and ushered her inside.

"Jin, at your service," the driver said. He was dressed all in black with a black and white hat.

"Thank you, Jin," Maya said as she entered the car. Anders and Derek handled the luggage. Anders sat next to her, and Derek went up to the front.

"There's bottled water in the center console if you're thirsty. The drive will be just over one hour," Jin said.

"Thank you," Maya said, and leaned against the side, staring out the window. The lights and colors of the city reminded her of the International Quarter.

Similar, but different. Let's hope I have more luck here.

The drive went by without incident. They talked little, and Maya was happy with that.

I'm enjoying the quiet. And I don't want to talk too much in front of Jin.

Eventually, they pulled up at a quaint hotel. It looked rustic yet modern with a grand entry.

"The New Atlantis Hotel," Jin announced as he parked the car. He immediately jumped out to assist with the luggage. An older porter slowly made his way over with one of those old-fashioned luggage trollers.

"Time for a new start," Maya said as she exited the vehicle.

"I promise that it'll go better," Anders said.

"Quite an easy thing to promise, isn't it?" Derek said. Anders chuckled.

"Doesn't matter, as long as we get the right outcome." Anders headed into the hotel.

"I've been meaning to ask, how did you get so well off?" Derek asked as they walked into the lobby.

"You mean my income?" Maya said with a laugh. Derek looked sheepish.

"Just curious. Bounty hunting isn't exactly a fountain of money. As Anders would no doubt attest."

"Oh, I know. I won the LifeDeath Academy tournament."

"The tournament? The one that's televised and hotly contested? That showcases the best new talent in the LifeDeath Clan?" Derek said, incredulously.

"Yes, that one." Maya leaned in close. "And I won the last round after they activated my Chakra bloodline."

"I see. I guess that explains how you mastered the first two Chakras in a week." Derek whistled with admiration.

"That's why I need to keep advancing. If I don't, they'll keep messing with me. I just know it."

"Well, we promised you a way forward. And tomorrow morning you'll get it." Derek smiled and nodded.

"Great. And I'll keep my promise too. You'll get another chance."

"I look forward to meeting the masters again. At your side." Derek bowed and Maya returned the bow.

"We all ready?" Anders said, returning from the desk. He held up a few room keys.

"We are now," Maya said.

"Good. Let's head up." Anders led the way to the elevators.

12

THE MODERN TEMPLE

Maya stood at the entrance to the temple. It looked hundreds of years old.

I can't believe they made it look like this. It's incredible.

They had created the temple for the school, rather than compromise an existing structure.

Maya stepped inside the massive entrance and noticed a large group of students all standing in a neat formation inside a central courtyard. Maya paused, watching the scene. One person stood on a stone platform and went through a kata. The entire group followed in perfect unison. Each one wearing the same uniform. A black tunic and black pants with white rope keeping the sleeves tied up.

Maya waited for the kata to finish, and the crowd to disperse. She wandered through the courtyard, looking for where to go. She eventually found her way to a tiny wooden room with a woman standing behind a desk.

"Can I help you?" the woman asked. She looked to be in her fifties with her black hair tied into a bun.

"You speak English?" Maya said, surprised. The woman nodded.

"Of course."

"Sorry, I shouldn't have been so surprised. I'm a new student. Maya Mills." She noticed the woman nod and review something on the desk.

"I have you down as an applicant. You must complete an entrance exam and initiation. Are you prepared?" the woman said, in a kind voice.

"Yes. I am ready now."

"Very well, I'll bring you some new clothes." The woman disappeared through a door cleverly hidden in the woodwork behind her.

Wow, that was surprising.

Maya let her eyes roam around the rest of the room. There were no decorations, and she didn't notice any other weird panels or depressions in the wood. Within a few minutes, the wall opened again, and the woman emerged holding a bundle of clothes.

"These will do." The woman handed them over. "Please find the change rooms off the main courtyard, and once you are changed, wait in the courtyard. Someone will come for you."

"Thank you," Maya said.

"Good luck," the woman said with a smile, and she gestured for Maya to leave the room. Maya nodded and turned to leave. After a short stroll, she found the change rooms. Thankfully, there were rooms for men and women. Inside was more amazing woodwork.

They've really built it like it was an ancient temple, only with clever modern enhancements.

Maya felt more at peace as she changed in the quiet and beautiful space. The wood seemed to convey a sense of time and calmed her mind. She found a set of lockers at the end, and one of them opened with a tiny keypad. It only took a few moments to figure out the mechanism, and she promptly locked her clothes away and left the room.

The courtyard was still empty, so Maya walked over into the center. She thought back to the kata she had watched, and it reminded her of what she had practiced back at the LifeDeath Academy.

That time feels so far away. Not to mention that I'm on the other side of the world now.

Maya didn't notice the man approach her. He turned up at her elbow and waited patiently for her to acknowledge him.

"Maya Mills?" he said. He looked to be her age, but he also seemed wise beyond her years. He had the manner of a kindly grandfather. He was dressed the same as everyone else.

"Yes, that's me."

"My name is Eiji. I will be your evaluator today." Eiji gave her a quick smile and gestured for her to walk with him. Together they crossed the courtyard.

"What's involved?" Maya asked.

"You shall see. A few quick and simple tests to assess your growth and potential. Nothing too harsh," he said. He ushered her through an enormous set of doors, and they continued through a long passageway.

At the end was a plain set of wooden doors. Eiji paused next to them.

"After you," he said. Maya pushed through the doors and entered the room beyond. It reminded her of the wooden room that Song had tested her in initially.

Hopefully, this goes a little better.

Eiji followed her in and padded over to the center of the room.

"Maya, what has been the extent of your experience?" he said.

"I've opened the first two Chakras. And I've also been able

to create a ball of energy and project it outside my body." Maya saw Eiji raise an eyebrow at this, but he said nothing.

"I see. And this energy ball, was it created before or after you made progress on your Chakras?"

"Before," Maya said, getting a sinking feeling in her stomach.

You probably shouldn't have said that. Who knows that he's going to assume now? Don't talk so much!

"Very well. Do you think you could recreate the energy ball now?" Eiji said.

"I haven't tried since I accomplished it. I can try?" Maya said, her voice tinged with doubt. Eiji nodded.

"Please, if I may observe you." Eiji stood still with his hands behind his back. Maya closed her eyes and tried to remember the focus that Anders had given her. The instructions she had memorized. She calmed her mind and retreated inwards. Maya felt the energy, her Life Force. This time it was a bit different. She could feel it swell inside the first Chakra point, and she let it collect there. As her concentration deepened, she felt the energy swell again at the second Chakra point.

How interesting, now that I've opened these up, they're acting like conduits. Will this change the outcome?

Maya continued to let the energy build, and then, like before, she visualized it leaving her body. Forming a ball of glowing and pulsing energy. The feeling became so real that she opened her eyes and saw the ball before her. It was hovering above her palm. It was humming with energy, and she thought she could see flecks of stone and droplets of water within it.

Wow. So, they're not just called that for nothing.

"Thank you. Is that as big as it gets?" Eiji asked. Maya shrugged.

"I think so. I haven't really tried to make it bigger."

"Please, try." Eiji continued to watch her. Maya closed her

eyes again. She tried to not only funnel more energy into the ball but also tried to increase its size.

Not just becoming denser, becoming bigger.

At first nothing happened, but over time her mind slipped into a new state. And what she had been trying to achieve happened all on its own. Startled, Maya opened her eyes again.

The energy ball had doubled in size. The hum was louder now, and the flecks of power were more obvious.

"I think that's probably it," Maya said.

"Thank you. If you don't mind, can you hit me with it?" Eiji said.

"Are you sure?" Maya said.

He can't be serious. I know it's probably small for him, but it's not nothing.

"I am sure. Whenever you are ready." Eiji closed his eyes and stood perfectly still. His hands were still behind his back.

This is what he wants. I need to do something with this ball anyway.

Maya stepped forward and slowly pushed the ball toward Eiji. He didn't react or flinch. Once the ball made contact, it contorted and started flashing brighter. The hum became louder, and the ball shrank.

What's going on?

Maya gave it one last little push and tried to release it. The ball flattened against Eiji, and then suddenly recovered its shape and hurtled back toward Maya. She was too astonished to do anything, and it was so close she had no time to react. The energy slammed into her with a tremendous force, and she felt herself blasted backward.

Maya lay on the ground, dazed. She slowly picked herself up and looked around. Her body ached, but that was it. The rest of the room seemed unchanged, and Eiji stood there, waiting patiently.

"What did you do?" Maya said.

"I merely reflected the energy back at you. Hurt, didn't it?" he said with no emotion. Maya couldn't help wincing as he spoke.

"Yes."

"It's good to understand the impact of what you can do to others. Come closer." Eiji beckoned for her to approach. Maya walked forward cautiously. Once she was close, Eiji reached out a hand. He placed it on her shoulder and closed his eyes again.

"This won't take long," he said. Immediately Maya felt a cold chill run through her body, and she shivered. Eiji removed his hand and put it behind his back again.

"And that is it." Eiji gave her a quick bow.

"That's it? What happened?"

"I've taken stock of your power and progress. You have a lot of raw power, in a strange form. You're new to training, aren't you?"

"Yes. How did you know?"

"The paths and channels that your energy uses to flow through the body. Over time they leave signs, much like a road or path that is well-used in life. Your pathways are new, especially those related to your Chakra points."

"Well, yes, they were a recent breakthrough as well."

I can't hide that from him, he seems to know already.

"I suspect that your next one won't take too long. But you'll struggle after that. Your raw power won't be a shortcut anymore." Eiji stepped around her and started walking to the door. Maya rushed after him.

"Where do we go from here?"

"You can return tomorrow."

"That's great. Thank you for giving me a place at the school," Maya blurted out, wanting to thank Eiji. He shook his head.

"No, I said you can return tomorrow. I do not give a place,

you earn it. Not easily, either." Eiji pushed open the door and kept walking.

"That's it? I just turn up?" Maya said.

"Yes. Easy, isn't it?" Eiji said, a wry smile on his face.

I don't like the sound of that. Not one bit.

Maya headed over to change and neatly folded her new outfit.

They didn't say I should give it back.

The courtyard was deserted once again, and after a last look around Maya left through the main gate. She found Anders outside, lounging next to a sleek black car.

"How'd you go?" he said casually. But Maya noticed the concern on his face.

That's sweet.

"Fairly well. I can come back tomorrow, which feels like a win." Maya flashed a hopeful smile.

"Sounds like a win to me. Let's go give Derek the good news. The poor guy has been a wreck all day," Anders said, unlocking the car.

"Really?" Maya said, surprised.

"No, but he did message me to ask how you were. It's all relative." Anders grinned and started the car. They sped through the streets, stopping at a nearby park. Derek was practicing a kata on the grass, his movements fluid and effortless.

For someone billed as a failure, he sure looks amazing.

"What's the news?" Derek asked as they approached.

"I think it went well. The evaluator had me create a ball of energy and then attack him with it. That was strange."

"Go on. What happened next?" Derek focused intently on Maya.

"He somehow rebounded it, and the blast knocked me down." Maya still felt a bit embarrassed as she retold it.

Knocked down by my power. Doesn't feel right.

"That's a standard lesson. Teaches you about the impact

your power has on others. Don't feel bad," Derek said. "What next?"

That makes me feel a bit better.

"He did some sort of test on me, and said that my strange raw power has helped, but after the next Chakra point it will not." Maya looked to Derek for a comment.

"He's right. You can't ascend further without making big breakthroughs. It won't be as easy as you've had it."

"That was easy?"

"Well, it's all relative. Isn't it?" Derek gave her a wry smile and winked. Maya couldn't help but laugh.

"Can't argue with that."

Things are going to get a lot harder soon. I better prepare myself.

13

FIGHT FIRE WITH FIRE

T he car came to a gradual stop and Maya took in a deep breath. The temple grounds were looming over her, and the morning sun was peeking over the gigantic walls.

"This is you," Anders said with a kind smile.

"This is me. It's my first day, and hopefully not my last."

"You've come this far. I have absolute faith. Go make something happen."

"And what will you get up to?" Maya asked, quickly putting the focus back on Anders.

"A bit of shopping, and a bit of research. There's an entire market of...alternative tech." Anders had a sly smile on his face.

"Alternative?"

"Yeah. Not officially sanctioned by the Master Sage and his minions."

"Aren't you one of those minions?" Maya said with a laugh. Anders looked sheepish.

"Yes, but I have a new employer now. Much better benefits." Anders tapped the steering wheel with appreciation.

"Seeing as there's no money coming in for the foreseeable

future, please don't spend it all at once. I don't want to discover you've purchased a giant robot," Maya said with a sigh. Anders grinned even more.

"If I find one, I can't promise anything."

"Fine. Just make sure it works." Maya opened the car door and stepped out. She felt a bit strange wearing the martial arts outfit, but it didn't make sense to come in her normal clothes and change again.

I need to treat this like it's my new life. Not something I'm trying on.

"Have fun, I'll be back later today," Anders called out from within the car. After Maya waved, he turned around and sped off.

There goes your way out. Better try to make this work.

Maya cautiously walked through the main gate. She noticed the courtyard was full again. Like the day before, there were students practicing a kata and following a single instructor on a raised platform.

This is my chance.

Maya slipped into the back row and started following along. All eyes were on the instructor which helped her feel less self-conscious. After a few minutes, the kata felt more natural, and she got into the groove. Just as she was getting comfortable, it all ended. The students bowed to the instructor who promptly left the courtyard.

The students all dispersed without a word.

"Excuse me," Maya said, but the woman in front of her looked right past Maya.

It's like I'm not even here.

Maya tried to subtly get in the way of another student, to ask for directions. But the man nimbly slipped past without paying her any heed.

"I just need..." Maya said but stopped. The students were flowing past and completely ignoring her.

Great. This is going to be fun.

Maya picked a student at random, a tall slim woman with short blonde hair, and started following her. The student expertly weaved through the other students, moving with purpose. She disappeared through some doors, and Maya rushed to catch up.

Suddenly the students before her all moved at the same time, closing off the path to the door. But the way they did it was astonishing.

It almost looks accidental. Almost.

Maya brushed past two other students and kept going. One stuck out a leg, but Maya noticed at the last second and stepped over it. Right before the doors, she lost her patience and physically shoved one student out of the way. The student did not resist and glided back into position like an inflatable toy that had been momentarily displaced.

The door did not resist as she charged through, and she glimpsed the student she had been following turning a corner at the end of a long corridor.

I'll catch up.

Maya broke into a run, charging down the corridor but trying not to make too much noise. With a little effort, the thumping from her feet on the wood became more muted. She whirled around the corner in time to see the student entering another room. Maya slowed to more of a power walk and strode along, entering the room with confidence.

It was full with rows of students standing in formation. An instructor stood at the front, staring at them.

Strange setup, this one.

The student she had been following was in one row with no sign of her having just arrived.

If it's a class, I'm going to try it.

Maya noticed that the last row was a bit shorter than the

others and found a place on the end. She stood still, like the others. The instructor paced around the room.

He's older than I thought.

Now that he was closer, Maya could see quite a lot of grey hairs. But it added to the rather powerful aura he was displaying. The instructor halted and stared intently at a student. When the student met his gaze, he slowly moved in closer and closer. After a tense thirty seconds, the student gasped and looked away. The instructor shook his head, and the young man left the room immediately.

It's some sort of test or challenge. I think I can handle a man staring at me.

The instructor resumed his meandering walk around the room. It was quite a while before he challenged another student. But like before, it happened very suddenly. He was closer to Maya this time, and she sneaked a better look at his face.

That's an intense stare. I wonder what it's all about.

Thirty seconds passed. The student maintained her composure, looking back at the instructor. He stopped and nodded. The relief on her face, obvious. But within a second the instructor was staring back at her, and she let out a little gasp. Immediately she bowed her head and left.

That was harsh. You really can't let your guard down.

Slowly but surely, the instructor worked his way around the room. And one by one the students eventually cracked and left. But not once did the instructor come near Maya.

Is he avoiding me too? That's most likely.

Before another thought could pass through her head, the instructor's face was inches from hers. The intensity of his gaze surprised her, and she barely held back a reaction. She stared back at him, at first with curiosity, and then with determination.

There was a strange power to his eyes, like they were radiating something. And within a few seconds she understood. It seemed like he was sending Chakra or energy from his eyes. And as she received it, an overwhelming pressure built up. She imagined she was pressed up against a giant rock, and a blazing sun was pressing ever closer, its heat increasing more and more.

Maya felt a bead of sweat well up on her forehead and trickle down her face.

Ignore it. It's all in your head.

Maya could feel her concentration dropping, and her will wavering.

This isn't a fair test. I shouldn't even be here. I'm not prepared for this.

The narrative went on and on. And she almost bought into it. She was about to tell the man off, when a thought struck her and broke through the stream of consciousness.

That's what he wants. That's what they all want. They want you to leave. Are you going to give them the satisfaction?

Maya redoubled her resolve and stood firm.

How do you fight fire? With fire!

She imagined herself to be a blazing sun of her own. Every time they stepped on her, every time they thrust her down into the darkness, she rose again. Stronger, and more determined. A thousand wrongs and injustices lay below the surface, and they could power her will. Her flame would burn stronger because she had endured more.

Try as you will, there's no win to be had here.

Maya projected the thought with her anger. She felt the intense heat withdraw to a safe distance. It was still there, threatening. But the heat was distant.

The instructor moved on like nothing had happened.

Don't lose your focus. Don't celebrate yet.

Maya kept a close eye on the instructor. He ventured close, but never quite came before her again. A few more students left the class, but Maya kept her vigil. The sound of bells rang louder and louder. The instructor finally stopped his rounds and bowed. He remained with his head bowed and his eyes closed. The students all filtered out of the room one by one.

Maya was the last one left. She walked over to the instructor and stood before him. He did not try to acknowledge her at all.

"What was that? What you did?" Maya said, watching the instructor with curiosity. He remained motionless. Maya kept waiting for an answer.

I will not be ignored. They can't lock me out.

"I'm going to stay here until you acknowledge me and my question," Maya said. There was still no response. She planted her feet and stared at him.

I wonder if I can somehow do that thing back at him?

The instructor moved, almost like he could hear her thoughts. He stepped past her and wordlessly crossed the room.

He's not getting away.

Maya followed him closely, leaving the room and keeping pace. The instructor wove through the building, taking corridor after corridor.

Wow, this place is a veritable maze.

He reached stone steps heading down and followed them without hesitation. Maya continued, only a few paces behind. The stairway spiraled down, and there were no torches or other forms of light. The lighting from the space above quickly dwindled until they were walking down in pitch black.

Maya reached out and felt for the wall to give herself some bearings. She paused and listened. The rhythmic steps of the instructor were still echoing through the stairs.

He's still going, so I'm still going.

Maya listened for the cadence of his footsteps and matched them. Within a minute, they were almost walking in perfect timing. He had advanced a bit further because of Maya's pause, but still seemed relatively close. Too late Maya noticed the change from stairs to a path, and she stumbled. But her hand pressed against the wall, and she steadied herself quickly.

I can't risk falling behind.

Maya kept up the same pace but continued to feel along the wall. It was all stone with nothing breaking up the blackness and monotony of the walk. Maya's foot stepped through something, and she dropped to the ground quickly.

What was that?

Cautiously feeling around, Maya realized that there was a stone missing and what felt like a rather sizable gap underneath it. The hole wasn't large enough to fall into, just enough to cause a fall.

Of course, there's traps in this pitch-black passage I've wandered into.

With a sigh, Maya hauled herself back up and took more care with her steps. After a few advances, she realized that there was a pattern to the missing stone. She escalated her speed, not wanting to lose the instructor completely. His footsteps were still audible, but faint.

A single point of light winked in the distance. Maya rushed toward it, not realizing how desperate she was to get back into the light. The missing stones started randomly appearing in new positions, but she didn't care. She just charged forward, altering her stride, or leaning on the wall for support. Finally, she reached the tiny piercing light.

It's coming from behind whatever this is.

Maya felt the stone before her, closing her eyes and trying to picture what it was.

It's a door. The light is behind the door.

Maya found a seam and pressed against it. The stone moved.

14

SEEKING TRAINING

Maya was assaulted by light and heat in all directions. She couldn't open her eyes. The sudden brightness was too intense.

"Open your eyes if you seek an audience," a voice boomed from somewhere nearby. Maya slowly forced her eyes open. The light was so bright she started seeing bright colors and shapes.

Focus. See past the light.

As Maya's eyes became more accustomed to the new environment, she noticed the multitude of mirrors around.

They must be bouncing and somehow amplifying sunlight.

"I seek an audience. I seek training," Maya said. She slowly scanned the room, not seeing any people but herself.

"If you want to train, show us the fire within," the voice said. It sounded male.

"You want me to open the Fire Chakra?" Maya said. There was no response.

"Return tomorrow and show us your Fire. We will offer you an opportunity to prove your worth." The voice rang with a certain finality. Maya listened out for more instructions, but there were none.

It's a good thing that I made it here. This feels like progress.

Maya turned and walked across the room, back into the dark corridor she had used. She had to wait at the threshold and let her eyes adjust to the darkness once more. Of course, she couldn't see anything, but at least the crazy colors and shapes were gone.

Maya retraced her steps with care, noting each path she had taken on the way.

I better be able to find my way back tomorrow.

Once she finally reached the main courtyard, she found another group practicing a different kata.

It can't hurt.

Maya found another spot at the rear and followed along.

It's nice to be a part of something. Even if they're all ignoring me.

Maya switched off the constant commentary in her brain and let the kata and movement overcome her. It was a welcome quiet that was relaxing and balancing. Once it was done, the group dispersed again. Maya didn't bother trying to speak to anyone, instead she weaved through the crowd and walked back out the main gate. With some relief, she saw Anders standing there, leaning against the car, and looking bored.

"How long have you been here?" Maya asked.

"No time at all. I literally just arrived," Anders said with a smile.

"Good timing, then. Did you get what you needed?"

"Even better. I got what I didn't even need." Anders grinned and entered the car. Maya sighed and followed him in.

"How was your first day?" Anders said with a chuckle.

"Hard work. But I can come back again tomorrow. I have some questions for Derek," Maya said. Her stomach rumbled, and she realized she hadn't eaten for a long time.

"I hear you. Don't worry, we've got you covered." Anders

sped off down the road. He asked no more questions, and Maya was happy to stare out the window and let her mind wander.

I need to know more about what they were testing. There must be a trick to it.

Anders parked the car and Maya looked out. They were on a quiet street, in front of what looked like a tiny restaurant. It even had red lanterns hanging outside, and an old-style tiled roof.

"This is a famous noodle place, let's see if it lives up to its reputation," Anders said.

"I sure hope so. Although, I'm so hungry just about anything will satisfy," Maya said. Anders laughed.

"We must come back when you're less hungry so you can appreciate it more." Anders waited for Maya to go ahead, and then he entered the restaurant. They spotted Derek sitting at a tiny plastic table in the corner. The restaurant was completely full. Derek waved them over excitedly.

"They were close to turfing me out. Lucky you finally arrived. Sit, sit." Derek gestured at the two plastic chairs and Maya and Anders eased themselves down carefully.

"You know the food is going to be great when the place is packed like this," Anders said, rubbing his hands together excitedly.

"I didn't take you for that much of a foodie," Maya said, giving Anders a sidelong glance.

"Oh, I'm not. But I love noodles. I think it's an offshoot of my obsession with those cheap packet noodles back home. They got me through some tough times." Anders stopped and watched as a server put down some cups of water and menus, disappearing before they could ask questions.

"Derek, that school is intense. And they tried to ignore me as much as possible," Maya said. Derek nodded slowly.

"They don't always make it easy for newcomers. Did they do any trials on you?" he said, sipping his water.

"I stumbled onto a class, where the instructor was staring at people. If they failed, they left the room."

"That's a classic. And the stare was hot?" Derek offered. Maya gasped.

"How did you know?"

"I'd wager you didn't stumble onto that class. They led you there," Derek said with a smile. Maya nodded.

"I needed to follow a student there. And she almost lost me in the crowd."

"Bingo!" Derek kept his eyes on her and raised his hand, trying to get the attention of the wait staff.

"They were testing you the whole time. And you went to the right class. The Fire Chakra is thematically linked to sight and movement. Not to mention fire."

"They knew what class I needed and drew me there?" Maya said incredulously.

"Must be an excellent school," Derek said. He noticed the server arriving and handed the menus back. "Two of your ramen specials, and vegetable udon please." The server accepted the menus, bowed, and hurried off.

"The first day they already tested you. It's not like hundreds of students turn up all the time. And many students need more effort to clear that Chakra point. Willpower is also important," Derek added.

"That explains the test of wills, the staring and heat. It's quite amazing when I think about it, that they've layered so much into one class."

"These things take time; they need to be efficient. How did you go?"

"I did well. I survived the intensity of the heat. The teacher's stare. I even tried to push it back with my Fire. So, to speak," Maya said. Derek whistled.

"You're definitely a natural. You're drawing on your

willpower and the Chakra's strengths already. What happened after?"

"The teacher left me alone after that. Once the class was done, I followed him through a pitch-black passage..."

"Sight again. Were there traps?" Derek interjected.

"Yes. And then at the end I found a..."

"Light-filled room?" Derek said with a grin.

"He's enjoying this way too much," Anders said with a chuckle.

"Sorry. Please continue," Derek said.

"Yes, a blindingly light room. I think they used a series of mirrors to concentrate the sunlight."

"Good. Another trial. How did that go?" The food arriving diverted Derek's attention. He directed the server on how to distribute the bowls and then sampled some soup with a spoon.

"I need to return tomorrow and show them my Fire," Maya said, watching Derek's reaction. He slurped his soup slowly and then looked up at her.

"That's your cue. You're going to be tested properly tomorrow," he said. Derek stared at Maya intently for a moment, then returned to eating.

"Tested properly?" Anders said.

"Yes, they're going to push you and see how far you've come. And when I say push, I mean not a gentle shove. They're going to hit you with a freight train. Metaphorically." Derek's voice had a casual tone, and he returned to his ramen.

It can't be worse than the Degeneration Field. Or can it?

"You ok there, Maya?" Anders said, his spoon paused halfway to his mouth. She nodded.

"Of course, just thinking everything over." Maya tried to focus on her noodles. They were quite delicious when she gave them the proper attention.

"I have every faith in you," Derek said. Once Maya looked

up, he continued, "Most students haven't had the life experience that you have had. They don't have that willpower, that determination. Just trust in yourself, and you'll keep advancing."

"Thanks. I think I just need to clear my head a little. I think I'll go for a quick walk," Maya said, standing up.

"Would you like some company?" Anders offered. He moved, but Maya waved him away.

"No, no, I'm fine. Please finish eating, I won't wander far."

"Alright, see you soon," Anders said with a wave. Derek waved too without looking up.

Men and their food, they're inseparable. I'll never understand it.

After walking through the room, Maya quickly glanced back. Anders and Derek were leaning forward, having what looked like a rather in-depth conversation.

I wonder what that's all about.

Maya stepped out of the restaurant and walked.

The next morning Anders dropped her off at the same place.

"You're going on another shopping trip?" Maya said. Anders shook his head.

"No, I have other business. An investigation."

"Oh, really? You guys working on a case?" Maya's interest was piqued.

"Nothing exciting like that. Just laying some groundwork for the next few steps of the plan. You're advancing so quickly; I don't want to get caught off-guard." Anders gave her a disarming smile.

He's hiding something. I must get it out of him later.

"Well, you enjoy that. I'll be off to get hit by a freight train," Maya said with a nervous laugh.

"Be gentle with the freight train, it won't know what hit it,"

Anders said with a grin. Maya smiled and started off toward the main gates.

As before, there was a crowd in the courtyard practicing another kata. Maya almost stopped and joined them.

No, don't delay things. Head back to that light-filled room.

She sighed and wandered past the group, heading back into the rest of the temple complex. She wove her way through the corridors and with great relief found the stairs down. As before, she took her time, the total darkness not seeming as black as before.

Am I getting more used to it?

Maya more gracefully stepped off the staircase into the corridor of darkness. She started counting her footsteps, waiting until she reached the missing steps.

Two hundred and four. Two hundred and... There it is.

Maya made note of how far she had come before the traps began and then continued ahead, taking care to avoid the pattern. She noticed the tiny point of light sooner this time, and before she knew it, she was ready to open the door again.

Here goes.

Maya pushed open the door, trying not to close her eyes as she entered the room. The light was a little less bright, but still overwhelming. She kept her eyes open, but they wept with the effort.

"We see you. Step into the middle of the room," a voice said. Maya couldn't see how far to go and walked slowly and resolutely until she discovered what they wanted. After a handful of steps, she noticed a stone pedestal and stopped.

"Take the key off the pedestal," the voice said. The sound bounced around the room, making Maya unsure of where it was coming from. She reached out and retrieved a golden key.

It's warm to the touch. And a normal size. Why is it important?

As she examined the key, the pedestal retracted into the

floor. Once it had completely disappeared, she saw a stone staircase heading down.

"Your task is to place the key into the door. Easy." The voice stopped talking and Maya waited around for further instructions.

I guess it's self-explanatory.

Maya gripped the key firmly in her right hand and descended the stairs.

15

THE FIRE WITHIN

Maya reached the bottom of the stairs and gasped. *This is impossible.*

She was in a gigantic room with channels of molten lava running along the sides. In the middle was a path of what looked like volcanic rocks. At the far end of the room were a few stairs and a large golden door. If it weren't for the stairs, her view of the door would have been blocked by the enormous boulder blocking the path.

The entire room is like a death trap, and the only way through is to push a massive boulder while not burning my feet off? Am I really ready for this?

Maya looked back at the way she had come. A rumble of stone surprised her, and the staircase rose back into the ceiling.

And now I'm trapped. And it's a boulder that I need to roll on a slight incline. I feel like Sisyphus, tricked into pushing a boulder up a hill for all eternity. Is this a punishment for advancing too fast?

Maya took one last look around the room and steeled herself for what had to be done. She slowly approached the volcanic path, feeling the intense heat from the flowing lava.

She reached the end of the safe path and peered at the volcanic rock.

How hot is it?

Maya removed her shoes and put a single foot on the heated path. It felt extremely hot, but just manageable. But the heat was not constant.

It's getting hotter. And fast.

Just as her foot felt agony, she pulled it up again. A quick glance confirmed her fears.

It's burning my foot. This isn't a trick at all. I can't ignore this.

Maya tried again with her other foot, stepping on the same part. It felt as hot as it had when she pulled her foot off the first time.

It didn't cool down at all.

While her right foot cooled off, she tried putting her left foot on a different spot on the path. As before, the heat slowly ramped until she couldn't handle it.

Is my tolerance for heat becoming exhausted too fast? Or are there hot spots that don't cool down?

Maya peered at the path, looking for another spot she could reach safely. She could step a bit further and try a patch she hadn't stepped on yet. Now that her right foot had recovered from the heat, she was ready. Cautiously stepping out, she placed her foot down and immediately confirmed her theory.

I need to keep moving; the path becomes too hot otherwise.

Maya retreated and mulled over the entire obstacle.

I need to shove that super heavy rock, or climb over it, but not stand in the same place for a long time. Fun.

Maya closed her eyes and imagined being somewhere else. It was a pleasant break for a few moments. With a sigh, she opened her eyes and gritted her teeth.

Time to make this happen.

Maya stepped out onto the super-heated walkway, dancing

from spot to spot, never staying still. She approached the giant boulder and put a hand on it.

Hot, very hot.

She pushed against it, feeling some resistance. But it gave way a little.

Before I shove this thing the whole way, I must try something else.

Maya searched for handholds and didn't spot any. She pressed a foot into the boulder, trying to give herself enough leverage to swing an arm further up and grasp a different spot. After three attempts she managed, but the intense heat from further up the boulder caused her to gasp and fall. The ground singed her arms, and she rushed back to the relative safety of the first few steps.

That's a no.

Maya examined her hands and arms. They were glowing red and felt burned.

I can't experiment too much from here on.

Maya stirred the Fire within her, the drive to get this done and prove herself. She threw herself back onto the path, using the strategy of moving around to keep her feet from burning away.

Movement is also a key part of this Chakra. Don't forget.

Maya pushed hard against the boulder. It rocked and moved ever so slightly.

More. Faster.

Maya leaned in, throwing her weight against the stone. However, her dancing footwork reduced the strength and stability she could use to push harder. Yet, steadying herself caused the path to heat tremendously.

Keep moving and find a rhythm. You need to keep trading stability and power for holding the momentum and not burning.

Maya alternated between pushing hard and merely main-taining enough pressure to prevent the boulder from rolling back. Small gains in distance gave her a fresh path to tread on and reset the 'hot clock' as she started calling it.

Sweat tinged her face and clouded her eyes. Her arms tired, and her feet grew weary. But she had only progressed one-third of the way through the room.

How do I even know that I can get past this boulder once I push it far enough?

The thought was depressing, and Maya discarded it and tried not to think about it. Her energy and enthusiasm were fading fast.

This is your chance. Don't give up.

She looked longingly at the floor. Sure, it was hot, but she could rest.

Did it feel restful when the level eighteen Degeneration Field was crushing your body?

The memory of that helplessness and the sight of Elias laughing and leaving triggered something within. Her Fire returned, burning hotter than ever before.

I'll show him. The Master Sage won't get away with this. I won't fail here. I can't.

Maya stopped the dance. She focused entirely on pushing the boulder.

There's no heat if I can't feel it.

She ignored her feet and pretended nothing was happening. She focused all her attention on pushing the boulder. It rolled a bit faster. The difference was minimal. Almost impossible to measure. But she noticed. And it was enough to keep going.

She couldn't feel her feet anymore. Something nagged at her, that this was probably terrible. But she had no time for that. Surging forward was her only recourse, the only path possible. The boulder rolled faster now. Her continued and increasing force had created some momentum.

Keep going.

Maya tripped on something and staggered to her knees. The heat was overwhelming, the middle of the room much hotter than she could have expected. Everything burned. Heat filled her completely.

Be the fire. Move through it.

Maya slowly stood again and used the heat. She used the Fire within, and the fire without. Binding them together, they were a fuel stronger than anything else. And she burned it for energy. Her muscles felt renewed, and she moved faster and faster. The boulder started moving again, and then it started rolling with speed.

The joy of motion seeped into her, but Maya didn't revel in it. She kept focused on the door up ahead. She kept that boulder moving; the stone moving of its own accord.

We're on the home stretch now.

Suddenly the boulder jolted still and then lurched to the side. It rolled off the path into the stream of lava, splashing fiery death everywhere. Maya ignored it and strode over to the door. She pulled out the key, thrust it into the door, and turned it quickly.

The lock clicked, and the door swung open slowly. Behind it was a bright light. Maya stepped into it and then fell into a heap. She felt hands pick her up and carry her away.

I feel so light. What's happened?

The sensation of being enveloped in light lasted for a few seconds and was then replaced with a perfect darkness.

Maya opened her eyes, not realizing she had been asleep. She lay in a dark room, only a few rays of sunlight peeking in through the wooden shutters. A man sat by her bed, his eyes closed, and his legs crossed in a meditation pose. His long brown hair fell to either side of his face.

"Am I still in the temple?" Maya said. The man nodded.

"You pushed too far, and your body needs to rest. But you made a breakthrough." He spoke without looking up, but his voice was not chiding.

He sounds kind. That's a change.

"The Fire Chakra," Maya said in an awed whisper. She closed her eyes and concentrated inside.

There it is. A source of fire, but also a path for it to be channeled through.

"It feels peaceful," Maya said, surprised. She looked to the man for confirmation.

"You feel peaceful because you have stopped fighting your spirit. You have embraced your own fire. It empowers you." The man slowly rose from the ground. He walked over to the bed, offering a hand. Maya took it, and he gently squeezed it.

"The rest of your journey will not be so forceful. From here on in, you need to step outside the bounds of fate. To embrace compassion and the true way." The man released her hand and stepped back, motioning for her to get out of the bed. Maya gingerly pulled back the sheet, noticing the many bandages covering her body.

This is going to hurt.

She swung her legs off the bed and let them rest on the ground. With a little nervousness, she put weight on one foot.

It's fine.

Maya tried the other foot, and when no shooting pains ran through her, she stood.

"You look surprised. Like I would encourage you to get out of bed if you weren't ready." The man had a wry smile on his face.

"It's more likely than you might think. I'm Maya. What's your name?" Maya said.

"Kancho. Nice to meet you, Maya." Kancho gave her a deep

bow and gestured toward the door. "Will you take a walk with me?"

"Sure. Wait, how much time has passed? I have friends waiting for me." Maya suddenly panicked, remembering Anders and Derek. The experience had been so intense and dreamlike, she had forgotten all about them.

"We already sent word that you were fine but recovering. Your friend left, a little reluctantly, but he will return to pick you up today." Kancho smiled and started walking.

"Thank you. Where are we going?"

"You'll see. Nothing like what you just experienced." Kancho led her down a corridor and into the sunlight. She was in a courtyard she hadn't seen yet.

"You heal exceptionally fast. Quite a gift," Kancho said, giving her a sidelong glance.

"Always have. It has served me well in this training so far. That last trial was quite extreme. I'm still debating if it really happened."

"I understand. To be honest, I think you surprised them. I expect they were trying to break you and humble you into taking the slow and steady road." Kancho chuckled, a deep and pleasant sound.

"Sure showed them, didn't I?" Maya said with a grin.

"They're not sure what to make of you. That's why I'm here."

"You get given all the troublemakers?" Maya said.

"Mostly. I suppose it's only fair, given that I was one once. Maybe I just understand them better." Kancho winked and opened a modest wooden door to the side of an extensive building. Maya followed him through and stopped immediately, letting out a gasp.

A giant, wide tree dominated the room. Surrounding it were other trees, moss-covered rocks, and an array of tiny plants.

I've walked into some sort of lost forest. It doesn't make sense.

"This is my favorite place in the temple. Come find a place to sit. We are going to contemplate life and all that's in it." Kancho carefully picked his way through the rocks, treading purposely. He selected a spot and stretched out, putting his hands behind his head, and closing his eyes.

"Don't be shy, make yourself comfortable," he said. Maya looked around and picked a spot.

This seems like the best place to be right now, may as well make the most of it.

16

A FRANTIC LEAD

Maya stepped out of the temple gates, spotting Anders instantly. He was lounging against the car, as he had before, but looked up sharply as soon as she approached.

"You look like you've been in the wars," he said.

"I think the technical term is a 'lava-filled boulder death room'," Maya said with a laugh.

"Glad to see you cheated death once more. Was it really that bad?" Anders said, opening the car door.

"Worse. But what doesn't kill me makes me stronger." Maya paused and added, "I think that's literally true."

"Agreed. Good to see you succeeded with the third Chakra," Derek said from the back seat. Maya looked over quickly with surprise.

"Derek! Why are you here?"

"Anders was concerned. I offered to wait with him."

"We're both happy that you are fine. How was the rest of your day? After the lava room?" Anders asked, starting the car up.

"Nice and relaxing. I have a teacher now, and we rested in

an ancient forest, deep within the temple." The memory gave Maya a smile.

"Sounds like an excellent teacher to me," Derek said.

"He seems good. I really need some guidance from here on. Not that you haven't helped, Derek."

"Haha, don't worry about me. I agree, you need a proper teacher."

"A near-death experience, another Chakra mastered, and a new teacher. Sounds like grounds for a celebration," Anders said.

"Sure. If I don't need to make a single decision," Maya said, leaning back in the chair.

"Done. Derek and I already planned it."

"Do I get to find out what I'm in for?" Maya said with a smile.

"No, it's a surprise. You'll have to wait." Anders gave her a wink and sped down the road.

"Don't worry, it'll be great. You'll see." Derek sounded excited too.

It will be nice to kick back and rest after all this. The forest wasn't enough; I need to take my mind off things.

Maya tuned out and let Derek and Anders talk about something else. After the intensity of the previous day, and the strange calm of the forest, she was fine with just having a blank mind. It felt good to be in the company of friends, but not having any requirement to take part. In what seemed like no time at all, Anders slowed down and parked.

"We're here already?" Maya said, looking around. They were in the middle of an entertainment district. She could hear the music of clubs nearby, and throngs of people out and about.

"There's a good vibe out there. So far so good," Maya said.

"You've seen nothing yet," Anders said. He grinned and stepped out of the vehicle. Once they were on the street, Maya noticed that the rest of the street was blocked off.

"Markets?" she said. Anders nodded.

"That's just the beginning. We can grab some exceptional street food. Do you eat sushi?" Anders asked.

"Yes, and I love other bite sized treats!"

"Great. We're going to just grab delicious things on our way."

"On our way to where?" Maya asked. Anders shrugged.

"You'll just have to see." Anders winked at Derek, who started laughing.

A few blocks later and Maya had snacked on some vegetarian gyoza, sushi, and a pancake. Anders had eaten twice as much and was even still eating a skewer of beef.

"So good. And here we are." Anders casually gestured to a building just past the end of the market stalls. The glowing neon sign showed an image of a microphone.

"Hang on. Karaoke?" she said.

I can't remember the last time I sang anything.

"It'll be fun. It's completely Derek's idea, and I'm willing to try it," Anders said. He looked over at Derek.

"Guilty. Anders is only responsible for driving us, I organized the rest. Have you done it before?" he asked.

"Just the once."

That was a disaster.

"Good. Nobody has a bad time at karaoke. It's just too fun. C'mon." Derek put an arm around each of them and playfully steered them toward the building.

Just as they reached the entrance, Anders paused.

"Wait, I need to take this." Anders answered his phone in hushed tones and waved them upstairs.

"He'll catch up. Let's get settled in." Derek led the way, speaking to the bored girl at the counter and then signing into a terminal. She handed him a key card, and he thanked her before setting off.

"You've done this before," Maya said, laughing.

"Of course. Just relax, it'll be harmless fun." Derek charged ahead, taking the stairs two at a time. Maya had to hustle to keep up with him. They moved on into a narrow corridor with doors evenly spaced on each side.

Reminds me of the facility that the Master Sage was running. Snap out of it, you need to stop reliving those times.

Derek sped through the hallway, stopping briefly in front of room twenty-one. He waved the key card, and the lock flashed green and clicked.

"And here we are." Derek pushed the door open, and they entered the room. To be fair, it was more of a booth. With a large screen mounted on the wall and a circular table surrounded by seating taking up the rest of the space.

"Skooch in and get comfortable." Derek eased his tall frame into the large booth cushion and moved around until he was in the corner. Maya stayed close to the door. Derek immediately started fiddling around with the panel in the center of the table, flicking through songs.

"There are some good options here. Any requests?"

"Something I won't have to sing by myself? I'm not familiar with a lot of the newer songs," she said. Derek nodded. He continued searching for a song. Maya was watching the screen, looking for something she recognized when she heard a loud knock at the door. Derek didn't seem to notice, so she slid over and stood to open the door. Anders was standing there, out of breath.

"Sorry, but there's a bit of a mini emergency." Anders pushed in past her, and Maya closed the door.

"What's going on?" she said, sensing his unease.

"It's a long story. But the short version is I just got a call from a contact in the city. Someone has been trying to sell a bloodline testing device." Anders looked over at Derek. "You're going to want to hear about this."

"Bloodline device? Not so suspicious, but I'm listening," Derek said.

"It doesn't work properly. Everyone is getting a zero reading," Anders said. Derek shrugged.

"So, it's malfunctioning? That's hardly an emergency."

"My guy got a look at it. It's not testing for the usual things." Anders looked at Maya. "Didn't you encounter one of those in the lab? My brother tested you with one and then destroyed it?" Anders said. Maya instantly froze.

He can't be serious.

"You think it's for the seventh bloodline?" Maya said, her heart racing.

"It has to be. And this guy selling it has a reputation for scavenging through old labs. It's his niche."

"If we can get one, we might find other people who have it. And see what powers they have. Or maybe even trace the device back to a lab, find the trail." Maya was suddenly lost in thought. She had ignored the seventh bloodline, the lab, and everything else. She had been so caught up in her own struggles, just trying to get her head above water. But this opportunity was something else.

I must investigate. This can't be a coincidence.

"Let's go buy it," Maya said.

"I arranged the deal. We should leave immediately," Anders said, opening the door.

"We're going to come back another time. Right?" Derek said. He looked forlorn for a moment before going back to his usual self.

"I promise you'll hear my awful singing another time," Maya said, her voice strained despite trying to be cheerful.

Why am I feeling so anxious?

Maya didn't really have time to dwell on her feelings. Within minutes Anders had pulled up outside a large warehouse with a shady alley nearby.

"I'm meeting the contact there. I don't want to spook her, so please hang back. I'll let you know if there's any issues." Anders looked at them both, his gaze serious.

"I'm fine," Derek said in a calm tone.

"I'll defer to your judgment on this one," Maya said reluctantly. Anders nodded and left the car. He walked past the warehouse and entered the sketchy lane.

I have a bad feeling about this.

Maya left the car and crept along the street. She turned back and motioned for Derek to stay put. He nodded and held his hands up. Maya continued, peeking into the alley. She could see Anders halfway down, standing close to a hooded figure that she couldn't identify.

So far, so good.

Maya scanned the rest of the alley. There was minimal lighting, and she had difficulty spotting anything useful. Suddenly something flashed, and Anders was on the ground. Maya sprinted over.

"Are you OK?" Maya said as she reached him. Anders groaned and looked up.

"Fine. I don't think it was a setup, we were being watched." Anders tried to look up. Maya followed his gaze and saw a shape on the roof.

"Stay here, I'm going to investigate." Maya ran to the side of the alley, spotting some bins she could climb on. From there she could reach a fire escape ladder, and leaped up, grabbing onto the bottom rung.

Keep going. You can catch up.

Maya hauled herself up the ladder and noticed the shape on the roof. It was a hooded figure, crouched low.

"Who are you?" Maya said, eyeing off the stranger. A woman's voice laughed, and then she disappeared. Or almost did. Maya saw some sort of light trail and the woman appeared on the next rooftop.

How is she doing that?

Maya shook her head in wonder and saw a way forward. She ran along the rooftop, aiming for a ledge that she could leap off to reach the next roof.

This is probably a trap. You better not fall off the roof.

Maya squashed the running commentary and focused on her speed. She knew she could make the jump and vaulted off the roof at top speed. Her fingers slipped off the handhold she was aiming for but grasped a lower ledge.

Breathe. Breathe.

After a moment, she climbed back up onto the roof. The woman was crouched there again. She let out another laugh and did the same streak into nothing. Maya saw the trail again and headed off in the same direction. After another less perilous roof leap, she was on tiles.

Heading into a residential area?

Maya had to adjust her footing and slipped a few times but maintained a good pace. She had no idea where the woman had gone but could only continue in the same direction. As she ran out of roof she slowed and looked down. There was a large courtyard below with a circular water feature in the middle. The woman she had been chasing was standing there.

The courtyard was better lit, and Maya noticed more details on the woman. She was wearing what could only be described as a ninja outfit with a hood. She was also carrying a nondescript box.

That could be what I'm after. I have to try.

Maya looked around and didn't see a good way to climb down.

I have to just hope my training is working.

Maya closed her eyes and took in some deep breaths. She focused on her internal energy, and the Chakra flow. She opened herself to the strength and resilience that was needed to reinforce her legs, and the will and strength to oppose the impact on her body. She leaped down with confidence, dropping into a crouch as she landed. But her legs did not buckle, and she broke nothing.

"Are you done running?" Maya said with way more confidence than she was feeling.

"Yes. But you aren't," the woman replied.

17

A CRUMPLED BOX

"Hand it over," Maya said, slowly approaching. The woman didn't move a muscle and kept watching.

"Why do you want it?" she said, looking Maya up and down.

"It has answers I need," Maya said, advancing further. The woman crushed the box with her hand, tossing the remnants to the ground.

"Now it doesn't. Do you still want it?" she said in a taunting tone. Maya's cheeks heated instantly, and she clenched her fists.

"That was unnecessary," Maya said through gritted teeth.

"From your perspective, perhaps. But you seem upset. Take it and walk away." The woman gave Maya a dismissive gesture with her hand and turned her back.

What's the point? She's clearly in league with the Master Sage, she might offer me something more.

Maya stepped forward, nudging the crushed box out of her way.

"Maybe you can help me instead," Maya said.

"Wrong answer," the woman said with a sigh. She disappeared again, the trail leading up to the rooftops again. As

Maya contemplated following, she noticed four shapes dropping around her.

Maya whirled to look at them all. Four men dressed in martial arts uniforms.

Probably Chakra bloodlines. They're not here for small talk.

Maya took the offensive, rushing the closest one. She launched into a kata, adapting it halfway by changing up the kicks and sneaking in an extra punch. The man easily blocked it all, countering at the end with a punch that knocked Maya back and forced the wind out of her lungs.

Need to be more careful.

She felt the fury rising inside her. Anger at being blocked again, at letting another opportunity slip away.

Use it. Combine it with your will to force a way forward.

Maya started focusing her energy. The four men approached from all sides.

They're probably stronger and better fighters. But you have an edge. You won't give up.

Maya approached the one that had already struck her. She whirled into an attack, trying to bait him into counter-attacking. Within moments, he capitalized on an opportunity. But this time Maya was waiting. She saw the strike coming and grabbed his arm. First with one hand, and then another. Before he could pull it away, she sent out all the energy she had been gathering through her hands.

The flash of blue was momentarily blinding, and it knocked the man back. His hands looked badly burned, and he reflexively held them against his chest, backing away.

They'll think twice before doing that again.

However, the other men didn't seem to be concerned about attacking from other directions. They used the opportunity to strike while her guard was down. The first hit landed on her kidneys, and then the back of her knee. She went down before she could retaliate. The blows kept coming.

Hold it together.

The sound of a sudden crack interrupted the flurry of attacks. Maya rolled away and looked up. Derek was standing there, smiling at her. One attacker backed away, nursing a limp arm. Within seconds, the entire group shuffled away.

"Good riddance!" Derek shouted after them. Once they were gone, he turned back to Maya.

"Are you OK? They landed some good ones." Derek moved in closer, getting a better look at her.

"Nothing's broken. I think they were more focused on beating me up. Thank you, I'm not sure how I would have turned the tide there." Maya let out a sigh, and as the adrenaline drained out of her all her injuries started speaking up.

"Looks like I missed the fun," Anders said as he shuffled over. "Everyone alright?"

"Ego's bruised, and I feel like a fool. But nothing major otherwise," Maya said. Derek slapped her on the shoulder.

"Don't worry, it's all part of the process." He bent down and gingerly picked up the damaged box and handed it to Anders.

"Is this what we were after?" Derek said. Anders carefully opened the box, sifting through the contents.

"I'd say so. I'll see what I can do and give Kora a bell. She might do something with it." Anders smiled, but his face told a different story.

What a waste.

"Did you see that woman?" Maya said to Derek. He nodded.

"Yes. A Speedster. Well, technically she's of the Haste bloodline. Moves too fast to see."

"Yeah, I figured as much. I could see something, though. Like a trail of where she had gone," Maya said, searching for the right words to describe it.

"That's handy. Must be because you have the ability, although it's untrained. Would you agree, Anders?" Derek said.

"Absolutely. Maybe you'll be a Speedster too, once you activate the bloodline," Anders said.

"I guess that's all we can do for now. I wish I knew who they were. We don't have any leads." Maya sighed.

"We might have had something, if you didn't charge off so quickly." Anders held up a black circular device.

"What's that?" Maya asked, reaching for it. She turned it over in her hands.

"Tracking device. Once it attaches, it shrinks and starts transmitting. Why don't you keep that one?" Anders said with a wry smile.

"Thanks. Next time, I promise," Maya said.

He's right, I really messed this one up.

"You know what would really cheer everyone up right about now?" Derek said, a hopeful and cheeky smile on his face.

"Sorry," Maya said, shaking her head. Derek acted like she'd wounded him. Then he quickly recovered and shrugged.

"That's fine, I had to ask. Let's head back to the car."

"I got to say, you get points for asking. You really love that karaoke," Anders said as they walked.

"It scratches a certain itch, but I knew it was over the second Maya ran out."

"I'm sorry. Thanks for coming so quickly. Things were going to get a lot worse before they got better."

I'm not sure I could have broken out of that. But there must have been a way. Lucky, I didn't have to wait for an answer this time. It could have been quite dangerous.

"You're welcome, I always take the opportunity to get a bit of exercise." Derek stretched his shoulder out as he walked.

"Maybe next time we can plan it a little better," Maya said.

"Don't beat yourself up too much. You sprang into action. We retrieved something. I guarantee Kora will discover something useful." Anders gently shook the box, but the resulting rattle did not sound promising.

"I'm going to hold you to that," Maya said. Anders chuckled and seemed to hug the box closer to his body.

Maya stood with hesitation outside the temple gates. Anders had sped off, and she didn't feel quite ready to set foot inside.

Is it shame? Do I feel ashamed of what happened?

She forced her feet forward, and soon enough she was inside the gates. Another group kata was underway, and Maya glided into a spare spot, glad for the distraction. She was soon lost in the motion, just enough exertion and focus to capture her attention and stop her brain from churning. With great reluctance, she completed the last moves and bowed with the rest as the instructor left.

I should find Kancho. Where will he be?

Maya started off, picking her way through the students milling around. She retraced her steps, looking for the way back to the strange forest building. The way back had been a bit of a blur, and she hadn't quite paid enough attention. But after a few false loops she recognized the area and moved quickly toward the room with a more defined purpose.

Easing the door open, Maya looked around. She spotted Kancho lying on a log, like he had never left.

"Have you moved at all?" Maya asked as she entered the room.

"Yes, and no. But I can see you definitely have." Kancho responded without even opening his eyes and stayed perfectly still.

"I had a bit of an adventure last night," Maya said, finding a space she could lie down comfortably. She purposefully selected a different spot to the previous day.

"What happened?" Kancho asked, in an indifferent tone.

"It's a long story. But I was investigating something, and

some strange woman jumped in and stole an item. I chased after her, but she moved differently." Maya paused, trying to describe it properly.

"Speedster?" Kancho offered.

"Yes, how did you know?"

"It was the most likely answer. Please continue." Kancho remained still and waited.

"Once I caught up with her, or more accurately she waited for me, she broke the item, and then her friends closed in to fight me." Maya paused again, and she noticed that Kancho's eyes were now open, and he was watching her.

"And?" he said.

"I damaged one, but another knocked me down from behind and they all piled on. It was only when a friend intervened that they scattered." Maya finished and waited for Kancho to respond. He closed his eyes for a while and then responded.

"You feel you made a poor decision. And you were not strong enough to win. Correct?"

"Yes. I feel a bit embarrassed by it. I ran off and was completely outmatched."

"It's not a matter of being outmatched. It's a matter of preparation. And making the best choices." Kancho sat up and chuckled to himself.

"What do you suggest then?"

"We use your recent failure. We meditate on it, here in this blessedly quiet wood."

"Is this your way out of getting out of doing something?" Maya said, suspiciously.

"It's called training. It's what we do here. You should try it, sometime." Kancho winked at her.

"Is this really going to help?" Maya asked.

"That is entirely up to you. I suggest that you make it so." Kancho lay down again and closed his eyes once more. Maya resisted the urge to complain more and eased back into a comfortable position. It took a bit of wriggling, but once she was wedged between a few tree roots and some moss it was relaxing.

"I can sense the change already. Let's do some training," Kancho said with a chuckle.

The hours passed strangely. Maya was at the same time not aware of the time passing, yet also acutely aware that she was lying around doing nothing. She oscillated between deep calm and timelessness, and a restless fidgeting that only annoyed Kancho. Well, she assumed it did based on the various grunts he let off. He never actually said anything.

"I think we're done for today," Kancho said out of the blue. He slowly rose and stretched out. Maya did the same, her muscles initially feeling quite heavy.

"Is it lunchtime?" Maya asked, suddenly feeling hungry.

"If you want to call it that. Dinner is more customary, though." Kancho smiled and started walking out of the room. Maya glanced around.

"But it's not dark yet," she said, confused. Kancho didn't respond, he kept heading for the door. Once he reached it, he left immediately. Maya rushed after him. Bursting through the door, she noticed twilight all around them. A chill permeated the air.

"You're right. We spent the entire day in there?" Maya said, shocked. Kancho nodded.

"It was a good start. But we need to do more. Come back here again tomorrow." Kancho made eye contact and then turned and walked away.

"How long will I be doing this?" Maya called out.

"As long as it takes," Kancho replied without turning around. Soon enough he had disappeared around a corner.

He seems to know what he's doing. For now, it's all I can do.

Maya's stomach grumbled again, and she hurried off through the temple grounds.

I hope Anders isn't worried that took longer than I expected.

As always, he was lounging against the car, playing on his phone.

"Long day?" he said as Maya approached.

"Longer than it seemed. Nothing to report either. How about you?"

"Too much. It's not even worth taking you through it. Tomorrow it'll all make sense." Anders paused, pointing at Maya.

"Was that your stomach?" he said.

"Yeah. I didn't eat all day," Maya said with embarrassment.

"I'd be hungry too, no judgment there. Let's get something quick." Anders jogged around to the driver's side and entered the car.

"Derek?" Maya asked as she sat down.

"He's busy on a few other things. We're keeping ourselves occupied while you train." Anders had a mischievous glint in his eye but said nothing more.

"How intriguing," Maya said. She resisted the urge to launch into a series of questions.

Maybe it'll be more fun to get surprised.

18

THE GENIUS PREVAILS

The loud knocking jolted Maya out of her reverie. She was sitting on the couch, sipping on her coffee.

"It's for you," Anders said from the other side of the room, not looking up. Maya carefully balanced her coffee and shuffled over to the door. She opened it slowly, peering at whoever was on the other side.

"Girl, you sure keep things interesting." Kora swept into the hotel room, placing a quick peck on Maya's cheek, and then continuing. She was dragging a black suitcase behind her and let it lean against the couch.

"Wow, this is a surprise. I thought you'd be helping remotely," Maya said.

"With the state your device is in? Not a chance. Now, where is it?" Kora said. Anders pointed to the box on the coffee table. Kora ran over, gingerly lifting the box, and cringing at the rattling and metal jangling sounds that came out of it.

"You just keep on testing me, don't you? Luckily, I always rise to a challenge." Kora sat down and opened the box, peering inside.

"Do you have a room organized?" Maya asked, suddenly wondering where Kora was going to stay.

"Anders has it organized; I'll move over there when it's set up appropriately. For now, I'll study this thing. Bag, please." Kora clicked her fingers and pointed at it. Maya set down her coffee and dutifully wheeled the suitcase over.

Wow, this is heavy.

"What have you got in here?"

"Just the really important stuff. Everything else is in my room." Kora opened the bag and started fishing out identical black satchels. She opened one up and laid out some tools.

"You're really prepared," Maya said.

"Oh, this is nothing. That's more Anders' game. But I'm too impatient to do it any other way. How certain are we that this was a testing device for the seventh bloodline?" Kora said, looking up at Maya.

"Not sure. That they ruined the device helps confirm it. Anders?"

"I'm fairly confident. Confident that it worked and wasn't a regular testing device. And that my contact couldn't identify it. But without it functioning, I don't know how sure we can be if I'm honest. There's a lot of misdirection surrounding this bloodline." Anders sighed and shrugged.

"Fine, fine. Why don't you both clear out of here? I need some space to think." Kora focused intently on the box in front of her.

"We should let the genius do her thing. Let's leave a bit early," Anders said.

"Sure. Good luck," Maya said, but Kora didn't seem to hear. She was slowly extracting tiny pieces from the box.

"Don't call me for updates, I'll call you," Kora said as they left the room.

"I think this is going to take a while. Lucky you have something else to occupy yourself," Anders said with a laugh.

Three painstaking days later, they received the call. Maya was overcome with a wave of relief.

"Finally! It was taking all of my willpower not to sneak into her room."

"You realize that would have been pointless. She writes nothing down," Anders said with a chuckle. He started the car, and they started driving away from the temple grounds.

"I know. But you need to understand. This training, it makes me feel so restless. It's agony. I'm rested enough. I need something to happen!"

"What's your teacher saying? Kancho?" Anders asked.

"He doesn't really say anything. He gives me a mysterious smile and reminds me to return tomorrow. I think he's satisfied?"

"I'm sure there's a purpose to it. You'll see." Anders opened the door to their hotel room, holding it for Maya. She walked through quickly.

"I bet I will. But for now, I'm ready for some good news." Maya ducked across the hall, and they were standing in front of Kora's room. Maya hesitantly raised her hand to knock and was interrupted.

"Enter!" Kora called out from within the room. Maya opened the door and gasped. The hotel room wasn't visible anymore. The space was entirely covered in electronics and machinery.

"I like what you've done with the place," Maya said as she entered.

"How else did you expect me to work here?" Kora was standing over a metal table in the center of the room. A metallic box stood before her.

"That looks...not broken," Anders said, closing the door behind him.

"It's not the original case. I reverse engineered it, and a lot of other things, actually." Kora walked over and yanked Maya's arm, dragging it over to the machine. She placed Maya's hand on top of the machine. It whirred and powered on.

"It works?" Maya said, looking over at Kora with a puzzled expression.

"Shh, just wait." Kora stared intently at the device, and then pulled out a fancy tablet computer and started reviewing the screen. Maya glanced at Anders, who shrugged back at her.

"I haven't built the visualization yet. I'm not even completely sure it's doing the right thing. When you experienced a machine like this before, what happened?" Kora spoke without looking up.

"Let me think. It was smaller than this, more rounded. It beeped after it scanned me. And then some lights lit up. I think it was three?"

"Hmm, that doesn't really help. I think the design is functionally different. If they are related, then this device is probably an older unit. Potentially even a prototype."

"What can you tell me about it?" Maya said.

"It's returning numbers, I'm still figuring out what they mean."

"Well, how does the number change for you? Or Anders?" Maya said. Kora didn't respond instantly.

"Good idea." Kora rushed over to Anders and dragged him over to the machine.

"I'm here to help. You can ask beforehand," Anders said.

"No time for that." Kora waited for the machine to power up and down, and then she consulted her tablet again.

"One series of numbers seems to be like Maya, and different to my results," Kora said, almost to herself.

"We're on to something. Anders' brother had the seventh bloodline as well. It might be in him too, in a dormant or blocked state."

"I don't have any powers. I always get a zero reading on those machines—" Anders started saying.

"No, Maya's right," Kora said, interrupting. "Scanning for the presence of the bloodline without checking for whether it is or can be activated. That's something different about this."

"Maybe this device wasn't to test if you had the bloodline, but more to test if you were a carrier. Whether it was in your lineage?" Maya said. She looked over at Kora, but the woman was deep in thought. Anders, too, seemed to be elsewhere. Maya continued, "We believe the Master Sage was trying to give himself the power as well, it would benefit him to be tracking the presence of the bloodline to help understand it better. And find more people that may have activated it."

"This is good. I can work with this. We can kick off our own bloodline investigation." Kora sounded energized.

"I am loving the enthusiasm, you two should focus on this." Maya forced a grin and Anders gave her a concerned look.

"You're not going to help?" Anders said.

"Oh, if I can, I will. But my focus for now needs to be on my training. I can't seem to make any more progress." Maya sighed.

"You can't force it. Even I can see that's what your teacher is trying to show you," Anders said gently.

"Well, it still feels like I'm behind. Look at what happened the other night? I ran in and got myself pummeled."

"There are always losses before a major win. Take this device for example." Kora pointed to the bloodline tester. "I can't remember the number of times it seemed hopeless these last few days. You literally gave me a box of scraps."

"Sorry about that," Maya said. Kora waved away her concern, annoyed.

"Don't be sorry. That's not the point. I'm trying to remind you to be persistent. Keep going. Suffer the frustration and pain and suck it up. The next breakthrough is just out of reach." Kora smiled then strode over and grabbed the box.

"Kora, I never picked you as the type for the inspirational speeches," Anders said with a chuckle.

"The box and I have more work to do," Kora said. Holding the box, she took it over to her mess of machinery. After a few moments of concentration, she turned around.

"You're still here? Anders make yourself useful. See you later Maya."

"I think that's your cue," Anders said before joining Kora.

"Good. I'll leave you to it then." Maya turned and left the room, closing the door gently behind her.

They're good people, and they're helping you. Go make that next step.

Maya headed over to the lifts and pressed the call button.

The walk to the temple was long and winding but gave Maya time to think.

How am I supposed to master this next Chakra? How long will it even take?

She didn't know anything about it, her faith was purely in Kancho and his teaching.

Can he help me in the way that I need?

The thought bothered her, as it was in opposition to how she felt about him, how he had treated her. His compassion and calm had helped her so much, despite her need to keep pushing forward. She resolved to finally ask him about the next Chakra, and what it meant. As she reached this decision, the large temple gates rose before her. She walked inside and joined the kata in progress. As she went through the motions she looked around, trying to spot any students that she recognized, but saw none. There was no sign of Kancho either.

He must be in his favorite forest as always.

As the kata finished, she felt refreshed and ready. Maya

walked through the dispersing students, finding her way back to the strange building with the forest. Before she could reach it, she noticed a group of students walking away from the building.

Curious.

Maya followed them. They headed in a different direction altogether, picking their way through a part of the temple complex that Maya had never explored.

I wonder where this will take me.

Maya kept her distance, not wanting to disrupt whatever was going on. She almost lost them in the winding between laneways, and strange shortcuts across hidden courtyards. Finally, they reached something different. There was a set of stairs heading down into a dark area, like a tunnel. There were already some students standing alongside the entrance.

What's this?

Maya approached them, taking a closer look. The students looked up at her.

"So, you're the new one?" a woman said. She had short brown hair and a slim build.

"Yes, I'm Maya."

"Yuko. We're here to observe another student." Yuko pointed down into the tunnel. There was a man standing inside, barely visible.

"Doing what?" Maya asked, curious.

"Experiencing the gloom tunnel," Yuko said in a matter-of-fact manner.

"I see," Maya said, looking back at the tunnel again. It did look gloomy now that she thought about it.

"Go on, see for yourself," Yuko said. She gestured toward the tunnel, and Maya started off. As she walked down the stone stairs, she felt a sense of foreboding. And once she reached the entrance, the feeling intensified. Something was off.

Maya took a step inside the tunnel. It hit her then. A wave of energy, dark and unsettling.

This feels so wrong, who would come down here?

Maya was about to turn back when she heard a noise. She peered further into the dark. It was the man inside. He had dropped to his knees and was sobbing.

I must help him. He will never get out of here by himself.

Maya walked forward purposefully. Each step immersed her more fully in the gloom, as she began to call it.

They weren't joking about the name.

The man was in the middle of the tunnel.

No wonder he's suffering, it must be worse back there.

Maya pushed again, resisting the feelings that surrounded her. It was a depressive atmosphere, like the problems of the world were too much. Maya stopped suddenly.

This is full-on.

She turned to look back, and the tunnel entrance closed.

No!

19

THE GLOOM TUNNEL

Maya swung back around to look into the distance. The far end of the tunnel still looked open. There was a faint light gleaming.

I could just run there.

The thought popped into her head and surprised her. The pull was so strong. She shook her head and focused on the man ahead.

He needs me. I can handle it.

Maya focused on the light ahead, using it to remind herself of the bright daylight beyond. Each step was heavier, she wanted to sink down. But a little voice inside reminded her of the man ahead. His situation needed help, and it was a warning of what might happen to her. There was little hope of recovering if she broke down like him.

Don't think about it.

Maya forged ahead, focusing on the man. He was curled up into a ball now, rocking back and forth. Pangs of sadness hit Maya and threatened to tip the scales. But she kept herself from falling and took a deep breath before continuing.

Sooner than she expected, she reached him. He seemed

oblivious to her presence. She dropped into a crouch to get closer.

"Hello, I'm Maya," she said. The man kept sobbing and rocking. He didn't seem to have noticed her.

"We need to go. It's unsafe for us to stay too long," Maya said. The man made no response.

"What's your name?" Maya said, trying a new avenue. He paused his movement, trying to speak. Maya waited.

"Toru," he whispered. The act of speaking seemed to pause whatever cycle he was stuck in.

"Nice to meet you, Toru. I'm Maya." Maya watched his reaction. He nodded slightly but did nothing else.

"Let me help you up," Maya said, offering a hand. Toru didn't move. His eyes were still closed.

"I'll help you to the tunnel exit. You'll feel much better," she said. Toru looked like he was going to speak again. After some effort, he forced a few words out.

"Too dangerous. Go back," he said.

"Alone? Maybe you're right. But we're together," Maya said. She almost mentioned the fact that the entrance was closed but stopped herself.

I don't want him to feel worse.

"Just try a bit, see how you feel," Maya said, holding her hand out. Toru opened one eye, looking at her.

"They're waiting for us outside. C'mon," Maya said. Toru accepted her hand and opened both his eyes. He stood slowly. As they both rose, Maya noticed that he was shorter than her. But not by much.

The oppressive dark feelings started to retreat.

"See? It feels different now," Maya said, hoping to capitalize on it. Toru looked around suspiciously. He wiped the tears off his face and nodded.

"Let's go while the going is good," Maya said. Maintaining his hand in hers, she gently turned him around and led him toward the light. There was an ease to the effort which hadn't been there before. And the gloom and oppression became smaller, not bigger. That puzzled Maya the most. In no time they reached the other end, and Maya pulled Toru out into the light.

Once her eyes adjusted, she noticed a small congregation of students. Yuko was at the head, and she walked over.

"Not your best day, Toru," she said. Toru smiled and nodded back to her.

"Thank you for your help," Toru said to Maya. He bowed. She returned the bow.

"Happy to help, you looked to be in a rough spot," Maya said.

"He's struggling with the Heart Chakra. Like you," Yuko said. Maya stared at Yuko.

"Heart Chakra?'

"Yes, it's the one after Fire. It's a turning point in your development. It's harder to obtain and requires a real shift in thinking. This tunnel has been built to assist with developing it." Yuko gestured to the tunnel behind them.

"But it's supposed to be something undertaken with an instructor," Toru said, his eyes dropping down.

"We wouldn't be Kancho's Leftovers if we followed the rules," Yuko said with a laugh. Maya gasped.

"Your teacher is Kancho too. But why are you called that?"

"Walk this way, I'll explain," Yuko said. She started walking off and Maya fell in beside her.

"Kancho doesn't always reveal a lot about himself. But he's always been a bit of a rebel. He was almost kicked out of the school for trying to accelerate his growth too much," Yuko said.

"I'm in trouble then." Maya sighed.

"Not necessarily. They realized that Kancho wasn't alone. They had lots of students who didn't fit the mold. That were odd, or unconventional. So, they allowed Kancho to push ahead on one condition."

"Which was?" Maya said.

"Once he mastered the sixth Chakra, that he return and be an instructor for all the difficult students. He agreed, and here we are." Yuko stopped and pointed to the building in front of her. It was the towering building that housed the forest Maya had been training in.

"How did you know I've been training here?" Maya said.

"We all started here. I'm not sure if that's just Kancho's style, or if it helps us the most. But this place centers you, it helps with whatever you need. It's probably the most critical for the Heart Chakra." Yuko strode forward and entered the building, Maya followed closely behind.

Maybe these students can help me take action finally.

Yuko picked her way through the forest, carefully. Maya kept looking around for Kancho, trying to spot him. But she was unsuccessful. They kept going, further than Maya had ever gone inside the forest. Finally, they arrived at an unusual clearing. It didn't look like people had cut the trees again, it was more like they just chose not to occupy that space. Yet, the space was oddly neat. Almost a perfect square.

"Here we are, the Leftovers Box. A place all our own," Yuko said with a grin.

"You're really owning this name," Maya said, chuckling.

"It's the only way. Come over." Yuko walked into the center of the space, stood in the middle, and waited. Maya strode over and stood opposite Yuko. They both bowed to each other.

"The Heart Chakra requires you to rise above. Above the pull of your lower emotions, above the struggle of your fate." Yuko spoke slowly and deliberately. Maya nodded along. Yuko suddenly lurched forward with a strike. Maya barely deflected it, almost losing her balance.

"You have to step aside from being immersed in good, or

evil. Or other absolutes. You must appreciate the two without being either."

"Why is that? Why can't I be good?" Maya asked the question but kept her eyes on Yuko. The other woman was circling around Maya, and then launched into a flurry of attacks.

She's so skilled. She could probably overwhelm me. Why isn't she?

Maya worked hard to block and dodge the constant attacks. The occasional palm strike or kick evaded her guard, and Maya grunted with every landed hit. Yuko showed no sign of letting up or answering Maya's question. Maya drew in a breath and remembered to use her Chakras.

Settling into her Root, she drew on Earth to increase her resilience. She stopped blocking a few hits and let them go. Next, Maya drew upon the fluidity and ease of Water, and her fear of Yuko and what she could do melted away. She ignited her Fire, drawing upon her power and fighting back.

"Better," Yuko said, on the back foot yet not looking troubled at all. "Being immersed in good without understanding evil is not enlightened. It is just childish." Yuko activated another level of speed, dodging all of Maya's attacks with ease.

"Choosing the right outcome without touching good or evil; this is the way. This is the truth." Yuko slipped into a new pattern of attack. With no difficulty at all. She was instantly faster and stronger than Maya's best attacks.

Blow after blow rained down. Maya could not keep up. She drew from all the power she had, pushing her muscles harder and focusing intently on Yuko. But the woman was too fast, too strong. Finally, with a strong palm strike to the chest, Yuko sent Maya flying across the space. She crumpled against a tree and her limbs drooped around her.

"You're down. You're fighting a superior opponent. You cannot win. What do you do next?" Yuko said as she strode over. Maya struggled to get up, but she rose to a standing position, wavering.

"I pick myself up. I don't give up," Maya said with a grin.

"You're resilient. That's a start. But it's not enough." Yuko stalked forward, a gleam in her eye. Maya tried to steady herself.

You need to pull something out. Don't just get hit.

Maya focused herself, trying to find a way to fight back. She put her hands up in a ready pose. Suddenly Yuko was in front of her, holding Maya's right arm.

"If I broke this right now, what would you do?" Yuko said.

"I'd keep fighting, one way or another," Maya said without hesitation. Yuko stared at Maya, not saying anything.

Is she really going to do something?

Yuko released Maya's hand and started walking away.

"Come back tomorrow. I'm going to recommend to Kancho that you're ready for a breakthrough," Yuko said. The rest of the Leftovers joined her, leaving Maya standing alone and watching them leave. She finally relaxed her arms.

Something just happened, but I'm not sure what.

After a few more moments, she started off. Slowly she made her way back through the forest.

Derek waved with excitement when he spotted Maya and Anders.

"Quick, get inside," Derek said. Maya looked past him, taking in the venue. It looked like an old-style house with a large entrance and black peaked roof.

"What is this place?" Maya asked.

"It's a Tea House. Very authentic. You're going to love it," Derek said with a grin. Maya's stomach rumbled in response.

"As long as they serve food as well," she said.

"I think Derek's met you before," Anders said dryly. Maya shook her head at him in mock disappointment and rushed ahead to join Derek.

They were greeted by a woman in a traditional robe at the entrance, who ushered them inside. The Tea House was busy, its simply furnished rooms full of people. However, the noise was less than Maya expected. The conversations were somehow muted. Rather than the roar of food and laughter she was accustomed to, it was more of a constant murmur.

They walked through until they arrived outside in a courtyard. A single table was set up there with a view of the gardens.

"Please make yourself comfortable," the woman said, before disappearing back inside.

"Here we are. Doesn't this feel nice?" Derek said, pulling up a chair. Maya sat opposite him, looking out into the garden.

"It is nice. Thanks for organizing this," Maya said. Anders sat next to her, his awkward movement causing a scraping sound on the floor as he fixed his chair.

"Sorry," he said with a chuckle.

"The Heart Chakra, then," Derek said. He looked at Maya, waiting for a response.

"I thought you would be the one talking," Maya said, a little awkwardly.

"I'll offer some comments. But I'd like to hear how you're going," Derek said. Maya sighed and leaned back in her chair.

"Mostly frustrated, to be honest. I seem to be finding ways to progress, but then nothing happens."

"Give me some examples."

"Well, I spent days relaxing and considering my progress with Kancho. It seemed quite rejuvenating, but I made no progress. I finally stumbled upon his other students, the Leftovers, and helped a man out."

"Seriously? That's a real name?" Anders said.

"They're quite proud of it. The man I helped was stuck in

some weird tunnel which seemed to enhance negative feelings. I thought it would be like the other challenges, ever-increasing until I reached a breakthrough. But the effect just faded away," Maya said. Derek nodded.

"That's fine. What was the other thing?"

"Then another student quizzed me on a few things and started explaining what I needed to do. She started fighting me, and I couldn't fight back. Not really. I was no match for her." Maya paused and took a sip of water.

"Then the strangest thing. When I was ready to fall over, she grabbed my arm. And asked me what I would do if she broke it," Maya said finally. She looked over to Derek for an answer.

"What did you say?" Derek said, watching her intently.

"I said I would keep fighting, one way or another. That's when she said to come back tomorrow, I was ready for a breakthrough." Maya sighed. "But it didn't feel like a breakthrough."

"That was the wrong answer to give, by the way," Kancho said, sitting down at the table with them.

20

THE BREAKTHROUGH

Anders rose to his feet suddenly, almost knocking his chair over.

"Who are you?" Anders said. He started readying something, but Maya put her hand over his.

"Relax, Anders. This is my teacher, Kancho. He's quite unorthodox, I should have expected him to turn up somewhere." Maya smiled over at Kancho and motioned for Anders to sit down. He eased down reluctantly, eyeing Kancho off.

"It's an honor to meet you. I'm Derek," Derek said, giving a small bow. Kancho returned the bow.

"The honor is all mine. I apologize for intruding on your evening," Kancho said. He waved at someone in the background, and a man came over with a tea tray. He placed simple ceramic-style teacups in front of each person and placed two ornate teapots on the table in front of Kancho. One was red, and the other was blue. He bowed to Kancho and then left with his tray.

"I took the liberty of ordering tea. One is for Maya and me, the other is for you two." Kancho picked up the blue teapot, pouring for Anders and Derek. He took great care with the pot, ensuring not a single drop spilled. Similarly, he poured for Maya from the red teapot, and finally poured his own from the same pot.

"What's the difference?" Anders said.

"Minimal. They're both a similar flavor, as you can smell. But it's tradition for a teacher and student to drink the same tea before undertaking a trial together," Kancho said, bowing before Maya.

"You said I gave the wrong answer. Why?" Maya said. She went to drink her tea, but Anders bumped her awkwardly.

"Sorry, my leg is playing up," he said. Maya set the cup down, her focus entirely on Kancho, waiting for his answer.

"Your answer was wrong, because you seem to have an issue with your mindset." Kancho picked up his cup and drank deeply. "You are tough and have willpower. That is fine. It's to be commended. But you so strongly associate your power with fighting. That is why you are wrong."

"I suppose that's true. But you can't blame me. After all I've been through," Maya said, quickly trailing off.

"Care to enlighten me?" Kancho said, taking another sip of his tea. Maya picked up her cup to drink.

"You're a Master teacher, aren't you? Tell us how she needs to adjust," Anders said, interrupting. Maya put down her cup, curious about Kancho's response.

"It's not that simple. I can tell you the answer, and you'll know it. In theory. But the real trick is coming to the answer. Understanding it so deeply that it becomes part of you," Kancho said. Maya stared at him intently. Anders fussed with his own cup, but Maya ignored it.

"You have to try. I need to move forward. Tell me," Maya said. Kancho nodded.

"All power, ours especially, is not about fighting. About combat. Because of our incredible feats, people wrongly associate Chakra with fighting. But it's not about that. It's about becoming enlightened, becoming one with your body, and rising above its limitations. It's not just growth in power, it's personal growth too."

"Let me tell you, I've had plenty of that," Maya said. Kancho nodded and took another sip of his tea. Maya did the same. It tasted a little bitter, but she ignored it.

"I can see that. But I feel that your struggle has been too focused on survival. On fighting for your life. You need a new perspective." Kancho paused and drank more tea. Maya matched him.

"His words ring true," Derek said. He took a deep drink of his tea. Maya had more as well.

"How am I supposed to do that? Become enlightened?" Maya said, unable to mask her frustration. Kancho laughed.

"I'm your teacher, I'm here to help. You're an odd student, lucky you found yourself an odd teacher."

"I guess I have had a strange path to unlocking my Chakras," Maya said with a chuckle herself. Kancho gave her a quizzical look.

"Maya, I realize that we're in Atlantis, training in a temple. But I have the internet, I know who you are." Kancho's face was expressionless as he poured himself more tea. Maya could only stare at him.

"What are you getting at?" Anders said.

"Maya won the LifeDeath tournament. Quite an odd feat for someone with the Chakra bloodline, no?" Kancho sipped his tea again. There was silence across the table.

"I have the sight, Maya. I can see your bloodlines. It was subtle, but the signs were there if you knew how to look," Kancho said.

"What signs," Maya said, her voice barely a whisper.

"The presence of your LifeDeath bloodline. Many would chalk it up to it being a latent power since it's not active. But I could see. It had been used before it was deactivated. Before you activated the Chakra bloodline." Kancho paused, watching her reaction. When she said nothing, he continued.

"It explains your enhanced physical recovery, and in part your exceedingly fast progress through the Chakras. The mindset of someone who has already mastered something makes it easier to master something else." Kancho smiled and poured Maya more tea.

"The fact is, however, that when I look again, there seems to be more. I see other bloodlines. I don't believe that they've been used, but I'm not going to write them off as dormant either. You're not a carrier for them. You have them. All of them." Kancho watched her with piercing eyes as he spoke. Maya felt a shiver go down her spine.

"You're just imagining things," she said quietly.

"Once you accept that fact, the rest of the puzzle fits neatly. It explains the struggles you've been through, and why you're so desperate to progress in your Chakra mastery. You fear for your own wellbeing, and the power you've already attained is locked away until you master Chakra." Kancho smiled triumphantly. Maya sank further into the chair. She looked around the table. Derek looked stunned, and Anders was staring into space.

"What if that was true? What then?" Maya said.

"Others would reject you. I suspect that's already happened, seeing as how you made it to my temple. But I'm not traditional like that. While you've been with my students, I've been planning. Figuring out how to push you forward." Kancho looked at Maya, and then turned his gaze to Anders.

"You're going to help me? Not send me away?" Maya said, the relief tumbling out of her. Kancho's expression didn't change. He kept intently staring at Anders.

"The thing is, Maya, the tea I poured for us was different. It contained a special poison. One that attacks the body," Kancho said in a matter-of-fact manner. Maya quickly knocked her cup over in horror. It spilled all over the table. Derek stood up and rushed over to Maya. Anders remained still, staring into space.

"How could you? How is this helping me? You tricked me!" Maya said, rising to her feet.

"But you've not been drinking it. Your friend has." Kancho gestured toward Anders. Anders nodded but looked sleepy and weak.

"Anders!" Maya grabbed him in a panic, staring into his face. He tried to shrug.

"Sorry," he breathed. Maya whirled around to face Kancho.

"What's the meaning of this? Where's the antidote?"

"There is none."

"Don't give me that nonsense. You drank it too, how do I fix him?"

"It wasn't meant for him. I will recover, in time. I am more resilient. You would have recovered too, over a longer period. But..." Kancho held his hands up, "who can say what will happen to him?"

"You monster. You're worse than the rest." Maya turned back to Anders.

"What's happening to you? Don't worry, I'll fix it. We'll make you better," Maya said, panicked. Anders nodded.

"His body is slowly shutting down. You're going to have to find help pretty quickly," Kancho said, standing up.

"You can't get away with this. Where do you think you're going?" Maya said.

"The school doors are barred to you now. We can't openly oppose the Master Sage. Not when we know his will. And the masters don't appreciate students lying to them. It leaves a bad taste in the mouth." Kancho sighed and started to walk away. Maya stepped in front of him.

"You're not going anywhere. You're going to help me fix this," she said.

"What are you going to do? Fight me? Is that your answer to

everything?" Kancho chuckled. Maya tensed her fists, her whole body taut and quivering with anger.

"I trusted you. How could you betray me like this?" Maya could barely get the words out. She looked back and saw Derek supporting Anders.

"I'm helping you, Maya. You're at a crossroads. I've given you a path. You should be thanking me," Kancho said.

"This. This is unforgiveable. I thought you'd be better. You've mastered the Heart Chakra and beyond. Shouldn't that make you a better person?" Maya said.

"You're thinking in the wrong terms. Good and evil. Right and wrong. Perhaps we can have a philosophical debate one day. However, I think the question you're really asking, is how I could have had these breakthroughs toward enlightenment, and then treat you this way. Is that right?"

"Yes. Out with it."

"Two reasons. One, the insights you experience from your journey are only temporary. You must reflect and internalize them over time. Your personality can override them if you are so inclined."

"And the other?" Maya said, fuming.

"I see things differently to you. You're still lost in the fog, I'm further up the mountain. What you see as betrayal, I see as something else. Good luck, Maya." Kancho smiled and stepped to the side. Maya reached out and grabbed his arm. Kancho looked at her hand, and back at Maya's face.

"You're going to try and stop me? Physically?" Kancho said.

"I told you before. You're going to help me. I won't accept no for an answer."

"Still, you fight. What would you do if I broke this arm?" Kancho said. Maya instantly recoiled.

That's what Yuko said. What are they on about?

Before Maya could think any further Kancho grabbed her arm with his other hand and in a smooth movement that was too fast to properly see, broke her right arm. Shock and pain ran through her, and Maya fell to the ground. She involuntarily closed her eyes.

"That's better. I wish you all the best, Maya. Don't worry, your LifeDeath power will heal that arm a little faster than normal. And your Chakra will help. You've got that going for you." Kancho stepped away and started walking. Maya forced her eyes open, watching him. He nodded at Derek, who helped Anders down to sit on the floor then rushed over to help Maya. She didn't have any words, just cradled her arm.

"Don't worry about him, we'll sort this out. At least he's right about your arm. It will heal faster," Derek said, looking over her arm.

"I can't believe this is happening. It's a nightmare," Maya sobbed.

"I'll make a few calls. With some help, we've got this. I promise you."

How could I have failed so spectacularly?

21

THE OUTCAST

Derek was driving like a maniac, even worse than normal. Maya cradled Anders with her good arm, trying to steady them against the car's turns.

"Don't worry, he's stable for now," Derek said for probably the tenth time. Maya just nodded and kept her gaze on Anders.

"You're going to be fine. Why did you switch with me?" Maya said. Anders coughed.

"I could tell something was up," Anders said weakly, forcing a smile.

"It was meant for me. Who knows what this poison will do to you?"

"I'm pretty tough y'know. I was prepared for this." Anders grimaced for a second, before relaxing his face. "It's very distracting, this whole mess. Try and search through my right pocket. You should find. A vial." Anders closed his eyes and rested. Maya braced against another wild corner and carefully tried to access his pocket. She felt something and retrieved it. It was a glass vial with a rubber stopper. She awkwardly held it up, noticing a pale-yellow liquid within.

"What is this?" she said. Anders answered without opening his eyes.

"It's a broad-base antidote. It counteracts most poisons and boosts your immune system," Anders said quickly. He drew in a ragged breath after.

"You keep this on you? All the time?" Maya said in amazement.

"You never know." Anders struggled to prop his head up a little to look at the vial. "That's it." He slumped back down again. Maya examined the stopper.

"Looks a bit tricky, I don't want to lose the whole thing." Maya peered up at Derek. "Hey Derek, any chance we can stop for a minute?" she shouted.

"Just a moment," Derek said, full of concentration. Suddenly the car lurched to a stop.

"We're here," he said. Derek turned to look at them.

"I want to try this antidote that Anders has," Maya said, holding it up. Derek reached out and took the vial, studying it.

"Can't hurt. I'll help." Derek leapt out of the car and came into the back, propping up Anders while Maya eased off the stopper. She gently poured it into his mouth, a little at a time.

"Tastes worse than expected," Anders grunted. But he swallowed the whole vial. Maya replaced the stopper and stashed it away.

"Where are we?" Maya said.

"A friend's place. I'm going to call in a big favor," Derek said.

"Off we go then," Anders said. Derek chuckled and gently eased Anders out of the car. Together with Maya, he supported Anders toward a quaint old house. It looked like a medieval cottage with an overgrown front garden and a rickety wooden fence.

"This place looks abandoned," Maya said.

"Purposefully. My friend doesn't like visitors," Derek said.

"I hope you're right about this," Maya said. She pushed the

gate open, and they stepped through tall grass up until the wooden door. Derek knocked twice, then waited. There was no response.

"It's Derek! Open up!" Derek shouted. Silence. Eventually, there was a shuffling sound and an unlocking sound. The door slowly swung open.

"Of course, you have to come at night, don't you?" A woman said. She looked to be in her fifties with long, brown hair and was wearing glasses. She was attired in a dressing gown.

"I'm sorry, it's an emergency, Evelyn," Derek said. Evelyn looked them up and down.

"So, it seems. Bring them in," Evelyn said. She sighed and shuffled into the house. It was furnished with antique furniture, some items covered in sheets, the others coated in dust. Evelyn guided them into a sitting room with an old leather couch, and two upholstered sitting chairs. She sat in a chair and pointed to the couch. They settled Anders down and made space for themselves.

"I'm Evelyn. I'm familiar with Derek. And you are?" Evelyn said.

"I'm Maya, and this is Anders. He's been poisoned," Maya said.

"I can see that. Who poisoned him? And with what?"

"We're not sure. It was Kancho, a teacher at the local academy," Maya said. Evelyn frowned. She looked at Derek.

"Did you get a sample?" she asked. He nodded. Derek brought out a takeaway coffee cup. He handed it to Evelyn. She opened it and peered inside. She smelled the brew and took a tiny sip.

"It's well masked. Let me see a moment," she said. Evelyn closed her eyes and concentrated. She sat very still. After a few moments, her eyes sprung open.

"I've not seen this for a while. Nasty concoction. I've never seen it used on a Normal, either," she said, looking at Anders.

"It was meant for Maya. I switched our cups," Anders said with a weak smile.

"Oh, that's very noble of you. Dying for your lady friend, who could have survived it," Evelyn said dryly. Anders visibly gulped.

"What do you mean?" Maya said.

"It's a debilitating poison. It attacks your Chakras. For one with training, it's a hindrance. And is sometimes used in questionable situations. But for one without that additional ability, it's fatal. Not immediately, but eventually."

"But you can help, right?" Derek said, panicked. Evelyn shook her head.

"No. I don't have multiple bloodlines. Chakra, as you would remember, is extremely limited in what it can do to others. I'm sorry," Evelyn said.

"But there must be someone who can help?" Maya said.

"I don't know of anyone. But theoretically, yes."

"How long have I got?" Anders asked.

"It's hard to say. Optimistically, a few weeks?"

"Can't you do more?" Derek stood quickly and started pacing.

"Derek, I am sympathetic. But look at me. I'm cut off, I'm an outcast. I have no connections. I just live in peace. Find yourself someone with LifeDeath and Chakra blended. At least you're in the right part of the world to do so," Evelyn said. She rose as well. "I wish I could offer more. If you'd like, you can stay the night."

"Thank you, it's fine. Is there a name for this poison?" Maya said.

"Clear Tar. It's odorless and tasteless, but it blocks your Chakras like tar," Evelyn said. Derek nodded.

"I see. We better get Anders comfortable. Thanks for your help," Derek said, bowing. Evelyn returned the bow. Maya helped Anders up, and they slowly made their way back to the front door.

"Good luck. Please let me know how you go," Evelyn said.

"Thank you, I will," Derek said. He opened the door, and they walked Anders out. As they reached the car, Anders spoke up.

"Well, that's a kick in the teeth. Death by tea. What a way to go," he said.

"It's not going to happen. I won't let it." Maya opened the door, and together with Derek helped him inside.

"Derek, drive a little slower this time?" Anders said.

"You got it," Derek said, as he turned on the car and pulled away.

Maya closed the hotel door behind her and walked over to Derek.

"He's sleeping now," she said.

"Good. He needs to rest. What are you going to do?" Derek said.

"I need to go for a walk, clear my head. Can you start hitting up contacts?"

"I already have a few in mind. Leave it to me." Derek started to walk away, and then stopped, turning back. "Are you OK?"

"I'm fine. Relatively. Go and do your thing."

"I'll check in with you in the morning." Derek waved briefly and strode off to the lift, his phone already in his hand. Maya wandered over to Kora's room and hesitated in front of it.

No. She deserves to know, but I can't do this now.

Maya waited for Derek to leave and then headed over to the lift.

Hours later, Maya found herself in a dimly lit park. There were only a few lights around the perimeter, and the inside was almost pitch black. She didn't mind, it matched her mood.

Look at this mess you've made. Anders is dying. You're denied further training. The Master Sage is waiting in the wings to do something else. What now?

Maya started thinking about the steps that had led her there. Her insistence of pushing ahead with the training, and her guilt at dragging Anders with her. He had other things to be doing, not just following her around. She stoked her anger, remembering how the Master Sage had hounded her, and that they were only in this situation because he refused to let her be. Negative emotion followed negative thought until she was kneeling on the ground, the darkness of the park mirroring her inner state perfectly.

You've made your own 'gloom tunnel'. Congratulations.

For so long, she drowned in those thoughts and feelings. Being dragged deeper and deeper. All the while there was a thought that kept trying to pop up.

Can't you rise beyond this? Didn't you pass the Water Chakra and the Fire Chakra?

She aggressively pushed it down, believing that she deserved the agony. Anders was dying because of her. She had to keep fighting. That was how to survive. How to be strong. But the thought kept coming back. And with it, a new realization dawned. Maya was lost for words.

She felt an opening in her chest. Not a hole, but an expansion. She breathed a deep breath, amazed at the lightness she was feeling. Somewhere along the line, she had passed through something. The darkness was subsiding. Replaced with something else.

Insight?

In this new state, she reexamined the events. They were bathed in a different light. Kancho had not betrayed her. He had seen where she was stuck and designed a way through it. Anders had interfered, but that also served the same purpose. Kancho had designed a problem that she couldn't fight physically. He had even broken her arm to reinforce the point. The same one that Yuko had made.

I don't have to fight everyone. Not everything is a battle.

With a moment of clarity, she knew what to do.

The rays of dawn tickled Maya's eyelids, and she opened her eyes. She hadn't slept a wink, but instead meditated for the entire evening. Or what was left of it, after her downward spiral.

Not going to recommend that to anyone.

Maya stood and stretched her legs. She carefully cradled her arm, remembering for the first time that she should have taken better care of it.

Time for that after I talk to Anders.

Maya sped off, walking at pace. She didn't feel tired, only light on her feet. The walk back through the city felt like a blur. She barely noticed the scenery. She was instead desperately clinging to the sense of peace she had found in the night. Not wanting it to go away but knowing that it would eventually.

When she arrived at their hotel room, Anders was awake. He had propped himself up in the bed.

"Nice try, but you still look terrible," Maya said with a chuckle. But she gave him a proper smile.

"You look better. Did something change?" Anders said.

"I achieved the Heart Chakra overnight," Maya said. She carefully showed Anders her right arm. Along with the rest, there was a new mark. It was a circle with a heart shape inside.

"Cute mark. Was it hard?" he asked.

"It was. But I'm better now. We've got a lot ahead of us, but I can see my path clearly." Maya sat on the bed and cradled her broken arm.

"What's the plan?"

"I'm going to cure you myself. We'll still look for someone else to do it, but I won't sit around waiting for that."

"That's a lot of pressure to put on yourself. Are you sure?"

"Completely. I've already passed the fourth Chakra. There's only two more."

"But they're a lot harder. And you don't have any teachers left," Anders said. Maya nodded.

"I know. But we'll find another way. I have to do this. It's just another problem to solve." Maya smiled.

"I've been thinking about that. You know how I found your old school back in the International Quarter?"

"Yes, you did the treasure hunt for me."

"Well, I made a contact in the process. And turns out he had an additional bloodline."

"Really?" Maya leaned in closer.

"Yes, it's not activated but he had the Haste bloodline. Seeing as how he doesn't want that little tidbit getting out, I hit him up this morning for some information. And I have a lead." Anders gave her a triumphant grin.

"Great. So, you let me go on a diatribe and you have an answer?"

"Not an answer, just a lead. It's an organization in the next city over, Nentis. It's a collection of different bloodlines which work together."

"That sounds cool. What are they? Like a club?"

"No. Actually, they're ninjas." Anders kept a straight face, but Maya burst out laughing.

22

ROAD TRIP

"Ninjas? Really?" Maya said. Anders nodded slowly. "Yes. They're strong, and they're independent. We won't have the same Master Sage issues as all the schools."

"Hmm," Maya said. She looked away as she thought. "We might find someone with multiple bloodlines who can help. Or at least I can find people with the Chakra bloodline who will help train me. This could work."

"I know. It's not going to be easy, though," Anders added.

"It never is. How do you even get an introduction to a ninja organization anyway?"

"They prefer clan. You have to do something noteworthy." Anders started to grin, but suddenly looked to be in pain.

"Are you OK?" Maya said, rushing closer.

"It's fine. I get these little rushes. I can't explain them," Anders said. There was a knock at the door.

"Maybe he can," Anders said. Maya walked through the bedroom, to the main room and opened the door. Derek was waiting there.

"I got the message. What's going on?"

"We're planning. Come in," Maya said.

"Wait, something's different," Derek said. He looked Maya up and down. "Heart Chakra?"

"That's the one. Very eventful day yesterday."

"I'll say. That's not an easy one to do. Congratulations." Derek bowed, and Maya returned it.

"C'mon let's go talk to Anders." Maya ushered Derek in and closed the door behind him. They pulled some chairs in from the compact dining table to sit around the bed.

"Derek, we have a plan. And we need your help," Anders said. He looked over at Maya.

"Oh, right. I'll explain. I'm going to join a ninja clan," Maya said. Derek nodded.

"OK. Which one?" he said.

"Wait. You're not surprised?" Maya said.

"No, it's the obvious choice. Nobody else uses people of different bloodlines so interchangeably."

"I didn't even know they still existed," Maya said.

"That's the whole point," Derek said with a chuckle. "But look it's an open secret in these parts. They exist for multiple purposes. Mastery of bloodlines, power by association, safety. They take on assignments for money in addition to their own schemes."

"So how do I join?" Maya said.

"You need to impress them. It's not like you attend an interview," Derek said. Anders laughed out loud briefly, before cringing in pain.

"Sorry," Derek said. Anders just nodded. "So, who are we targeting?"

"The Hanzo clan. I have a contact with connections there," Anders said. Derek scratched his chin and leaned back in his chair.

"I think that could work. What's the idea? Breaking and entering?" Derek said. Maya laughed.

"What?"

"You need to impress them at their own game. Infiltration is a prime way," Derek said.

"I have his address. I think we can do this," Anders said.

"Where are we headed?" Maya said.

"Nentis," Anders said. "Maybe someone other than Derek can drive us?"

"Fine. I'll make the arrangements. You better start packing." Derek stood to leave.

"I better fill in Kora first. Let me know when everything's in place," Maya said. She stood as well and walked Derek to the door.

"I assume you're going to push ahead with your mastery?" Derek said as they reached the door.

"Yes. Ideally, we find someone to heal Anders. Otherwise, I'll do it."

"Good. Maybe this clan can get us both into the Lost Lands as well."

"Maybe. One step at a time."

"Indeed. I'll call you." Derek headed out and Maya walked over to Kora's door. She knocked twice.

"It's open!" Kora called out. Maya opened the door and walked inside. The hotel room looked immaculate. Several large suitcases were lined up, and Kora was sipping coffee and working off a laptop.

"Are we ready to go?" Kora said.

"What do you mean? A lot has happened," Maya began. Kora interrupted.

"Yes, I know. Anders is poisoned, we're finding ninjas. It's all very exciting. When are we leaving?" Kora said with a smirk.

"But how?" Maya said.

"You think all this kit is for a laugh? I know what's going on. I see and hear everything." Kora winked and closed her laptop.

"So, you'll help?" Maya said.

"I've already got the plans for the apartment you need to infiltrate."

"I guess that's a yes. Thank you."

"Don't mention it. I've always wanted to travel more; this is the perfect excuse. And I'm intrigued to see what tech these ninjas are sporting. Should be good."

"I'll see what I can get for you. Any progress on the bloodline sensor? For the seventh bloodline?"

"I've been able to replicate the technology into my own device. The next step would be creating a device that tests for it explicitly. Like a normal bloodline sensor."

"You think you can get there? With what you have now?"

"Did you even need to ask?" Kora shook her head with disapproval.

"Sorry, I shouldn't keep being surprised by your genius," Maya said.

"It's more fun that way, anyway. Call me when you're ready." Kora opened her laptop and was suddenly immersed in it once more. Maya saw herself out.

A few hours later, all their equipment was packed into a van. Maya tested the makeshift sling that Derek had provided her.

"That will do until we can organize something better. Oh, and sorry about the seating, this is the best we can do at short notice," Derek said. There were two seats up front, and two more in the rear of the van.

"Let's sit Anders back here where the seats recline." Derek helped guide Anders back there, and together they settled him into the chair.

"I'll sit back here," Maya offered. Derek nodded and she made herself comfortable in the other chair. Derek sat up front with Kora.

"I hope these kids are well-behaved," Derek said to Kora. She laughed.

"If you fight back there, you don't get any ice cream when we arrive," Kora called out. Anders managed a weak grin, and Maya chuckled. With that, Derek started the van, and off they went.

The trip was pleasant enough. Derek, true to his word, drove normally and Maya was able to adjust Anders enough to keep him comfortable. Once they were within Nentis proper it was the afternoon. Maya drew in a deep breath.

"Wow, this is huge. So many people," she said. Huge throngs were gathered on the streets, waiting to cross.

"It's peak hour," Derek explained. Maya marveled at the height of the buildings too.

"These skyscrapers are amazing," she commented.

"Wait until you see them at night," Derek said. Maya remained quiet for the rest of the trip, observing Anders, and taking in the city. They parked outside a tiny apartment block.

"We're here. I picked us something a little more discreet and out of the way." Derek turned off the van and jumped out, heading straight for the back. He opened the doors and then disappeared into the reception area.

"Hey, we're here," Maya said to Anders. He opened his eyes slowly, taking in the surroundings.

"Good," he said, and his eyes drifted closed again. Maya looked around for Derek. He was back soon, flashing some card keys, and they made the slow and deliberate act of moving Anders into the apartment, and then their belongings.

"Kora and I are across the hall, there and there," Derek said, pointing out rooms. "Once you and Anders are settled, come over to Kora's room and we'll discuss the plan. We'll need to hit that apartment tonight."

"Sure, see you soon." Maya returned to her apartment, checked on Anders, and then readied herself.

Kora, Maya, and Derek sat around a table of sushi and sashimi. Maya helped herself to another sushi roll as Kora spoke.

"This is the device you'll use to enter the room. If it doesn't work, then you'll have to improvise," Kora said.

"Doesn't work? I thought your stuff always worked."

"It will work. But I haven't seen what they have. This guy might have something I haven't catered for," Kora explained.

"The target is named Mikael," Derek added.

"Sounds European," Maya said. Derek shrugged.

"That's the information Anders got for us."

"I've figured out more of his background, but it's unnecessary for the job. What you'll be looking for is something like this." Kora turned her laptop to show Maya the screen. There was an emblem of a stylized fire.

"This is a token?" Maya asked.

"Exactly. Each clan member has one. If you take it, that's your way of showing initiative and skill. Mikael will be forced to introduce you."

"Sounds easy enough. Do you know where it is?" Maya said.

"I'm not a miracle worker. I don't have feeds inside his place. You'll have to figure that out yourself."

"Any other gadgets?" Maya asked.

"Take one of these stun wands from Anders. And here's a smoke bomb." Kora retrieved the two items and handed them to Maya.

"Smoke bomb?"

"You know, ninja style," Derek offered.

"If you need to escape, it'll cause a distraction," Kora said with a grin.

"So, I just throw it?" Maya said, turning the device around.

"That's the one. It's Maya proof," Kora said.

"Fine, I get it." Maya stood and pocketed the items. "Let's go."

"Oh, one last thing." Kora stood and pinned a tiny brooch to Maya's jacket.

"Is that for luck?" Maya said.

"You could say that. It also has a video and audio feed." Kora waved her away and Derek laughed.

"I'd say call us, but I don't think that will be necessary. Good luck and we'll be watching," Derek said. He stood and walked Maya to the door.

"Listen, I'll be close. If things go south, I can help."

"Thanks. Let's hope it doesn't get to that." Maya held up her sling. "I can't exactly fight my way out."

"No, you can't. Take care." Derek opened the door, and Maya left. She turned back to wave to Kora, but the woman was already engrossed in her laptop. Maya chuckled to herself.

A walk and a train trip later, Maya was close. She approached the building and double-checked on her phone.

"This is it. I need the ninth floor." Maya approached the building and watched the people streaming steadily in and out.

How many people live here?

Maya walked up confidently and entered the lobby without incident. The lobby was busy but not packed, thankfully. There were only the lifts and a few chairs. Maya crossed over and called a lift. The button lit up immediately.

That's a start.

When the lift arrived, she waited for the people to step out. Maya ushered some others into the lift and followed behind them. They presented their access cards and pressed floors ten and twelve. Maya stepped out of the lift and let it go, the other passengers appeared puzzled.

"I'll get the next one," she said. They still seemed puzzled, but the lift disappeared, and she waited for another. Thankfully, the next one was empty, and there were no people going in with her. Maya immediately pressed the close doors button and then retrieved her device. It was about the same size as her phone. She held it up to the reader and it flashed a few times before beeping. All the lift buttons lit up. Maya pressed number nine and relaxed.

Glad that worked. One step closer.

The lift sped up at incredible speed, and suddenly the doors were opening again. Maya was not ready. She stepped forward and searched around. It was a long corridor with lots of doors.

Look for number 912.

Maya headed down one direction, observing the numbers. She quickly determined it was the wrong way and turned back in the other direction. A woman walked past her but didn't pay her any attention. Maya slowed her footsteps and then stopped outside the door.

This is the one. But I can't just go inside.

Maya leaned in closer, trying to listen. She couldn't hear anything from outside.

May as well try.

Maya fumbled the device out of her pocket again. She held it up to the door reader and waited. The lights flashed as before. Then kept flashing. Maya looked around; nobody was there. Her pulse raced as the device kept flashing. Finally, it stopped. The lights were red. Maya swore under her breath. Just in case, she slowly tried the handle, but the door was locked.

Time for plan B.

23

SURPRISING A NINJA

M aya walked back through the corridor, thinking.
*I can't get in the door, there must be another way.
A window?*

She parked that thought, not wanting to get too out of control. A safer option would be to find another way to disable the door lock or some sort of master key. Prowling through the corridor, all she could see was more rooms.

The room next door.

There could be something there she could use to get in. Maya rushed back to the apartment door and sidled over to the next one over. Again, she listened in, and couldn't hear anything on the other side of the door. Maya retrieved her hacking device and held it up to the door. It started flashing once more and continued flashing.

C'mon, just work.

The lights suddenly became green, and she heard the door unlock.

It worked.

Maya turned the door handle gently and entered the apartment. Her initial assessment was that a total slob lived here.

There were clothes in piles, papers everywhere, and just stuff. The couch had boxes on it with space for a single person to sit. There was a computer and desk with piles of stuff on either side. But at least it seemed empty. Maya wandered through, looking for anything that stood out. She didn't notice any air conditioning ducts or odd doors that went nowhere. It was simply the main living room and kitchenette, a tiny bathroom, and a bed nook.

This is a bust.

Maya was about to leave when she spotted something. Past the couch with junk, it wasn't a window. It was something else. She approached quickly.

Sliding door. There's a balcony back here.

That had promise. She carefully navigated back there, almost knocking over a pile of clothes. She opened the door and heard another noise. It was the tell-tale sound of the front door opening. Maya rushed through the sliding door onto the balcony, closing the door as quickly as possible and trying to hide. She crouched down on the slim balcony and waited.

She could hear footsteps in the apartment. She kept listening. The steps paused and restarted a few seconds later. They seemed to be getting closer. Maya's heart rate started to climb, but she took a deep breath.

You got this.

The steps stopped. Maya poked her head up, trying to sneak a peek inside. There was a man in his twenties sitting on the couch now. He was watching the TV.

What now?

Maya turned her attention to her surroundings. She was standing on a polished concrete slab with a glass railing. Across from her was the balcony for the neighboring apartment.

That doesn't seem too far.

Maya crept closer and evaluated. If she climbed up, she could probably step over to the balcony.

Only it's a long drop, and you've effectively got one arm.

Her only other option was to reenter the apartment she was in, deal with or neutralize the man there, and leave.

You can do it. Complete the mission.

Maya used her good arm to steady herself, boosting herself up, and then lifting a leg up onto the railing.

Could really use my other arm right about now.

She leaned against the wall on her right shoulder, steadying herself that way. She started to look down but stopped. Focused completely on the other balcony, she stepped forward with her right foot and put it down on the other railing. She wobbled. Fearing a loss of balance, Maya went all-in, swinging her other leg over.

Her balance failed her, but she had enough momentum to carry forward and she tumbled down onto the concrete floor of the other balcony.

I had to land on my bad arm, didn't I?

But it was better than landing on the street. She rolled over and came up to a crouched position, looking into the other apartment. It was the same size and layout, but completely different. There were lots of bookshelves, neatly organized, and not a single thing out of place. She also couldn't see anyone inside.

Let's go.

Maya tried the handle for the sliding door. It wouldn't budge. Locked. Maya tried her hacking device. The lights didn't light up at all. She examined the lock again and swore.

Mechanical lock. Need an actual key.

Maya looked around for another way to force an entry. There wasn't one.

This is the only way. Make it work. The lock probably isn't that strong.

Maya grabbed the handle with her good arm. She focused on her breathing, entering a simple meditation. She needed to focus and draw upon her power, to have the strength to yank the door open, breaking the lock mechanism in the process. She imagined what it would look like, the door resisting and then suddenly rushing open as the lock gave way.

And then she did it. It all worked as she had imagined. Except the sliding door had way too much momentum and tumbled off the rails it was on. Maya had to think quickly and adjust her hold before it crashed into her head. Carefully setting it down, Maya squeezed her way through the opening and into the apartment.

This is taking too long.

Maya started looking around to find the emblem. She searched through the bookshelves, checked the desk. Even rifled through the drawers. Nothing of interest. And barely any clutter.

This Mikael is too organized. Where would he put it?

Maya wandered through the apartment, looking for anything unusual. She decided to check under the bed. There was a metal box. She pulled it out and had a look.

Combination lock. Must be something good inside.

Maya retrieved her hacking device again, holding it up to the area near the keypad. The lights started flashing and she held her breath.

That Kora. I'm going to tell her about it failing on the door. It better work now.

The lights flashed green, and she heard the box unlock. She gently opened the lid, looking inside. There were some papers, some keepsakes. And at the bottom was the emblem. It was the right fire symbol but made from glass. It was orange and red. She grabbed it and put it in her jacket pocket, closing the lid on the box.

As she slid the box under the bed, she heard the front door unlock.

Great. Just super.

Without too much thought, Maya readied the smoke bomb. As a figure walked through the door, she threw the smoke bomb at the ground near the entry. As soon as it landed, acrid smoke billowed out, causing the person entering to cough and stumble back.

Maya ran over, pushing the person out of the way and running through the door. She made it to the hallway before realizing that the lifts were a bad idea. She instead ran the other direction, hoping to find stairs.

Of course you're going for the alternate escape route. Next time don't even pretend that things are going to go smoothly..

She was familiar enough with the look of the apartment doors to know she had to keep running.

"Hey!" a male voice shouted from behind. Maya didn't look back. She found an odd-looking door and paused. She tried it and noticed a stairwell.

Bingo.

Maya glanced back and saw a blond man running her way. She ducked into the stairwell.

It was long a way down, and very compact.

This is not going to work for a chase, he's too close.

Maya decided to wait behind the door and readied the stun wand. A bead of sweat appeared on her brow, but she ignored it. She focused all her tension into readying that wand. The door opened and the man burst through. Maya quickly shoved into him with her body, knocking him off balance and thrusting forward with the stun wand. It made contact and the man dropped to the floor, grunting.

Maya used the opening to run down the stairs, using the next door to enter another floor. She ran along this one, sprinting for the lifts. She called one and waited. Her eyes were glued to the stairwell door.

Don't recover yet. Don't recover yet.

She wasn't in the condition to fight. The lift chimed and she jumped in, pressing the 'G' button. The doors slowly closed and as the lift roared down, she slightly relaxed.

You're not out of this, but you're close.

The lift arrived and she strode out of the opening doors. Maya didn't look back, she just kept pushing forward. A block away from the apartments she almost ran into Derek.

"Easy there," Derek said with a chuckle.

"Derek? You were here?" Maya said with a mix of relief and surprise.

"Why wouldn't I be?" Derek said quickly. "Come this way." Derek led Maya away. They walked down an alley, into a strange area. It looked industrial and deserted.

Is this a way to sneak out without drawing attention?

Derek guided her into a tiny building attached to a series of factory units. It was a non-descript concrete block.

"They won't track us in here," Derek said. Maya nodded and pushed the door open. She stepped into a darkened room with only computer monitors lighting up the space.

"A bit dark, don't you think?" Derek said, flicking a light switch. Powerful fluorescents beamed around the room, temporarily blinding Maya. As her vision recovered, she noticed two people sitting amongst the computers. Kora and another man. One she recognized after a few moments.

"What's going on? Why is he here?" Maya said, confused and looking around for answers.

"Take a seat, Maya," Kora said. She pointed to a nearby office chair. Maya walked over to the chair, wheeling it closer to Kora and sitting down. At this distance, she could see the screen.

"That's my video feed." Maya looked over at the man.

"Did you like my apartment?" Mikael said without any emotion. Maya was thrown.

"But I saw you enter, I stunned you," Maya said.

"Did you really?" Mikael nodded to Kora, and she manipulated the footage on the screen. In the frame before the smoke bomb exploded you could clearly see the man in the room. He had blond hair and a similar build to Mikael, but very different features.

"I see," Maya said.

"I knew you'd never get a good look at him. Don't worry, he recovered quickly," Mikael said, again without any emotion.

"What's going on here?"

"This was your test," Derek explained. "Did you bring the emblem?"

Maya reached into her jacket, retrieving the emblem. As she removed it, she could see a large crack through it.

"Here. It's a little damaged," Maya said sheepishly. Mikael accepted it, looking the emblem over before crushing it in his hands. He left a pile of fine powder on the table.

"Were you supposed to..." Maya said, pointing to the powder and trailing off.

"It was only a prop; it served its purpose. The question is, will you?" Mikael said, looking Maya in the eyes. He had an intensity she didn't expect.

"So, you were watching me the whole time. Seeing me flounder." Maya looked over at Kora sharply. "Was that even your device? It failed completely on the door." Maya's voice started to rise in volume. Kora shrugged.

"Sorry, part of the test. But you should be prepared for tech failing," Kora said.

"Well, tell me already. Did I fail?" Maya said, looking at Mikael. He nodded.

"Yes, but we will accept you. You achieved the result and escaped, despite your injury." Mikael let his eyes wander over to the cast and sling.

"Hang on. I can join you?" Maya said.

"We have a place for you. Luckily for you, your contacts

were strong enough to make the difference. I'll have to train you myself, to ensure you can succeed.

"You?" Maya said.

Oh, nice one. Insult your new boss.

Mikael rose up. Looking her up and down, his presence suddenly felt different. He radiated a kind of power.

"My name is Mikael Sedlecki. I am known in the Hanzo clan as 'Shadow Step'. You would do well to not underestimate me." Mikael turned and strode away.

"Wait," Maya said, rushing after him.

24

A BIG DEAL

Mikael didn't slow at all, emerging into the night. Maya stumbled but caught up to him.

"Where are you going?" she said.

"To headquarters."

"Why are you taking me in? I'm sorry that I made a mess of your apartment."

"That wasn't my apartment," Mikael said without looking at her.

Hopefully, it was part of the test. And I didn't just throw a smoke bomb in someone else's apartment.

"What bloodline are you? Chakra?" Maya asked, falling in line with Mikael's pace.

"That's not something you're supposed to ask. But no." Mikael turned the corner, heading toward the cluster of factory units Maya had spotted before.

"What drew you to the Hanzo clan?" Maya asked.

"You need stillness. Hold your tongue before you cause further trouble," Mikael said. Maya's face started to heat up, and she swallowed her next words. They continued.

The factory units were a jumble of featureless concrete

buildings. There were car parking spaces and driveways assigned to each one, but oddly not a single car was parked.

Maybe because it's after dark?

They approached one building, and Mikael opened the door. He held it open for a moment before continuing. Maya rushed forward and stepped inside. They were in a compact office space. Without any real furnishings. There was a single door and Mikael was already opening it. Beyond that door, they were in what looked like an elevator.

"Is this..." Maya began to say when the room suddenly dropped. They were plunging at an incredible speed. Maya looked at Mikael and he had no reaction. If anything, he looked bored. Just like that the lift suddenly halted, and a set of doors opened. Mikael walked out and Maya almost forgot to. Beyond the doors looked like another city.

"What?" Maya said, stumbling out of the lift doors and taking it all in. They were in a city underground. With simulated sky, tall buildings, and people bustling everywhere. Those that waited near the lift noticed Mikael, and they bowed immediately. It was like a wave as he walked, the bowing people tracking his progress.

He seems like a big deal.

Once they passed through the initial throng, the bowing ceased, and they were lost in the crowd. Maya stopped gaping at the sheer scale of the place and focused on following Mikael. They navigated a few streets until he stopped outside a cute cottage. It had a red tiled roof and simple cream walls. It looked completely out of place. Mikael walked up to the front door and opened it.

I didn't see a key.

Maya followed him in, closing the door behind her. The house was simply furnished, but in an elegant style. Classic European furniture, and not a speck of dust.

"This is my house. Your room is down here." Mikael walked through the main corridor, stopping in front of a room.

"I'll live here?" Maya asked, as she reached the room. It contained a simple bed, wooden desk, a mirror, and a wardrobe. "Cozy."

"You'll stay here while you're under my guidance. It's too dangerous for you otherwise." Mikael said nothing more and continued through the house. Maya took one more glance around her room and then rushed to catch up. At the back was a kitchen. Mikael threw open the doors and stepped into the backyard. It was covered in grass with a tree in the middle. Mikael walked over and sat under the tree.

"Mind if I join you?" Maya said. Mikael pointed to ground next to him and nodded. Maya carefully walked over and sat down. She gazed up at the tree.

"It feels like we're outside," she said.

"It's all relative. In a way, we are," Mikael said. He closed his eyes. Maya remained still for a moment, thinking. But there were too many questions.

"What do we do now? What's the Hanzo clan do?" she asked. Mikael kept his eyes closed.

"We wait for our next mission. The clan does as it needs to survive. That is why it succeeds."

"We wait? How long will it be? I'm not sure if my friends briefed you, but Anders is sick. He's been poisoned."

"Clear Tar. I'm aware," Mikael said. Maya shuffled her position, so she was facing him.

"Exactly. Have you dealt with it before?"

"Yes, I have. For Normals, there is usually no cure. I've heard of machines that can slow the process."

"Great. Can we get one for Anders?"

"Expensive. You'll need to earn one."

"Let's start now." Maya stood and started pacing around the grass. Mikael was motionless.

"Speed is not about constant motion," Mikael said. Maya stopped and regarded him.

"What do you mean?"

"Speed is about taking the shortest time for the best result." Mikael opened his eyes and looked at Maya. After a moment, he was gone. Maya whirled around and saw Mikael standing behind her.

"How..."

"That's my talent. Haste. There are different types, but I'm often referred to as a silent Speedster. For obvious reasons."

"That's something else. No wonder you're a ninja," Maya said. "I've not encountered the Haste bloodline much at all."

"You'll see more of it. I can see that you need to be occupied." Mikael paused, thinking. "I can't specifically help you with your Chakra training, although I do partner with others who do."

"Can you share anything to help me?" Maya said. Mikael assessed her, considering.

"You cleared the Heart Chakra?"

"Yes, that's it. Just two to go. Well, maybe three total?"

"Correct. The seventh Chakra is rare. The Space Chakra is next for you. It's located here." Mikael pointed to his throat.

"How do I train for it? I don't have to sing do I?" Maya said, chuckling.

"It can help," Mikael said, no humor in his voice. Maya gulped.

"Well, I'll do whatever is necessary."

"I think there's some books you can read while we wait."

"Wait?"

"For the mission. They don't give me any old mission."

"But my friend, Anders. He doesn't have time."

"They won't let him die. Come." Mikael walked off, each step deliberate.

I thought a Speedster would just be instantly everywhere. He seems to make a point of taking his time. I wonder why?

Mikael led her back through the kitchen to another room. Mikael paused and gestured to the door.

"After you," he said.

"Thanks." Maya turned the handle and entered the room. It was a library. There was a single leather seat, a tiny side table, and the walls were lined with books.

"Will this suffice?" Mikael said.

"Wow. This is incredible. Yes. Yes." Maya rushed over to the nearest shelf, scanning through the book titles.

"Enjoy," Mikael said, before walking off. Maya barely noticed him going. She had already spotted three books about the Chakra bloodline.

I can finally catch up now.

Days passed quickly. Maya spent most of her time in the library. Derek kept her updated on the phone. Anders was stable and getting treatment that would keep him that way. She was free to focus on her training and working with Mikael. But Mikael seemed to enjoy doing nothing and being still. It reminded her of Kancho, which was still a strange memory to process. So, Maya occupied herself in the library, making up for lost time.

A week into her stay, Mikael stepped into the library. His eyes took in the room.

"I see you've been busy. Are you a scholar yet?"

"I made scholar years ago. This library is amazing. Have you read them all?"

"Of course. They're not for show."

"Can you read faster?" Maya asked. Mikael nodded.

"You're a quick study. Most don't come to that conclusion so quickly." Mikael walked into the room and picked a book off the ground, returning it to the shelf.

"We have a mission," he said. Maya closed the book she was reading and looked up.

"Finally. What is it?"

"You'll see. Come." Mikael turned and walked out of the room. Maya rose and rushed after him. Mikael walked through the house, retrieving a letter, and handing it to Maya. She eagerly read it.

"It's on paper, that's great. I thought everything was digital these days."

"Not everything." Mikael watched her read the letter. Once Maya was finished, she handed it back.

"Rescue mission then? We go in and retrieve a man. Shouldn't this be easy?" Maya said.

"You are to lead and plan the mission. I am a resource at your disposal," Mikael said. Maya spotted the slightest hint of a smile. The first example of any emotion.

"Me? But you're the legendary, super ninja," Maya said.

"Who better to assist you?" Mikael said.

"Well, you'll have to tell me more about what you can do."

"You already know that. I'm sure the first book you read was about the Haste bloodline."

"You're right. And you told me what type you are," Maya said, thinking out loud. Mikael nodded and turned to leave. "That's it?"

"There's a laptop in the library you can use to gather additional data," Mikael said, watching her reaction. "I can see you're formulating a plan now. Let me know when we're ready to leave."

"But we can't wait around. We need to save this man, Shin."

"Then you better stop talking and start planning." Mikael kept walking. Maya took the letter into the library and read it again.

Time to figure this one out. I can't rely on Mikael to do it. But I can use his skills.

Hours later, Maya returned to the kitchen with the laptop.

"I think this will work. We start tonight and—" Maya said, about to launch into a discussion. Mikael cut her off with a gesture.

"This is your plan, we're not brainstorming. Let's go." Mikael stood, picking up a bag, and slinging it over his shoulder.

"We have access to transport, right?" Maya said nervously as they walked through the cottage.

"For you, I'll make an exception. I'll requisition one," Mikael said.

"Thanks. I'd rather not walk."

"That was a joke. We have freely available transportation," Mikael said as an aside, and opened the front door. They walked in silence through the strange outdoor space, quickly arriving at the lift. Mikael called it and they zoomed upward, the speed still surprising Maya.

This probably seems slow to him.

The doors opened and they walked through. A few people waved at Mikael, and he nodded to acknowledge them. Instead of exiting the complex, he turned right and headed for one of the units. They stopped outside a colossal roller door. Mikael held up his right hand to a sensor on the side, and the giant door started rolling up.

Let's see what they consider transportation.

Once the roller door was up, Maya could see inside.

"I wasn't sure what to expect. But it wasn't this." Maya looked over the vehicles. They were all black vans. Completely nondescript and uninteresting.

"You wanted a sports car? Not our style," Mikael said. He walked over and opened the door on one of the vans.

"Keys are inside, let's go." Mikael waited for Maya to step into the driver's seat and turn the van on. Then he leaned over and pressed a button on the dashboard. The large side door of the van slid open. Curious, Maya stepped out to look.

"Wow," Maya said. The van was completely kitted out. Other than a few seats, the back was packed full of equipment. Computers and monitors, weaponry and other tools, and some storage boxes.

"Good luck fitting all this in a sports car," Mikael said, stepping in, and making himself comfortable in one of the chairs.

"I'll let you know when we get there," Maya said with a sigh.

"Great. You've picked things up so fast," Mikael said. Maya shook her head and returned to the driver's seat. She pushed the same button again, and the side door slid closed.

I really hope this works.

25

THE MISSION

M aya parked the van. Steering would have been uncomfortable with her broken arm, but thankfully the self-driving feature worked well, and she hadn't needed to do anything. Not that she was relaxed enough to take her eyes off the road, either.

"Climb back here, and brief me," Mikael said. Maya looked around the cabin and the dashboard, pressing a button that said 'Rear Access'. A panel slid back, giving Maya access to the back. It was an awkward squeeze, but she pushed herself through and crouch walked into the back of the van, sitting down in one of the chairs.

"Mission leader, what's the plan?" Mikael said. He was fully attentive and didn't look to be joking around.

"As you know, Shin is in that warehouse. We don't know where, or how many are guarding him," Maya said. Mikael nodded toward one of the computers but said nothing. Maya whirled around and turned on the computer. It revealed a satellite map of the area with red dots superimposed over it.

"I presume these are people?" Maya said. Mikael nodded. Maya considered the image for a few seconds.

"I know why you're doing this, being so passive. It's to help with the next Chakra," Maya said.

"Amongst other things. Please continue," Mikael said.

"You'll infiltrate the warehouse, entering through the roof. You'll work your way down, looking for the target. Once you've found him, you'll exit the building, and I'll drive the van up, giving you an escape," Maya said. Mikael watched her patiently.

"That's it?" he said.

"Yes. We'll manage contingencies as they come up."

"And you?"

"I'll be monitoring from the van."

"Very well. What about audio-visual support?" Mikael said.

"You should wear a camera and microphone kit," Maya said, looking around. Mikael selected a black pin from a drawer and handed it to Maya. Next, he stood up, and became a complete blur. He stopped moving but was now wearing a black combat uniform. Head to toe he was covered in black.

"Nice," Maya said with approval. She handed the black pin back to Mikael and he clipped it into something on his head.

"Good luck," Mikael said, opening the van door.

"Hey that's my line," Maya said. Mikael turned back to look at her for a second, before disappearing. Literally. Maya scrambled to turn on the other computer, fumbling around for the AV program. Within a minute she found it. She could see and hear from Mikael's perspective on one computer, and another one had the surroundings mapped out.

"Here we go," Maya whispered. She could see that Mikael was moving slowly.

Must be saving his speed for when he needs it.

Still, Mikael was skillfully navigating around patrolling guards. He approached the warehouse. Maya realized she had been holding a breath, and let it go in a big exhale. Mikael walked around the perimeter of the building. Maya glanced back at the map.

"There," she whispered, pointing out a spot. It was an area with no patrolling guards nearby.

"The northeast corner of the building is a good place to ascend," Maya said. There was no response. She brought up the AV controls and realized there was a button to push to talk.

"Lucky there's nobody here to see that," Maya said. She pressed the button and spoke again.

"The northeast corner of the building is a good place to ascend."

"Acknowledged," Mikael whispered. Maya nodded with approval. She turned back to the map, seeing Mikael's location approaching the safe area. She glanced back at his camera feed. It paused for a moment, then became a disorientating blur. When it settled down, the view was spectacular. Mikael was on the rooftop, looking out across the city.

"Ascent successful. Looking for a suitable entry point," Mikael said. He started walking.

"Acknowledged," Maya said. She kept her eyes on the map, watching all the red dots signifying enemies. They seemed to be consistently following a pattern.

"Located access point," Mikael said. Maya saw through the link that Mikael was standing in front of a door. It had a keypad attached. Mikael attached a small device onto the keypad. There was a series of flashing lights, then the door unlocked.

Of course, his one works properly.

Mikael retrieved the device and stepped through the door, entering a stairwell. Maya switched over to the map, trying to associate the enemy locations with Mikael's position.

"I can't get a good read on enemy positions inside the building. Proceed with caution?" Maya said.

"Acknowledged. Proceeding to the basement," Mikael said. He started off down the stairs. Maya kept switching from watching his feed, to watching the map image. She couldn't see anything important changing from an enemy perspective.

This is so tense.

Maya leaned back in the chair, stretching a bit.

"Entering the basement," Mikael said. Maya quickly alerted herself and watched his feed. Mikael was walking through a very dark space. She had trouble making out what was in it.

"Target located," Mikael said. He stopped moving, and Maya could see a faint definition of a chair and a shape sitting in it.

"Shin?" Mikael said, leaning in. There was no response. Maya heard a ripping sound.

"Yes, it's me. Took you long enough," Shin said.

"Why'd they take you?" Mikael said, untying Shin.

"Politics. Making a statement. Who knows, really?" Shin sighed.

"Nice work. Let's get you out of there," Maya said. She looked over at the map. Something was off. A cluster of red shapes was forming. Inside the building.

"The enemy is advancing in a group. I think they're onto you," Maya said.

"We're going to need support getting out," Mikael said, looking around. A bright light suddenly filled the feed. Maya looked back at the screen. The room was perfectly illuminated. It was an almost bare concrete room. Featureless except for the chair Shin was sitting in.

"Ask him how long he was sitting in there," Maya said.

"Ask him yourself when you get here. This is your mission after all," Mikael said.

"What? I can't do that. I'll find you an exit from here," Maya said.

"Why do you think I brought you along? You need to prove yourself, and get mission experience."

"What can I even do? With my arm like this?"

"Make us an exit. I walked the perimeter, there's only the main doors. They're not going to be open unless you intervene. I'd rather not throw Shin off the roof."

"Point taken." Maya looked around the van.

There must be something here I can use.

Maya grabbed a few supplies, took one last look at the map, and left the van.

This is just super. Infiltrating an enemy base with a broken arm and no support.

Maya crept forward, using the same route Mikael had taken. She looked out for enemy patrols and only saw one.

The rest must have gone inside.

Maya clipped the comms pin to her jacket.

"Mikael, can you hear me?" she said.

"Affirmative."

"I'm on my way."

"We're still in the basement. We've left the room but are looking for somewhere to evade detection."

"I'll come find you." Maya suddenly ducked behind a mid-height concrete wall. A guard passed by, not noticing her.

You're in no condition to fight. Make sure they don't see you.

Maya slowly stood, watching the guard's patrol. He was wearing a similar outfit to what Mikael was.

Ninjas. There you go.

Maya crept around and continued ahead, the warehouse building looming over her. She spotted two bored guards manning the front door.

They don't appear to be alert. Maybe they don't know about the breakout.

Maya found a spot to hide, behind some large crates. She looked over what she had retrieved. A door hacking device, two smoke grenades, a stun wand, and an unidentified cube.

Anders would know what this is.

Maya peeked out at the guards. They weren't moving anytime soon.

I doubt I can distract them long enough to break in. I need to do something else.

"We've reached the main level. But our hiding spot is not good. We'll be spotted soon," Mikael said.

"Trying to sort out the guards at the front door," Maya said.

"I'm sure you can handle two. There are at least twenty circling in here," Mikael said.

No pressure.

Maya considered the smoke grenades. She steeled herself and then crept out of hiding. Aiming carefully, she threw the first smoke grenade. It flew past the guards and smashed nearby. They were suddenly alert, but the smoke didn't affect them at all.

"Go check it out," the first guard told the other.

"Fine." The second guard strolled over to investigate the source of the smoke.

Maya crept forward, pulling the stun wand out with her good arm. The second guard was completely focused on the smoke and his companion. Maya continued creeping as she closed in. The guard turned suddenly. As he started to speak Maya jammed in the stun wand. It crackled, and he dropped to the ground.

That worked. One charge left.

Maya kept going, heading for the smoke.

We both won't be able to see, maybe I'll have an edge with the element of surprise.

She advanced into the smoke, holding the stun wand out in front. She almost coughed as she entered and held up her left arm to cover her mouth. Suddenly a hand reached out and knocked the stun wand away. Maya stumbled back. She quickly exited the smoke cloud, drawing in three gasping breaths of fresh air.

The guard stepped out of the smoke, holding the stun wand. His eyes darted over her broken arm.

"They're sending in one-armed ninja pretenders now. Talk about desperate," the guard said. Maya stepped forward until she was inches from his face.

"I only need one arm," she whispered. He gave her a curious look. Before he could do anything else, Maya closed her fist and hit him from close range. The guard dropped instantly, the stun wand clattering onto the ground.

Hmm, I'm getting better at harnessing my Chakra.

Maya bent down and picked up the stun wand. She tucked it into her pants before turning to the door. There was a keypad on the side. Maya retrieved the hacking device and attached it. It flashed for a few moments before turning to green lights. She removed it and pushed against the weighty doors. They opened and she stepped into the building.

Be smart. You can't take on twenty more of these guards.

Maya assessed the space. She was in a foyer, which branched out in two directions. Both the left and right path seemed to be long, winding corridors.

"I'm inside, on the main level. Which way are you?"

"Good. We're at the back, either way is fine," Mikael said. Maya nodded to herself. She turned right and headed down. There was a series of doors along the corridor. Maya tried the first one, slowly turning the handle. It was empty but looked like lab equipment.

Curious.

Maya closed the door and rushed ahead. There were no signs of the guards yet. She continued around the perimeter, coming to what seemed like the middle of the building. On her left, instead of a door, there was another corridor. At its end was a larger door.

Big room in the middle?

Maya considered it for a moment but kept going. She heard

guards approaching and ducked into the nearest room. She didn't take in the surroundings, focusing on the sound of the guards walking down the corridor. They paused nearby and Maya waited. Straining to hear.

"Taking your time?" Mikael said.

"Shhh," Maya said back. There was no reply. Once the footsteps continued, Maya sighed. She glanced behind. There were two people, a man, and a woman, lying in beds attached to medical equipment.

What is this?

Maya walked closer to investigate.

26

SECRET SAMPLES

M aya stood over the sleeping man. He seemed to be at rest, motionless. The woman was the same. Maya looked over the rest of the contents of the room. Mostly medical machines. She noticed a chart at the bottom of the bed. She rushed over to grab it, skimming over the contents. It looked like records of some sort of measurement. It fluctuated, the number rising and falling over different measurements. Maya pulled out her phone and took some snaps of the chart pages. As the different clues came together, Maya felt a rising panic.

They're testing something. I can't ignore this.

Maya whirled around the room, looking for something to take. Some evidence. She noticed a metal box on a table in the corner. Lifting the lid, she saw a row of blood samples in glass tubes. She picked up the first one and read the label.

Subject 1 - Day 53

Maya replaced the tube and looked through the others. She discovered the other days had sequential numbering.

They must be collecting samples and then taking them offsite for testing. I should borrow a few.

Maya carefully retrieved the first two tubes and inserted them into a padded pocket inside her jacket. After a last check, she returned to the door, opening it slowly. The guards were nowhere to be seen. Maya closed the door quietly behind her and continued down the corridor. She passed more identical doors but didn't go inside.

Stay on mission.

"Status update," Mikael said.

"I'm approaching the rear. What room are you in?"

"We're not. Look for an air vent," Mikael said. Maya looked up and noticed a grey duct, bulging a bit further down.

"I think I can guess where you are. How do you get out?" Maya said.

"We'll emerge in one of these rooms. Hold on."

"I'll wait." Maya heard some banging from the ducting and then followed it along. She picked the nearest room and tested the door. It was unlocked. Maya slowly turned the handle and peered inside. It was another medical room with a bed, but it was empty. There was a large air vent on the wall. There was a clank, and it clattered to the ground. Mikael smoothly jumped out and landed on his feet with ease. He was followed by another man with short black hair. He was similarly dressed but didn't land quite as elegantly.

"Maya, meet Shin," Mikael said.

"Nice to meet you," Maya said.

"She's the help? She can't even fight," Shin said, pointing to her arm. "No offense."

"None taken. Let's go."

"She's avoided capture so far with only one arm. More than I can say about you," Mikael said. Shin swore under his breath.

"No time for that now. I don't want to stay a minute longer." Shin walked up to the door and opened it slightly.

"Is it safe to let him go ahead?" Maya said.

"It's fine. He's got LifeDeath, all they can do is slow him down."

"Sure, would be nice if my arm fixed itself as fast as it used to. Oh well, let's go." Maya followed closely behind Shin, and they all emerged into the corridor. They crept forward, Mikael constantly checking behind them. As they passed the side passage leading to the central room, Mikael suddenly appeared in front of Shin.

"Large group approaching. We should hurry up."

"Don't need to tell me twice," Shin broke out into a run. Maya tried to keep up, feeling awkward with her arm cast and remembering the vials of blood in her jacket. They sped down the corridor, their footsteps ringing out and telegraphing their presence. As they neared the main doors, there was a blur and they stopped. A woman stood before the doors. Maya gasped as she recognized the woman.

It's her. The one who had the bloodline seven detector box and broke it.

"Oh, we meet again. How delightful," the woman said, looking over their group.

"Move aside, Valerie," Mikael said. Valerie laughed.

"Why would I do that? I'd prefer if you stayed. And the help are hot on your trail," Valerie said. She locked eyes with Maya.

"Now you are a surprise. New addition to the Hanzo clan?"

"Nice to meet you, Valerie. We need to stop running into each other like this," Maya said.

"She's stalling us," Mikael whispered.

"If you can slow her down, I can inflict some damage," Shin whispered, keeping his eyes on her. Mikael nodded. The next instant he was next to Valerie.

"Mikael, you're so predictable," Valerie said. She revealed a cube that she had pressed into him. He looked down at it in horror.

I have that same cube.

"What have you done?" Maya said.

"He won't be moving anywhere soon. Now I can take care of the rest of you," Valerie said.

"It's a Binding Cube. Replicates the LifeDeath ability. He's going to be frozen for a time," Shin explained softly. He readied himself for a fight.

"Catch her and do the same. It won't work on you, right?" Maya said. Shin nodded.

Valerie was suddenly a trail of light. Shin lashed out but missed. The two of them seemed to be having some sort of battle, but Maya couldn't quite follow it. She turned to look behind. The formation of guards was catching up.

I need to wrap this up.

Maya put a hand in her pocket, feeling around for her cube.

You'll have one shot. Don't mess it up.

Maya ignored the ongoing fight and made her way over to Mikael by the main doors.

"Don't worry Mikael, I'll get out and get help," Maya said. She turned to open the doors and noticed a flash of light.

"Not so fast," Valerie said, suddenly appearing before Maya and blocking the door.

"That's my line," Maya said. She revealed the Binding Cube that she had pulled out a second earlier, as soon as she'd noticed the flash. It was too late now. Valerie instantly froze, a furious glare the last expression on her face.

"Can we fix Mikael? Or should you just carry him out?" Maya said.

"An electrical shock would do the trick, but I don't have the right equipment," Shin said. He glanced back at the approaching guards.

"I got it," Maya said. She stepped over and pulled out the stun wand.

"Sorry," she said as she activated and pressed it into Mikael.

He seemed to tense even more with the shock, but after a moment started to move.

"Thanks," he said and gave her a short bow.

"And to finish up," Maya said, pulling out her last item. She hurled the smoke bomb at the group of guards. As it exploded and filled the room, the three of them pushed through the doors.

The two guards were still stunned on the ground. Mikael walked past them and nodded.

"Nice work. Let's speed this along." Mikael put a hand on Maya, and Mikael, and then the world suddenly lurched. Maya had the strange sensation of light rushing past and then they were outside the black van. Mikael sagged, exhausted.

"I'm going to need to recover after that. Let's drive," Mikael said. Maya opened the doors and ushered Mikael and Shin into the back. She jumped into the front and started the engine, pulling them away. She checked the mirrors but didn't see any pursuing forces.

"That was a success. I was a bit worried there for a minute," she said.

"You impressed me. Shin, not so much," Mikael said.

"Hey, I kept that woman at bay. That counts," Shin said.

"And what did you achieve at this location? Before you were captured?" Mikael said.

"They're doing research. Blood related. I couldn't get samples out," Shin said.

"We left you there for days," Mikael said, sighing.

"Valerie kept showing up and shipping off the samples. I'm not a miracle worker," Shin said, defensively.

"Any idea what they were after?" Maya asked. She turned the corner and kept speeding.

"We think the Shogun Clan are trying to create more bloodlines. Supplement their numbers," Mikael said.

"Interesting. And what bloodline are they after?" Maya said.

She had to brake suddenly, waiting at a traffic light. They seemed to be far enough from the danger now, so she had to start obeying traffic rules.

"Could be anything. Shin, what do you think?" Mikael said.

"I couldn't say, they were very tight-lipped about it."

"Fine. It wasn't a complete waste of time at least," Mikael said.

I need these samples. Valerie was the one smashing that seventh bloodline testing box. It could be related.

Maya continued driving, her mind working through the implications and connections to the secret bloodline.

She parked the van with the rest, and slowly extracted herself from the vehicle. The exhaustion and weariness from the mission had come all at once. Mikael and Shin quickly appeared from the side door. Shin came up to Maya.

"Thanks, I owe you," Shin said. He gave her a slight bow. Maya returned it.

"You're welcome. Glad I could help." Maya gave Shin a smile. He nodded and walked off.

"Not one for conversation, is he?" Maya commented as Shin walked away.

"No, not really. What do you want to do now?" Mikael asked. Maya hesitated, then answered.

"I think I'll go meet up with my friends. See how Anders is going," she said.

"I expected that was the case. Please wait an hour before you go. I need to report this and come back," Mikael said.

"OK. I'll be at the cottage," Maya said.

"Good. See you soon. Oh, and good work today," Mikael said. He bowed and then walked off.

"Thank you," Maya said after him. She watched him for a

moment, before walking over to the super-fast lift. Her mind was instantly on other things.

The time passed in a flash. Maya hadn't really done anything of note when Mikael walked through the front door of the cottage. He was carrying a large case and set it down in the library.

"Usually this is more formal, but I thought you'd prefer it to be quicker and with fewer people." Mikael rotated the case until it faced Maya. He pressed some latches and the case sprung open.

"In recognition of your service today, Maya, you are officially inducted into the Hanzo clan." Mikael walked around and retrieved a flame emblem medallion from the case and presented it to Maya.

"Thank you. It's metal," Maya commented.

"Of course. The glass ones are only for testing," Mikael said with a chuckle. "Keep this on you. Show any other member of the clan, and you'll receive help. No questions asked."

"This is an honor," Maya said.

"You served us today and earned our trust. There is one other thing." Mikael bent down and retrieved the other bulky thing from the case. It was an indeterminate shape, hidden within a cloth bag. He slowly removed it, showing Maya. It looked like a black cast or tube.

"What's that?" Maya said.

"It's a specially designed restorative cast. It will enhance your arm and allow you to use it safely while it heals. Try it," Mikael said, offering it to her. Maya accepted the cast awkwardly, not knowing how to put it on. Mikael reached over to help her. He removed the old cast like it was nothing, expertly clipping on the new one. It automatically tightened around her arm, squeezing with warmth.

"Seems like you've done this before," Maya commented.

"Many times. Healing is something I need help with."

"Do you have any specialists here? People that are from LifeDeath and Chakra? That can heal anything?"

"For your friend, Anders?" Mikael offered. He stepped back while Maya tested her arm. It felt stronger, like she could rely on it.

Wow, this is something else.

"Yes, he needs help."

"Don't worry, I'm aware. We did have someone once, but they returned to China to further master their Chakra ability. We're not in contact anymore," Mikael said.

"Did you have a name?"

"Miko."

"And how hard is it to get into the Lost Lands?" Maya asked. Mikael laughed.

"If they don't want you? Very hard."

"Good to know," Maya said. Her mind started working overtime.

There's someone out there who can fix him.

"Thank you for everything so far. I'm going to check on Anders," Maya said.

"Very well. Return quickly. Now that you're a full member we have more work for you to do," Mikael said. He closed the metal case and left the room without another word.

27

OFFICIALLY A NINJA

M aya opened the door, not knowing what to expect. She found herself in a basic hotel suite with minimal furnishings.

"Honey, I'm home," Maya called out. Derek emerged from the bedroom with a smile.

"Nice cast," he said, approaching.

"It's actively healing my arm." Maya demonstrated by moving her arm freely. Derek nodded.

"Sounds like you've won them over. Come see Anders," Derek said. He started to walk away but Maya grabbed his arm.

"What do I need to know? Have things worsened?" Maya whispered.

"Only slightly. He's stable for now."

"For now?"

"There will be a tipping point soon."

"And?"

"More rapid decline after." Derek gently freed his hand and continued to the bedroom.

I can't waste any time.

Maya put on a smile and walked into the bedroom.

"How's it going?" Maya said as she entered. Anders was propped up on the bed. He was trying to read something.

"How's my favorite ninja?" Anders said. His voice was weak and cracked a little. But he smiled.

"I've been officially inducted," Maya said, flashing her flame emblem.

"Well done. That's no easy feat, according to Derek," Anders said.

"It's a big step. What else have you learned?" Derek said, turning from Anders so the concern on his face was not obvious.

"Two things. The most useful one is that the Hanzo clan used to have a woman called Miko. She had both LifeDeath and Chakra bloodlines. But she left to go to the Lost Lands to further her training, and they no longer have contact." Maya watched Anders' reaction. He seemed to be buoyed by the news. But Derek shook his head.

"Well, it's a good lead. I'll look into it," Derek said. His eyes told a different story.

"It will give me something to research too," Anders said.

"And the other news?" Derek said.

"This one will probably be more exciting for Kora. You remember that Haste ninja that broke the bloodline seven scanner?" Maya said.

"Yes," Anders said. Maya moved closer to the bed.

"Her name is Valerie. I encountered her on a job with the Hanzo clan. She was there collecting blood samples from test candidates." Maya retrieved the vials and presented them.

"I brought a few with me," Maya said with a grin. Anders stared at them intently.

"You think they have the secret bloodline?" Anders said, weakly. He began to cough, and then settled down in the bed more.

"I suspect so. But we'll need to do some tests. Where's Kora?" Maya said, looking at Derek.

"Close by, in her own room. She's deep into something right now, don't ask," Derek said. Maya handed over the blood samples.

"Make sure she gets these. And I'll send over some images too." Maya pulled out her phone and transferred the photos she had taken of the patient charts and notes. Once she was done, she put her phone away.

"It's been a while. I'm sorry, but I've been making progress," Maya said. Anders nodded slowly.

"It's an exciting update. Why don't we let Anders rest a bit?" Derek said, guiding Maya out of the room.

"Back soon," Maya said to Anders and waved. Once they were back in the main room Derek pulled her aside.

"How's your training going? The Space Chakra?" he said, urgency in his voice.

"It's progressing," she said.

"You're going to need to speed that up." Derek anxiously glanced back at the bedroom.

"What's wrong?"

"He's declining rapidly. I'm not sure how to slow it down," Derek said. The concern in his voice was obvious, and Maya gasped.

"Why didn't you say anything sooner?" she said.

"We had it under control. There was no reason to rush. But now, things are different. You need to be ready."

"But I have this lead now. Miko."

"The value in that is giving Anders hope. Otherwise, it's useless."

"What am I not understanding here? She can heal him. That's incredible," Maya said. Derek shook his head slowly.

"Look, each bloodline clan is wary of the others. They're generally distrustful of MultiBloods and tolerate them, at best.

The Chakra bloodline clan is probably the biggest purists, in that way."

"I realize that. We'll need to sneak into the Lost Lands or find some excuse. It's the plan," Maya said in a matter-of-fact way. Derek sighed.

"It's not just that. There's no way a MultiBlood person would go to the Lost Lands to further her training. Willingly."

"What are you saying?" Maya leaned in.

"Most likely she embarrassed the elders, or they feared her becoming too powerful and prominent. She will be hidden away. Guarded. In the hopes that she's never found, and people forget she even existed." Derek furtively looked back at the bedroom.

"I can't let you delay your own training chasing this. You need to keep making breakthroughs."

"Is that even possible? Am I going to end up the same if I even make my way there? Shunned and a prisoner of the elders?" Maya said. Derek gently took her hands into his.

"No, you're stronger. You need to rely on yourself. Win that way and save Anders with these hands." Derek gave her a short bow and released her hands, walking back to the bedroom. Maya followed behind him. She could see Anders settling back down into the bed. Exhausted.

"I'm going to head off. You're looking great, keep it up Anders," Maya said. Anders nodded weakly and turned onto his side. Derek nodded at her, and then sat at the bedside.

"I'll visit again soon," Maya said and left the room.

Maya walked through the door of Mikael's house and saw him standing in the corridor, waiting.

"How was your visit?" he asked.

"Good," Maya said, faking a smile. Mikael nodded. "I'm

glad. Come with me." Mikael turned and walked down the corridor. Maya followed him to her room. She noticed a dark ninja outfit on the bed.

"Now that you're officially one of us, you'll need to dress like us," he said. Mikael smiled and looked over Maya's jacket.

"This jacket isn't exactly ideal for infiltration," he said. Maya stepped over and looked at herself in the mirror. The red of the jacket stood out, and the awkward way it hung on her right shoulder since her cast couldn't fit inside seemed to accentuate her injury.

They'll spot you a mile away.

Maya laughed.

"I guess this means I won't be sitting in the van next time?"

"You won't. Find me in the library when you're ready." Mikael left the room. Maya walked over to the bed, examining the clothing.

Let's see how this goes.

Maya reluctantly removed her red jacket, folding it neatly and placing it on the bed. The more she moved her broken arm, the more she realized that it wasn't resisting. She tested it a few more times, twisting and turning it gently.

I can move it normally. Wow.

Maya still took care but tried to dress normally. With some effort she pulled the ninja outfit on, including the soft boots, and looked in the mirror.

You look like a ninja.

The form-fitting suit wasn't shapely, adding extra bulk in places to disguise her body type. She nodded with approval and left the room. She walked over to the library, finding Mikael lounging on a chair and reviewing a tablet.

"What's next?" Maya said. Mikael glanced up at her, and then gestured to the chair next to his. She sat and looked over at the tablet. He was reviewing satellite images and handed the tablet to Maya.

"Shin is more useful than he may appear. He discreetly placed a tracking device on Valerie before we left the warehouse. We tracked her to this location," Mikael explained. Maya was looking at a fortress, built into the mountains.

"Where is this?" she asked.

"Atlantis Alps, on the edge of True Atlantis. We'll need to fly in close and trek the last miles."

"What's the plan?" Maya said, while zooming in and trying to look at the building. She could see a main building surrounded by walls and turrets.

"We infiltrate, discover what they're doing there, and we extract some evidence," Mikael said. He put his hand out and Maya returned the tablet.

"Sounds like spy work. Who else is going?"

"Just us. Easier that way." Mikael tucked the tablet into his clothing and rose from the chair.

"Okay then. When do we leave?" Maya said, standing as well.

"Now." Mikael strode out of the room. Maya rushed after him.

"Shouldn't we prepare?"

"We can do that on the flight. They found the tracker, so every moment we delay our chance of finding something reduces," Mikael said without turning back.

"Right we are," Maya said, following Mikael through the house and out of the front door. They turned a different way, not walking toward the main lift.

"Where are we going?" Maya asked.

"Aircraft hangar," Mikael said. He started walking faster, and Maya scrambled to match his pace. As they walked, nobody paid them any attention. People seemed to have their own jobs to rush off to. Mikael turned a corner, and they could see a giant building looming above them. Maya started to gasp but forced it down. Instead, she kept pace with Mikael as they approached what seemed like a tiny door in comparison to the gigantic structure. Mikael leaned in and scanned his eyes before the door unlocked.

"After you," he said, holding it open. Maya stepped through the door, finding herself in a dark corridor. She continued, walking toward a light in the distance. As she emerged into the brightness, she had to shield her eyes. Humongous circular lights blazed like the sun. Once her eyes adjusted, she noticed several aircraft parked in a cavernous space. Multiple jets of different types, and a few helicopters.

"This way," Mikael said, walking past Maya. She quickly followed, looking ahead to see what he was aiming for. Within moments it was clear. They were heading for a compact helicopter. It was all in black with the Hanzo flame crest emblazoned on the side in white paint.

"This is our ride," Mikael said. He opened the side door and hopped in. Maya carefully eased herself up. Her right arm held up fine. Once inside she noticed two chairs and a cabinet built in. Mikael began to fasten his seat belt, and Maya looked for hers, copying him.

"Get the door, please," Mikael said. Maya pulled the door closed and then Mikael handed her a headset. Maya popped it on and heard a bright voice speaking to her.

"Greetings, this is Takeshi and I'll be your pilot today," Takeshi said.

"Ayame not available?" Mikael said.

"Unfortunately, yes. But I promise your ride will be equally smooth," Takeshi said. Maya looked around trying to see where Takeshi was sitting.

"He's not in here. It's a drone helicopter," Mikael said. Maya nodded.

"Just wait a moment, I'm organizing a spot on the helipad," Takeshi said. Maya looked around, wondering how they were going to leave the facility.

We're still underground. How is this going to work?

The helicopter suddenly pivoted and began to move along the ground. Maya looked out of the window, trying to puzzle it out. She noticed a track snaking ahead of the helicopter.

"I see now," she said, pointing to the track.

"We need to be clever to make this work. Tracks help us position the aircraft easily and safely," Mikael explained. The helicopter soon passed through a giant set of doors and onto a helipad.

"We're about to lift off," Takeshi said. The helicopter powered up, and Maya heard the groaning of machinery. She tried to look but couldn't see anything other than walls.

"This is the fun bit," Mikael said. Before Maya could ask a question, the helicopter began to rise. She frantically looked for how they were going to emerge from underground. But there were no hints visible through the windows. The helicopter picked up speed and suddenly they were in the sky. The lights of the city illuminating the darkness.

"There's a special helicopter shaft. We only use it at night," Mikael said, a slight grin on his voice.

"You enjoyed not telling me, didn't you," Maya said.

"It's important to savor the small things," Mikael said, as the helicopter soared off into the night.

I hope I'm ready for this.

28

THE ALPS FORTRESS

Maya assembled a few minimal tools on the flight, but mostly she stared out at the sky. Mikael and Takeshi didn't offer any conversation, and that was fine by her.

I need to use this mission to push forward my Chakra progress. I need to tackle the Space Chakra. I don't have time to plateau here.

Maya looked down at her hands. They trembled slightly. She hid them away, hoping Mikael didn't notice. Despite her success at the last mission, she still felt rattled. Anders being sick, and her injury. The lack of progress on mastering the next Chakra. It rolled up into one thought. One emotion.

Failure. Powerless.

Maya tried to shake herself out of it.

"Approaching our descent now," Takeshi announced. Maya held onto the chair as the helicopter began to descend. They were slowly lowering to a clearing in the middle of a forest. The helicopter started touching the ground, lifting up and down a few times as Takeshi eased it into a landing position. The rotors were still spinning when Takeshi spoke again.

"Last stop, mountain forest. I hope you enjoyed your flight," Takeshi said.

"Are you going to wait here?" Maya said.

"Sorry, I can't. But call me when you want a pickup and I'll return."

"Go," Mikael said, pointing to the door. Maya thrust it open and shielded herself as she stepped out of the helicopter. She rushed over to the cover of nearby trees. She turned back and watched Mikael effortlessly step out, seemingly unconcerned by the rotor wind. He casually strolled over to her, not looking back as the helicopter rose back into the sky.

"Good luck," Takeshi said.

"Thanks," Maya replied. In moments, the helicopter was gone. Mikael revealed a watch from under his suit and tapped it a few times.

"This way," he said. Mikael disappeared into the forest and Maya followed. The forest was thick with trees and the occasional rocks and shrubs reminding them they were on a mountain. The climb was not harsh, but constant. Maya started to sweat, surprised by the effort it was taking. She stopped to catch her breath.

"Should have packed water," she said.

"There's a reserve in the suit. Reach behind your neck," Mikael said. Maya felt around and found some tubing. She pulled on it and took a cautious sip. Clean water filled her mouth.

"Wow," she said.

"There's not much, you should be careful," Mikael said. Maya took a few more sips then stashed it away.

"Done. Let's keep going." Maya took another step, navigating around a large stone. The forest was quiet as they ascended, and Mikael didn't talk. Maya focused on the mission. And wondered how much Mikael knew. He seemed to have more information that he wasn't letting on.

~

An hour later, they paused on the edge of the forest.

"We're here," Mikael said. They peered through the last of the trees and saw a massive structure. It was a Japanese-inspired black castle, made from concrete instead of stone. There was a large gate and ramparts with four square turrets sticking out. A central building towered above the walls. Maya counted several guards roaming the ramparts.

"They seem to be expecting us. I don't suppose we can just knock?" Maya said.

"Be my guest," Mikael said, keeping a straight face. Maya sighed.

"Maybe not. We're going to have trouble climbing those walls, or even getting close enough to climb them," Maya said. Mikael nodded.

"The guards up there will be Haste bloodline. They'll be ready to counter any speed-based infiltration or attacks.

"What should I do?" Maya asked.

"You're the mission leader. You tell me," Mikael said. Maya swallowed her frustration.

"How would you infiltrate with these guards?" Maya asked. She looked over at Mikael and noticed a wry smile.

"The simplest things are often the best. Create a distraction."

"That I can do." Maya scanned the walls again, taking in options. "Why don't we target that far turret as our entry point."

"Certainly. Your suit has a built-in grappling hook to help with the ascent."

"Great. What's the range on that?"

"Not a lot. Twenty-five yards."

"In meters?"

"Less. Just over twenty?" Mikael said. Maya nodded.

"Alright, I'll make a distraction in that vicinity. You can help surprise them and we'll ascend into that far turret. Agreed?"

"Agreed. Good luck," Mikael said. He disappeared into the forest.

"Great. Awesome," Maya said under her breath. She reviewed her tools. One Binding Cube, a smoke bomb, and a stun wand. She started to formulate a plan as she moved through the forest to get closer to the target spot before exposing herself.

Once in position, Maya took a deep breath and stepped out into the clearing. At first, there was nothing. She kept walking, one hand behind her back.

Easy does it. Just keep advancing.

Suddenly two men appeared in front of her. They had similar ninja dress, just like those she had seen at the warehouse where Shin was captive.

"State your business," the first guard said.

"I have a delivery," Maya said. The guard shook his head.

"No. You're a rival ninja. Are you here to surrender?" he said.

"No. It's really a delivery. Look." Maya slowly brought back the hand she had hidden behind. It was a smoke bomb. They both looked at her in surprise.

"What is this?" the guard said dismissively.

"The delivery. It's special. It doesn't smash when you throw it on the ground." Maya quickly threw it down, but it just appeared in the guard's hand. He laughed.

"Nice slow-motion throw," the second guard said. But the first guard didn't say anything. Or move. He was frozen solid.

"Huh?" the second guard said. He leaned in and took a closer look. Maya used that moment to thrust her hand at him, smacking the guard in the chest with a fully charged Chakra strike. He dropped to the ground, winded. Before he could move, Maya leaned in and followed up with another attack, knocking him out. She stood up and admired her handiwork.

Not bad. Not bad at all.

"I disabled the other two wandering the ramparts," Mikael said, looking down at the two guards. Maya carefully retrieved the smoke bomb, ensuring that the Binding Cube underneath it was undisturbed.

"Nice trick. How'd you manage that without disabling yourself?" Mikael said. Maya retrieved the stun wand from within her cast.

"This was giving me a constant jolt of electricity. Not pleasant, but beats the alternative," Maya said with a grin. Mikael smiled.

"I like it. Let's get away before these guards are missed." Mikael turned and started jogging toward the walls.

"Have you ever maxed out your power? Drained it completely?" Maya asked as they ran.

"Yes. Only once. Why do you ask?" Mikael said.

"It's just that you are always so careful to ration out your power. I expected people who had the Haste bloodline to just zip around everywhere.

"Some do. It varies a lot depending on the type of user, and their level of power. For me, I hate the idea of being forced to be slow. Others are different."

"So, you willingly choose to be slow, knowing that you can be fast whenever you need?" Maya said.

"Exactly." Mikael paused as they were reaching the walls. Up close Maya could see that the walls weren't completely sheer. There were horizontal grooves evenly spaced up the length of the wall.

"Those should work as hand holds, in a pinch," Mikael said. He aimed his wrist at the wall above one of the grooves and a metal dart fired out. It burrowed into the wall and held firm.

Mikael tested it, before scaling the wall. The device seemed to be reeling him in at the same time.

"Impressive," Maya said. She quickly looked for the mechanism so she could do the same. She found some controls woven into the sleeve. Aiming her arm, she pressed the first button and the dart fired out. Even though she was expecting it, she almost jumped from surprise.

"Bit more kick than you expect, isn't it?" Mikael said. He fired again, continuing his climb once the line was secured to a higher point.

"Couldn't you just run up the wall?" Maya said.

"Yes," Mikael said.

"Right. I'll stop asking useless questions." Maya continued her ascent, struggling more than he had. But by focusing her energy, she was able to plant her feet against the wall and gain some stability.

"With the right training, you could just run up the wall too," Mikael commented. He was almost at the top now.

"True." Maya sighed and readied the grappling dart again.

Not about to experiment halfway up this wall.

Apart from a few close calls, she soon pulled herself over the top of the wall. Maya sat for a moment, catching her breath. She looked over at her broken arm.

"I couldn't have done that without this amazing thing," Maya said. She was still marveling at the cast.

"The wonders of modern technology. Let's get to that turret and out of sight before we attract too much attention." Mikael started off again, faster this time. But Maya could still see his movements. She dragged herself up and ran after him. The first turret they encountered was thankfully empty. There was nothing inside, just a few slits to see out of, or perhaps even fire something.

"Next," Mikael said softly. He took off at greater speed,

Maya struggling to keep up. The next turret had a guard, but by the time Maya arrived he was unconscious on the ground.

"Last one," Mikael said. Maya nodded, but he was already off. She ran again, soon enough reaching the furthest turret. It was also empty. Mikael was waiting.

"Here we are. What's our next move?" he said. Maya stepped outside the turret, peering at the courtyard below. It was empty, save a path leading to the main building. Her eyes roamed over the building, looking for entry points. She spotted a few windows, higher up.

"Ignore the courtyard. We're going to do a window entry," she said.

"Very well. But I'm afraid it's too far to grapple to. We'll have to descend and climb again.

"Or do we?" Maya said, mostly under her breath. She looked down at her feet, her mind calculating.

"What are you dreaming up?" Mikael said.

"I've been doing a lot of reading up. A person with my skills should be able to do more with my body. Among all the fun stuff, is jumping."

"Correct. Have you tried this before?" Mikael said.

"No," Maya said, doubt creeping into her voice. As she spoke, the main doors of the central building opened, and a formation of soldiers poured out.

"Looks like we've been detected," Mikael said.

"Yes. The courtyard is off limits now," Maya said.

Now you have to do it.

Maya focused her Chakra, building a connection with the earth. She focused her strength on her feet and legs. Amplifying the muscles and power.

I probably should have moved before doing this.

Maya dismissed the thought and kept focusing. Once she had amassed enough, she pushed in, and then off. In the same instant she jumped with her legs, she reversed her connection with the earth. The idea was for it to repel her equal and opposite to the previous connection and attachment. It worked. Mostly.

Maya flew awkwardly, tumbling like she was trying to claw her way up. As she passed through the air, she realized that her jump wasn't going to make it.

This is going to hurt.

After a few images of broken legs flashed through her mind, Maya had a better idea. She steadied her arm and aimed at the building. She pressed the button and hoped. The dart fired again, connecting with the building. She started reeling herself in fast. It was working. But she didn't have time to right herself and brace for the impact. She thudded into the building, her broken arm bearing the brunt of the force.

The sharp sudden pain caused her to cry out. She stifled it almost instantly. But it was too late. The soldiers looked up. And started to mobilize.

Moments later, Mikael was nearby. He grabbed her arm and pulled her up to a ledge.

"It almost worked," he said.

"At least that window is open," Maya said. She shook off the pain and climbed through it.

29

GLASS TUBES

I nside the building was like a lab. Top to bottom. Concrete walls, floors, and ceiling. They had entered a bathroom. Maya glanced at her appearance on the way past.

You don't look like a complete wreck. Excellent.

They moved silently through the bathroom, entering a corridor.

"They know we're here. At least we've got a slight head start," Mikael said. Maya nodded.

"This way," she said, heading right. The corridor was featureless concrete with only minimal lighting. At the end of the corridor was a set of double doors. Maya rushed over to it, thrusting the doors open. Another corridor was beyond with another set of double doors at the end. They ran ahead, not worrying about being quiet. Although, Mikael was still silent. As they burst through the next doors, Maya suddenly stopped.

They were in a glowing blue room. The source of the light was a series of vertical tubes. They were filled with a strange blue liquid. And inside were people.

"Suspended animation?" Maya said, surprised. She walked closer to inspect them.

"I've not seen this," Mikael said. A low hum of machinery was the only sound in the room. Maya circled around one of the tubes. It was a woman. She seemed to be asleep. There were tubes and wires connected to her. Maya traced the path of the wires with her hand, seeing that they lead to a machine nearby.

"There's no terminal. I can't see what they're doing," Maya said.

"Entirely on purpose," Valerie said from across the room. She strode toward them, smiling.

"I suppose I shouldn't be surprised," Maya said, turning to face Valerie.

"I should hope not. Seeing as how I led you here. And gave you ample time to mobilize. I even left a skeleton guard outside to entice you in. Aren't I a great host?" Valerie chuckled. Mikael tensed up, ready to pounce.

"Sorry that we left you in a bit of a bind, before. It wasn't personal," Maya said. She noticed a flash of anger before Valerie composed herself.

"I underestimated you before. But not again. Where's your cast?" Valerie said.

"Replaced it with something better. I won't go so easy on you this time," Maya said.

"Really? Let's see here." Valerie suddenly became a blur. Maya felt a tug, and then it was over. Valerie was across the room again, holding Maya's new cast. Immediately Maya felt the pain surge through her arm. She clutched it, wincing.

"My, my. Quite the interesting technology here. Did you supply this, Mikael?" Valerie said. Mikael nodded. Valerie laughed.

"But it's not yours, is it? Someone gave it to you," Valerie said.

"I didn't see who left it. It was with the uniform," Mikael said. Valerie walked closer, a grin on her face.

"We left it for you. It was to test a little theory of ours. One that you've now proven." Valerie tossed the cast on the ground and stepped on it, shattering it.

"I think you need to see someone about your vision. You keep stepping on things," Maya said, trying to make light of it. The pain was increasing even more.

"The thing is that wasn't a healing cast. It was a suppression device. It works by isolating and suppressing the Chakra bloodline." Valerie started walking closer again. Maya backed up against the glass tube,

"Not sure what you're getting at," Maya said.

"Your arm was better, because your LifeDeath power was seeping into it, faster than usual. And that confirmed for me exactly who you are, Maya Mills." Valerie was triumphant.

"That doesn't matter. I'm nobody," Maya said.

"You have multiple bloodlines then," Mikael said, shocked. Valerie laughed again.

"Now that we've confirmed this, our special guest would like to make an appearance." Valerie stepped aside and doors at the far end of the room burst open. A man casually walked through, oozing command. He had blond hair and piercing eyes. And Maya immediately recognized him.

"You again," Maya said.

"Hello, Maya. We should stop running into each other like this," the Master Sage said.

"Is that..." Mikael started.

"Yes. The Master Sage," Maya whispered back. She could sense Mikael shrinking back a little. The Master Sage advanced.

"I was content to let you run off and find yourself. Even though I did make life a bit harder for you."

"The schools in the International Quarter," Maya said. The Master Sage nodded.

"But you just kept meddling. You couldn't help yourself."

"Not my fault you keep leaving a trail," Maya said. She

glanced around. There was nowhere to run. The Master Sage advanced again.

"You know what? You seem so interested in what we're doing here. Maybe you can take part. Fancy being in a lab again?" The Master Sage said, roaring with laughter. Before Maya could reply, she saw him before her, and suddenly she crumpled into a heap. Pain and blackness everywhere. She looked over at Mikael and saw him the same way.

Not again.

Maya awoke to a strange glow. Her eyes took time to adjust. But she felt a strange tugging at her whenever she moved. And the light was strange. Blurry and muted. As her eyes improved, she had a terrifying realization.

I'm in a tube. I'm in a tube.

Maya fought the urge to flail around. She seemed to be breathing something, somehow. She was otherwise fine. Just restrained. She tried to look beyond her tube but couldn't see clearly.

Hopefully, Mikael is safe. Got to get out. Maybe there's a way from inside.

Maya carefully tried to feel around, for anything that might be a release lever or valve. But the tube was completely feature-less, apart from the tubes and wires.

There must be a way.

Maya tried stretching out her legs to put pressure on the tube. Her limbs were heavy, and whenever she tried to put pressure on the glass her feet slipped. Again. And again. She tried her arms instead. It was easier to reach and press on the walls, but nothing happened.

They're so thick. Ugh.

Maya tried lashing out with a fist. It bounced harmlessly off the wall. But then she had a realization.

My right arm. It's fine now.

Maya tried moving it again, twisting and turning it slowly. Whatever had happened, her arm was better. One piece of good news in an otherwise horrible situation. With renewed enthusiasm she tried banging on the glass with both arms, lashing out with her legs as well. The weight of the liquid and the various cables hampered her efforts, and every strike just bounced away harmlessly. She leaned back against the tank.

What can I do?

The gravity of the situation began to dawn on her. Truly. Anders was getting worse by the minute; she was captured in a lab by the Master Sage.

I can't lose another twenty years!

Only this time she was also awake. And Mikael was either dead or captured as well. Would anyone know to send help? Could they even help?

No. Nobody can help. And it's all my fault. I involved Anders. Now he's dying.

Darkness began to overtake her. There was no way out. She banged the wall with her arm again out of frustration. If only she had made better choices. If only she was stronger, had progressed further in her mastery of Chakra.

But what if I was further along? What would I do?

Maya retreated into herself, bringing back the meditations she had been practicing. She let the frustration melt away. Slowly she built her energy, starting at the Earth Chakra and going up. She reminded herself of all her success, the way she had creatively solved problems in her way. She had won the LifeDeath tournament with no LifeDeath power. She had ascended through the Chakras through hard work. And rescued Shin with a broken arm and a few tools. This was no different.

Maya started to feel a lightness, and focused clarity. She realized that while her current prison was strong, that a single point of weakness would cause it to fail. And she knew just what to do. Maya focused on a point and reinforced her Chakra. She slowly launched a precise strike on a particular spot. The force shook the tube. She retracted her arm and did it again.

The next strike was faster, but just as precise. And again. She repeated the strikes, hitting harder and faster every time. Hitting the exact same spot. She worked into a rhythm. The tube reverberating with the force. The glass began to crack. Maya didn't celebrate, she kept with the rhythm. Again, and again.

The sound of the glass shattering was like a symphony of bells. The water and Maya burst out of the tube. She lay motionless for a moment on the cold stone floor. Naked.

Right back where I started.

Maya slowly pulled herself to her knees before standing up all the way. After a moment of discomfort, she felt fine. She roughly removed any leftover cables or tubes, tossing them aside. She took in the room around her. It wasn't the same one she had been in. But there was another glowing tube to investigate. She walked closer, focusing only on the tube. There was someone inside.

Mikael.

Anger threatened to bubble up, but Maya pushed it away. She had no use for it right now. She picked a spot on the glass and gathered her Chakra. She built it up slowly, ascending through the Chakra points in her body. When ready, she unleashed a controlled and focused attack on the glass tube. It shattered instantly, the fluid gushing out. Mikael tumbled out at the same time, but Maya caught him. She gently moved him away from the broken glass and lay him down on the ground.

Breathing, but still asleep.

Maya stood, looking around the room. She ignored the medical equipment for now, her eyes roving until she saw a row of lockers. She strode over, flinging them open as soon as she arrived. One of them contained her ninja outfit.

Bingo. Let's go.

Maya quickly dressed and then found Mikael's suit. She carried it back and crouched over him.

"Hey Mikael, that's enough beauty sleep," she said. He stirred but remained asleep. She tried again.

"Mikael, you're free now. Wake up so we can get out of here." Maya leaned in, listening to his breathing. It was even and not labored.

Need to try something else.

Maya placed a hand on his head. She gathered her Chakra again, this time gently releasing a little into his head. Mikael's eyes shot open, and he looked around quickly.

"It's Maya. Let's get you dressed and out of here," Maya said. Mikael locked eyes on her and nodded slowly. Maya turned and heard a rustling sound.

"Ready," Mikael said. Maya turned back and saw him fully dressed.

"Good. Let's find a way out. We can talk about this mess later."

"Agreed." Mikael started walking through the room, taking it in as he went. He paused and then spoke again.

"Our tools and comms are gone. We'll have to find our own way home."

"I think we'll manage. I'm not leaving here empty-handed though."

"Then we should find ourselves something on the way out." Mikael continued to the door and opened it slowly. He waved Maya over. She dashed over.

There was a corridor outside, like the ones they had seen when entering the castle building.

"There's a good chance it's the same place. Likely the basement," Maya said, looking around. Mikael nodded. A guard entered the corridor from a far-off door. Before he could acknowledge their presence, he was in a heap on the ground with Mikael standing over him. Maya walked over as Mikael searched the guard.

"Gloves are off now, eh?" Maya said.

"I'm not sure what's going on here. But I can't afford to hold back." Mikael retrieved an earpiece and slipped it into his ear. Within a few seconds he nodded at Maya.

"I'm patched in. I'll let you know when they're onto us."

"Until then, it's time for a treasure hunt." Maya headed over to the door the guard had used.

Why was the Master Sage here? I wonder what he's hiding.

30

INTO THE FOREST

Maya closed the door behind her. They were in a room full of computers and monitors. She scanned the content of the monitors as she walked by. They were mostly surveillance footage. She stopped before one screen. It was the room they had broken out of.

"This explains why the guard was up and about," Maya said.

"Doesn't sound right that he'd come to confront us alone. Why isn't there more chatter?" Mikael said. He looked concerned as he prowled through the room.

"This room," Maya said. She pointed to one of the monitors. The picture was a server room, full of cooling equipment and racks of computer hardware. Mikael walked over and took a closer look.

"There has to be something there. Look at the room code in the corner of the screen." Mikael pointed to the tiny white text in the top right corner. It said 'B2S1'. Maya glanced back at the room they had been in. It said 'B1T2'.

"One level down?" Maya said to Mikael. He nodded. They left the room through a different door and were in a different corridor. They strode down quickly, checking each door. Most were empty offices or storage. Finally, Maya found the stairs.

"Bingo," she said.

"After you," Mikael said, looking back at the corridor. Maya descended the stairs, two at a time. When she reached the B2 door she tried the handle, and it was locked.

"Allow me," Mikael said. He held the handle and it suddenly vibrated, and the lock fell out. He pushed the door open with ease.

"Nice trick." Maya stepped through the door and entered yet another corridor. She sighed and started walking.

"Based on what I saw, it's likely a corner room," Mikael said.

"Somewhere to start." Maya eased into a run, heading straight for the end of the corridor. She tried two rooms, and they were full of computer spares.

"You try all these, I'll skip to the next corner," Maya said. She didn't wait for a reply, instead running ahead. She reached the door and noticed a metallic label above the handle.

"B2S1. Got you," she whispered. She tried the handle, and it was locked. There was a card reader next to it.

I wish Kora was here. Oh well.

Maya gathered her Chakra and focused it intently. She channeled it into a palm strike, knocking the door off its hinges. She stepped into the room, surveying it.

"Let's go find some evidence," she whispered with a smile.

"Maya, whatever you did stirred them up. They're mobilizing," Mikael said as he approached the room. He took one look at the broken door and nodded.

"It won't take long," Maya said. She ran through the room, looking for something she could use. She spotted a terminal in the corner with a keyboard.

"Could you check the supply rooms for a computer drive? Or storage?" she said. Mikael didn't reply, and Maya assumed he had heard her. She tried logging on to the terminal. It was password protected.

"Allow me," Mikael said. He had appeared behind her without Maya noticing. She stood aside and let him go. Mikael pulled out the keyboard and was a flurry of motion. Maya couldn't follow what he was doing. The screen flashed different colors and finally it slowed down.

"I'm in," Mikael said. Maya gasped.

"How did you do that?"

"I have my ways. Don't forget that I'm not just good at running fast." Mikael inserted a small thumb drive into the terminal and started copying files. As soon as he was done, he removed it and entered a second drive.

"Is there that much material?" Maya asked. Mikael shook his head.

"Better to have two copies." Mikael finished up the transfer and then handed one of the drives to Maya.

"Don't lose this," he said. Maya nodded.

"We better get out of here before they swarm us." Maya headed to the door and looked out into the hallway. A formation of guards was approaching from both directions.

"We're in the corner, right?" Maya said.

"Yes. What are you thinking?"

"We make ourselves an exit." Maya dashed back into the server room, scanning past the rows of equipment. She found a suitable stretch of wall and steadied herself.

"Are you sure about this?" Mikael said.

"Mostly. You might want to distract them." Maya took a deep breath and focused on her energy. She slipped into a meditation, focusing, and building her Chakra. Part of her started to think about how she needed to speed the process up, but she swept the thought away. Her focus was entirely on building and focusing her Chakra. She could hear some commotion behind her but blocked it out. She couldn't handle the distraction.

Visualizing her fist exploding through the wall, Maya opened her eyes and punched. Her fist impacted the wall like a cannon, a shockwave rattling the room. Dust and debris flew everywhere, obscuring what had happened. As the dust cleared Maya could see a large hole in the wall. There was a crawlspace behind, and what looked like the outer wall.

"You might need to be quicker next time," Mikael said. Maya looked back and saw him standing nearby. The entry of the room was blocked by guards slumped on the floor. Maya quickly turned and strode toward the other wall. This time she didn't pause, she merely brought back the image of the attack in her mind and struck again. The impact was less spectacular, but she did crack a hole in the wall, big enough to fit her head through.

"Almost there," Maya said. She grabbed the edges of the wall with both hands, infusing her hands with Chakra as she struggled to rip the hole open wider. After some initial resistance, she succeeded, and the hole was now big enough to awkwardly squeeze through.

"Ladies first," Mikael said as he closed in. The server room was empty now with a new set of guards streaming in with armed rifles. Maya ducked through the hole and tumbled out the other side. Mikael followed closely behind, having an easier time of it.

"Can you speed us away?" Maya asked. Mikael shook his head.

"Too risky, I burned way too much power back there."

"Take my hand." Maya held out her hand to Mikael. He took it without hesitation. Maya crouched and forced herself into an awkward leap. They sprang through the air, arcing through and landing twenty feet away. She immediately launched them again, this time landing ten feet away. She used whatever additional power she could muster into running as fast as possible.

Mikael kept pace with her. The guards were firing in the distance but struggling to land a hit. Maya heard a helicopter nearby and looked up.

"It's not ours," Mikael said, before a wave of gunfire swept the ground nearby. He pulled her hand sharply to the side, helping her dodge.

"We just need to get to the tree line," Maya shouted, pointing. Mikael nodded and the world became a blur again. They suddenly stopped, surrounded by trees. Mikael dropped to a crouch, breathing hard.

"Can you walk?" Maya said. Mikael nodded. Maya offered him a hand, and he stood up with her help. He looked unsteady on his feet.

"The further we get, the better. They have to know we took something," Maya said.

"Definitely. With any luck they'll assume that we've been extracted and not do a proper search." Mikael spoke calmly, but Maya could see the discomfort on his face.

He's pushed himself too far. How many guards did he take out?

Maya guided him past a few bushes onto a makeshift path. There was a sudden whoosh of movement and Valerie stood before them.

"I knew I'd find you," Valerie declared. Her stance was strong, and she was clearly blocking the way.

"Don't worry, I'll take care of her," Maya said to Mikael. He nodded and leaned against a tree.

"What makes you think you can handle me?" Valerie said.

"You're just an order-taker. You don't have any creativity or true strength." Maya smiled, hoping her words would set off Valerie. She didn't need to wait long. A fist slammed into her chest, knocking Maya back. Valerie looked furious.

"You're nothing. Just a lost girl trying to play with the adults." Valerie was all tense, ready to strike again.

I think she's too fast for me.

Maya tried to look out for the attack, but she didn't get any warning. A slight twitch from Valerie, and then Maya was suddenly hit again. She placed a hand over her chest, feeling the injury.

It's not bad at all. Maybe I don't need to be as fast as her.

"You know, I've learned a few things recently. You'll never be fast enough to win," Maya said with a smile. She focused her Chakra, reinforcing her Earth Chakra. Hardening her body. Valerie didn't even respond. Maya noticed a series of blows striking all over her body. But Maya didn't focus on the individual hits. Or even what Valerie was doing.

Be still. Be strong.

Maya kept her focus and strength, closing her eyes. She continually reinforced her body with her Chakra, preventing the strikes from doing harm. The attacks suddenly stopped. Valerie stopped, nursing her right hand. It looked bruised.

"Have you been punching a wall?" Maya asked innocently. Valerie glowered back at her.

"Fine, you've learned something. But it doesn't matter." Valerie reached into her pocket and became a blur again. Maya didn't try to track the woman. Instantaneously she was bound up by a strong rope and dropped to the ground.

This isn't good. I'm completely disabled.

"Now I can just drag you back. All you did was waste my time," Valerie said, her voice mostly sounding satisfied. With something else mixed in.

She's really distracted. Something else is going on.

Maya looked over at Mikael. He was standing patiently. Acting like nothing was unusual. He almost got away with it. Maya turned her attention back to the rope binding her. It was tied in multiple knots; it wouldn't be something she could untie. And she couldn't slip out.

I can't let her take me back. Not now. I'll never be confined again.

Maya frantically searched her mind for all the things she read up on the Chakra bloodline and abilities. She gasped as she realized what to do.

"Figuring out the futility of your situation now?" Valerie said, laughing. She leaned over Maya, turning her over roughly. Maya ignored the woman. She needed to focus. She opened her mind to meditation, focusing her Chakra differently. Before she had used it as a weapon, to heal and guard, or to supplement her strikes. But this use was different. More precise.

She radiated out Chakra from her hands. Only this time, she focused the Chakra to have a cutting edge. To be sharp. At first, nothing happened. Valerie grabbed Maya's arm and started dragging her along. The movement was disruptive, but Maya pushed it away. She reminded herself of the wind tunnel. She could keep her focus. Suddenly it worked. The rope fell away from her hands. Maya quickly dropped her arms down to her legs, keeping the Chakra constant and severing the ropes at her feet.

Valerie was shoved back, surprised. She started to move in again, but Maya held out a hand. Valerie connected with it, and she recoiled in horror. Blood started to gush from an open wound.

"What?" Valerie shouted out, clutching her hand. Maya pulled herself up to a standing position.

"I've almost mastered the Chakra bloodline. I've done it faster than anyone. You'll need more than that to capture me again." Maya stared at Valerie, challenging her. The other woman maintained the stare. Pain and Hatred directed at Maya. She softened her gaze.

"We don't have to be enemies. Don't trust what the Master Sage says," Maya said. Valerie turned away.

"This isn't over. I'll let you go this time." Valerie disappeared into the distance.

"Let's not waste this opportunity," Mikael said. Maya turned and nodded.

"This way." Maya picked a path through the forest and Mikael followed behind.

31

PARTING WAYS

They walked in silence. Maya lost in her own thoughts, and Mikael was happy to offer nothing else. After a few hours, they finally reached a rough wooden cabin. It was empty but had a bench inside.

"Let's stop here for a moment," Mikael said. He sat on the bench and waited for Maya to join him.

"This a rest stop, for those travelers who need a break either before or after their ascent," he explained.

"Why's it empty?" Maya asked.

"We're out of season. Other times of the year this place will be a busy place. With staff passing out useful supplies, there will be vendors around, serving snacks and drinks." Mikael gestured out beyond the cabin.

"I'm glad it's free," Maya said, feeling a shiver go down her spine.

"This place has such an important purpose. Yet the rest of the time, it's vacant. Waiting. It's needed for only a short time. Then it's free, as you put it."

"What do we do now?" Maya said. Mikael sighed.

"I'll stay here. Give the cabin a purpose for now." Mikael smiled.

"And me?" Maya said.

"You have somewhere else to be. A different purpose."

"Can we stop talking in riddles?" Maya said with a sigh. Mikael turned and looked at her directly.

"We're cut off from the Hanzo clan, there's no communication. I can't tell you exactly what's going to happen. However..."

"The mission was compromised. The Master Sage knows I'm here. You know about me. The others probably do by now as well..." Maya said, her voice trailing away.

"Yes. Bad news travels on wings. Our time was well-spent. Go to your friends now."

"Thank you for your help. Will you be OK?" Maya said. Mikael nodded.

"You deceived me also. Yet I managed to escape with some evidence," Mikael held up the portable data drive and winked. Maya patted the other one in her pocket.

"This is really it, isn't it?" Maya said.

"Send word when you master the Chakra bloodline. And if you ever want to master the Haste bloodline, come find me," Mikael said with sly grin.

"How did you?" Maya said quickly.

"I didn't know for sure, until your reaction confirmed it. But why else would the Master Sage take such an interest in you? You won't be able to hide in the shadows forever, the world will come to know you. Maya of the many bloodlines." Mikael gave her another cryptic smile.

"For now, I'd rather keep that under wraps."

"Enjoy it while it lasts." Mikael closed his eyes and waited.

"Goodbye, Mikael," Maya said.

"Goodbye, Maya. And good luck." Mikael kept his eyes closed. Maya stood and took a few steps away, before turning back one last time. She waved and kept walking. She felt the breeze stir and found a red leaf in her hand. She pocketed it and continued down the trail.

Hours later she reached the bottom of the mountain, entering a gravel carpark. Maya noticed a single car parked there. The one that Anders had bought. Her heart leapt for a moment.

Anders. Is he better?

The driver's door opened, and Derek stepped out. After one look at Maya, he ran over, almost knocking her over with a hug.

"Maya, you're OK. I knew it, but we were so worried. We didn't know what to think," Derek said. He leaned back, looking at her for a second, before hugging her again.

"What happened?" Maya said. Derek released her and started to explain.

"Kora was monitoring their communications, because well she's Kora. The first thing we noticed was that suddenly comms were down. The Hanzo clan were scrambling to get a team mobilized."

"Nobody came for us," Maya said.

"Exactly. Let's get moving in case they come here." Derek stopped talking as a helicopter flew overhead. Derek opened the car door for Maya and then hurried over to the driver's seat. He turned the car on quickly and started driving as Maya buckled up.

"There was another communication. It said you were a spy, were hiding another bloodline, and trying to use the Hanzo clan to get information. Within the hour they dropped off all your things."

"Wow, they didn't waste any time. At least they returned my stuff."

"I think it was the option that was the least risk."

"How long have I been gone?"

"Over twelve hours. What happened to you? "

"Long story. But the Master Sage was there. They had people in tanks. And I ended up in one too." Maya shivered as she thought about it.

"But you're OK? You look OK." Derek stopped the car and looked her over again.

"You've changed. You passed the Space Chakra?"

"I did. Does that make us equals?" Maya said with a chuckle.

"In theory. But considering how quickly you got here, I don't know how to classify you." Derek started driving off again.

"I had a good teacher," Maya said.

"You sure did. And now we're out of lessons. It's a bit of a drive, do you mind telling the story as we go?"

"Not at all. Maybe you'll think of something I didn't pick up on." Maya leaned back in the chair and prepared to take Derek through it all.

Maya added the last touches as Derek parked the car. She had told the whole story multiple times, jumping back, adding extra detail, and answering Derek's questions. He hadn't given anything away, just probed for more and more. They left the car and entered the hotel lobby, Derek flagging the lift and using his access card.

Soon they were back in Anders' room. Maya rushed to his side and held his hand. He was sleeping, his breathing uneven and ragged.

"He's even worse," Maya said, looking back at Derek, sharply.

"I'm sorry. The Hanzo clan withdrew their equipment, and things are getting worse. Kora is trying to source something else to help."

"What can I do?"

"Sit with him a minute, and I'll get Kora." Derek dashed out. Maya turned back to Anders. She stroked his forehead, leaning in to give it a quick kiss.

"Hang in there. I'm so close. I promise I'll save you. Like you saved me." Maya heard the front door open and close, and she got up, moving back to the living room. Kora and Derek were standing in the doorway, Kora clutching her laptop in one hand.

"Glad to see you back. Derek said there was a close call with the Master Sage?" Kora said.

"Yes. I don't even know what he did. I was powerless." Maya sighed.

"One problem at a time. You have something for me?" Kora said. Maya dug out the data drive and handed it over. Kora accepted it carefully and walked over to the coffee table. She opened her laptop and plugged in the drive.

"No encrypted files, nice. This will be easy." Kora began exploring the drive immediately.

"She's going to need a minute. Have you thought about what to do next? I have some ideas," Derek said. He took a seat on the couch and Maya followed him.

"There's only one option. We go to the Lost Lands. Together."

"I agree."

"We do the challenges, we master the next Chakra, and I come back to save Anders." Maya glanced back at Anders' room.

"Just the small matter of getting in. I was hoping that the Hanzo clan could help. But we will need to find another way," Derek said.

"I have money. Surely, we can find someone to smuggle us both in. And Kora can keep an eye on Anders."

"They're doing bloodline testing. Mixing bloodlines," Kora said. Derek smiled at Maya and shrugged.

"Nice. Keep digging," Maya said. She looked back to Derek.

"The core plan is good. Let's focus on how to get to the Lost Lands. Once we're there we need to get ourselves onto the 'Hopeful's Path'," Derek said.

"What's that?"

"It's literally the road you must take. Every hopeful who wishes to test themselves against the masters takes it. There are trials on the way. If you succeed, you'll arrive at the hidden temple."

"That's where it happens?"

"Yes. There are no exceptions. I don't know of a person who has achieved the Command Chakra in any other way."

Maya was about to speak when she noticed Kora walking over.

"I couldn't help overhearing you have a problem," Kora said.

"Potentially," Maya said, looking at Derek.

"You need to get into the Lost Lands quickly, that's a problem. Fortunately, I have some people who owe me a favor or two." Kora winked and smiled at Maya.

"Do I want to know why?" Maya asked. Kora shook her head while still smiling.

"Should I make some arrangements?" she said. Maya glanced over at Anders' room.

"Do it," Maya said. Kora nodded and turned to head back to her laptop.

"You better start preparing yourselves," Kora said. Derek and Maya rose and walked to the front door.

"What am I going to need?" Maya said to Derek.

"Minimal things. Just make sure you have some essentials, and I'll organize the rest," Derek said as he opened the door and started to leave.

"Back soon," Derek said as he closed the door behind him. Maya turned to see Kora right there, clutching her laptop.

"The wheels are in motion. Come to my room when you're ready," Kora said. She grinned and left the room. Maya watched the door close.

Alone again.

She hesitated for a moment, before heading to the bedroom. She walked over to the bed and reached out for Anders' hand. She grasped it gently while she focused on her Chakra.

Feel how he is. Connect with him somehow.

Maya started her meditation, building her Chakra slowly. She tried to focus on his Chakra, not hers. She couldn't picture it, not quite. But she felt blocked. The flow of energy was stopped suddenly. Maya let out a tiny gasp.

This is bad.

Maya opened her eyes and watched him breathing. He seemed a little less labored.

"Anders, I'm going to go very soon. When I return, I'll have the power to heal you. Please, you need to wait for me. Can you do that?" Maya stared at Anders, hoping for some sign of recognition. But there was nothing. She sighed, and gently released his hand.

"Don't you dare die on me, Anders. If I get back here and you're gone..." Maya let the words go and turned to leave before the tears started.

32

HASTY EXIT

Maya ascended the ramp quickly, catching up to Derek. As she entered the cargo hold the ramp began to close behind her.

"Are you sure this is safe?" she shouted at Derek over the noise.

"Completely. This is our best shot." Derek navigated through the neatly stacked crates, tied down against the cargo racks. Maya followed close behind, having to steady herself as the plane lurched forward.

"We better get seated before this takes off," Derek said. He stopped suddenly and Maya stood beside him. At the back of the cargo area there were two chairs with seatbelts. Pure metal, no padding whatsoever.

"This is us," Derek said. He gestured at the chairs and waited for Maya to select one. She sat in one immediately, working on strapping herself in. Derek wasted no time sitting in the other chair and doing the same.

"It's going to get pretty cold in here, but we'll be fine with these outfits," Derek said. Maya nodded, eyeing off her clothing again. It was a modified black suit, like the one the

Hanzo clan had given her. Despite the conditions, she didn't feel any cold.

"Here we go." Derek leaned back in the chair as the plane started to rapidly accelerate. Maya braced herself.

Never flown this way before. Where did things go wrong?

The plane sped up more and more. Back here the roar of the engines was deafening. Maya closed her eyes and concentrated. She tried to focus inward, blocking out all the noise. It was partially successful. The strange lurch when the plane left the ground was even more accentuated than she remembered.

She glanced over at Derek and he gave her a reassuring smile.

Relax, you can do this. Just another plane ride.

Maya took a few deep breaths and relaxed. The plane kept ascending for a few minutes before it settled into its flight path. Once that happened she slowly allowed herself to relax a little.

The noise made it impossible to talk to Derek, she didn't even try. His eyes were closed anyway.

Must be meditating. It's a good idea.

Maya closed her eyes and began a meditation. There was nothing else to do, and for a while it would take her mind off Anders and his labored breathing.

Hours later, Maya felt a stirring. Something was different. She opened her eyes and looked over at Derek. He was alert and looking around too. The plane seemed to be descending.

Is it time already?

Maya continued looking around the cargo bay. She shivered, a chill registering despite her insulated suit. Nothing within the bay seemed disturbed, but Maya did notice a red light flashing in the corner.

Maybe that's something.

Maya unbuckled her belt and removed the straps. She stood carefully, walking around the bay. She looked back at Derek and motioned for him to follow. He quickly removed himself from the seat and walked over. Maya pointed to a nearby door and started toward it. It had a large lever handle. She leaned on it hard, and the door quickly opened. She stepped inside immediately, Derek closing it behind them.

Maya found herself in an antechamber with another similar door. The noise was a little less in here.

"Something's not right. We need to go look," Maya said.

"I feel it too." Derek stepped past her and opened the next door himself. They were in a narrow corridor when the plane suddenly lurched to the side.

"I don't like how this is playing out," Maya said. Derek didn't respond, instead he began to run down the corridor. Maya followed him closely, adjusting her balance as she ran to avoid toppling over. The plane was making erratic movements now. Derek opened the next door, holding it for Maya before they both entered.

They were inside a tiny passenger cabin. There were four empty chairs.

"Surely we could have traveled here instead?" Maya said. Derek shrugged.

"Not my biggest concern right now." Derek stalked through the cabin and tried the next door.

"It's locked," he said.

"Break it," Maya said. Derek nodded and took a step back. He swung at the door with his fist, bending it near the lock. With a little force he pried the door open and looked beyond. There was a small chamber before a closed door labeled cockpit.

"Let's go say hi," Derek said.

"It's just manners," Maya said. She gestured to the door and Derek knocked first. After a few moments, he hit it with his palm. The door reverberated but didn't break as easily. After two more successive strikes, the door started to buckle. Derek threw his shoulder into it, and the door broke down. Maya gasped instantly. There were no pilots.

"Drone plane?" Maya asked. Derek searched the cockpit.

"Possibly. But the seats are still warm. There were pilots." Derek kept checking the instruments. Maya noticed that the steering controls were flapping about without any control. She peered out of the windows, seeing only ocean rapidly approaching.

"Derek, we're going to crash," Maya shouted, pointing at the window. He looked up and swore under his breath.

"Parachutes in the cabin," Maya shouted. She turned and ran back to the passenger cabin. Checking under the seats she found only life vests. She threw them aside.

Useless. Find something else. Anything.

Maya returned to the chamber before the cockpit, looking for compartments.

"There's a slide that extends out," Derek said. Maya shook her head.

"That's not going to work. We need to get out before it crashes." Maya ran back to the cockpit. She could glimpse land in the distance. She ran over to the controls and tried yanking them down to pull the plane up. Nothing happened.

"If we time it right, we can survive a fall, right?" Maya said, running back to Derek. He looked up at her, a puzzled expression.

"In theory. You've more chance than I do."

"I don't see any other way of getting out of here. And we're running out of time." Maya looked at Derek, watching him think. He nodded slowly.

"I think you're right." Derek walked over to the airlock and quickly yanked the handle down. The door came off and was instantly pulled out of the aircraft. Derek and Maya clung to the walls, staring out at the ocean.

"Less time than we thought. We should leap that way," Derek shouted, pointing with his arm.

"Done. Follow closely behind me," Maya shouted. She carefully maneuvered past Derek, peering over the edge. The plane was descending fast now, the ocean quickly lurching closer. Maya tried to gauge the distance.

The sooner you jump, the further away the plane will be. But the harder the ocean will hit you.

Maya closed her eyes for a moment, thinking back to challenges she had surpassed to unlock her Chakras. Strength, stability, resilience, and letting go. With all those, she could do it. Maya shut away her thoughts, focusing only on the jump before her. She cleared her mind and pushed out.

The freezing wind whipped her from all directions, threatening to disorient and distract her. But Maya was focused on a small piece of ocean. She guided herself there, preparing her legs for entry into the water. A small panic rose as she fell, but it was momentary.

This is not your time to die. You have a greater purpose.

The thought was comforting. An instant later she broke the water. Feet first, she entered the ocean like a torpedo. The icy cold was a shock, but the impact was manageable. Her head went under the water, but she quickly surged upward. She kicked her legs out and they worked. Forcing her head above water she saw Derek falling behind her. He impacted moments later, dropping under the surface as she had. A wave crashed into Maya's face, blinding her. She opened her eyes again and saw Derek next to her.

He's OK.

Her attention was quickly diverted to the plane. It was finally crashing into the water. Giant waves surged away from the impact. Maya grabbed Derek's hand and pulled the two of them under the water. A few moments later they resurfaced. The plane was skidding away, pieces fracturing apart with incredible speed. Maya ducked them both down again, waiting longer this time. She could feel a wave of heat pass by.

That's not good.

She resurfaced and looked again. The plane was now a complete wreck with debris everywhere. And multiple fires. She peered into the distance looking for land. She thought she could see something, but it was too dark.

"Can you swim?" Maya said to Derek.

"Yes," Derek said. He didn't look too confident, but he was steady in the water. Maya released his hand and started to swim toward the wreckage. Without going too close, she kept an eye out for useful wreckage. Off to the side she spotted what looked like a door, and some aircraft panels.

"This way," Maya said. She swam over quickly, securing the door and passing it to Derek. He held onto it, resting for a moment. Maya found herself a panel and leaned on it too. She felt a moment of relief.

"How much did we pay for this?" Maya said. Derek let loose a chuckle.

"Too much."

"Figures. Let's see if we can finish the journey ourselves." Maya let the waves carry her along for a minute, before kicking her legs and propelling herself forward. She checked back and saw Derek following.

The next hour was slow and frustrating. They had to constantly dodge wreckage, the surging waves, and minor rest breaks. But slowly they progressed toward what was land. The aircraft wreckage was so spread out, they kept finding it. Even when they had left the main pieces behind. As they drew closer to the shore, the tide helped them along. And eventually, they stumbled onto the ground. Maya threw herself onto the rocky ground, lying on her back and looking up at the stars.

"We made it. We actually made it," she said. Derek flopped down beside her.

"Welcome to the Lost Lands. I think," he said. They both burst out laughing.

"It had to be this hard, didn't it?" Maya said.

"Of course. But we're here now. We just need to make it onto the path.

"Path of Hopefuls?"

"Exactly. Once we're on there, there's no more interference. We get our shot."

"You make it sound easy," Maya said with a laugh.

"If only it were. I think by the end you'll be wishing for another plane crash," Derek said. He sighed and sat up. Maya forced herself up as well.

"We need to find our bearings and keep moving. We might have a long way to travel, depending on where we landed."

Derek rose and started walking. Maya stood and took one more look out at the ocean.

One step closer. You can do this.

She turned and followed Derek.

33

FINDING THE PATH

Derek wandered back from a tiny house. He was carrying a backpack and jingling something in his hands. Once he was closer, he tossed it at Maya. She caught it and noticed it was a keyring with car keys.

"You got us wheels?" Maya said.

"And something to eat. We've got a long drive ahead of us." Derek walked over and stood by the car. It was a tiny box car, navy blue.

"Are you sure it works?" Maya said as she rounded the car.

Looks like somebody had a fight with the car.

"It should. And it'll help us avoid attention. Can't exactly fly in on a helicopter, you know?" Derek waited by the passenger side and Maya walked around to the other side and unlocked the car.

"You can drive, right?" he said.

"Yes. It's been a while."

"Have you driven on the right side before?"

"No."

"You'll catch on quickly." Derek entered the car and Maya sighed before opening the door and getting in. She spent a few moments adjusting the seat and checking the mirrors. Derek was already munching on some dumplings.

"Care for some?" he said, offering the bag. "They're vegetarian," he added. Maya grabbed one and stuffed it into her mouth. It was still warm, and completely delicious.

I really needed that.

Maya turned on the car, and to her surprise the engine started without incident. She turned on the headlights and looked over at Derek.

"You're navigating I presume?"

"Head right," Derek said. Maya pulled the car out and started driving. After a few turns they were onto a minor freeway. Endless road stretched out ahead of them.

"Where are we heading?" Maya said.

"Mount Emptiness," Derek said.

"Never heard of it."

"Oh, it's lovely this time of year. Well, any time of year."

"It's a temple, right?" Maya said. She slowed and kept her eyes on the road as a car sped past them.

"It's many temples. But at the peak, there's two temples. One represents the present, the other the future. They're very sacred."

"Interesting. And that's where the masters are?" Maya said.

"Correct. The Path of the Hopefuls is the way we wind our way up, and the challenges we must face. Three in total."

"Only three? That's not so bad."

"Oh, and they say there's over nine thousand steps to reach the peak." Derek popped another dumpling into his mouth and grinned.

"Of course. Silly me," Maya said, chuckling.

"It can't be too easy. At the end of this process, you unlock the Command Chakra."

"And I'll get my LifeDeath powers back," Maya added.

"Here's hoping," Derek said, stuffing his face again. Maya stared at him and almost stopped the car.

"Here's hoping?" She quickly returned her eyes to the road.

"It's generally accepted that mastering the Chakra bloodline means opening up the first six Chakras. As far as I know, only the masters have opened the seventh."

"Anders doesn't have time for that," Maya said.

"I know. We're on a good plan. I'm just saying that I hope your multiple bloodlines works that way. Hinging on the six Chakras, not all seven," Derek said, staring out of the car. Maya was quiet for a minute before responding.

"All this effort, for a chance. No guarantees," Maya said softly. She kept her eyes forcibly on the road, not looking back at Derek.

"It's unknown territory unfortunately. There's no book on how multiple bloodlines work. Just hearsay. But the reassuring thing is that there's people out there like you. Maybe not quite like you, but all the same they've unlocked the use of more bloodlines. Not one story said they had to master the seventh Chakra. That's something."

"It's definitely something," Maya said, staring off into the distance.

Every few hours they switched drivers. The radio didn't work, so they either listened to songs from Derek's phone or drove in silence. The rest of the day was spent this way, driving. And as dusk approached Derek suddenly pointed to a turn-off.

"Take this one, quickly."

"Hang on," Maya said, slowing and turning, the car slightly skidding with the sudden shift. They were onto a gravel road, heading up to what looked like a quaint cottage.

"Do we have time for this?" Maya said as they pulled up.

"We're not too far away, but you need a little rest. You haven't slept."

"But..."

"This is not a simple exercise. We don't simply do a hike and collect the prize. You're going to be pushed harder than you have in your life. You need to give yourself a fighting chance," Derek said, his voice full of passion. He quickly turned away.

"Otherwise, I'll fail," Maya said, completing the thought.

"You can't underestimate this," Derek almost whispered. Maya pulled into the drive, parking outside the main building. It was modeled after an English-style cottage with a thatched roof. Derek disappeared inside a little side building and Maya stared out of the window. There was nothing around, just dark countryside with the twinkling of lights in remote houses.

How did I end up here? What am I doing?

Maya chuckled and shook her head. If she stopped to question things, it all sounded crazy. But she knew what she had to do. She had to save Anders. Derek darted back to the car, entering.

"Got keys. Let's head in," he said. Maya left the vehicle and followed Derek onto the front porch. He unlocked the door with a key card and switched the lights on. The cottage was incredibly sparse. Maya spotted two single beds, a TV, and a bathroom.

"It's what we need, and nothing more," Derek said. Maya lay on the first bed. The minute her body touched it she felt like lead weights were dragging her down. Derek was saying something, but she couldn't really hear him. Moments later he shook her awake.

"Maya, we need to leave," Derek said. Maya quickly sat up, disoriented. She looked around and saw the beginnings of daylight peeking through the windows.

"Is everything OK?" she asked.

"All fine. You slept, and now we need to go," Derek said. He opened the front door and held it open. Maya stumbled out, trying to finish waking up. Derek thrust a cup of coffee into her hands.

"I'll drive first, you wake yourself up." Derek walked over and unlocked the car, starting it quickly. Maya entered the car and focused on her coffee. Each sip woke her up a little more.

"I really needed that I suppose," Maya said.

"Yup. Don't worry, there will be plenty of opportunities to run yourself into the ground once we reach the Path," Derek said with a chuckle.

"Good. I don't want you to get the wrong impression." Maya smiled and took a long drink of the coffee.

They drove for the rest of the day, taking turns, and stopping only when necessary. At twilight Derek parked the car in a gravel car park.

"This is as far as we can drive," he announced. Derek left the car quickly, staring out into the darkness beyond.

"Where are we exactly?" Maya asked.

"Parklands. We'll have to hike over to the starting point. It's not far from here, but we couldn't exactly park at the front gate. I can imagine they're looking for you." Derek started off to a path at the end of the car park. Maya quickly followed.

"Got a solution for the dark?" Maya asked.

"No, we can't announce ourselves. Just follow closely and let's stick to the track," Derek said, walking into the forest. Maya followed right behind. With each step they found less and less light. Soon enough, it was pitch black.

I can't explain this feeling. It's like being stuck in a cupboard, but we're outdoors.

As they went, they fell into a rhythm. The flatter sections they picked up speed, but for any hills they had to take more caution to avoid tumbling up or down. Eventually, there were lights in the distance.

"That's the main gates ahead," Derek said. Maya nodded and kept an eye on where he was directing her. As they emerged from the trees, she could see them finally. Large ornate wooden gates, in a decorative style. In front of the gates stood four people. Two men and two women. They were in martial arts uniforms.

"We even have a welcoming party," Maya commented.

"You're a celebrity. You just need to find a way past them. Once you're on the path, you're subject to the rules of the trials. They can't interfere again," Derek said.

"Did you make it this far?" Maya said.

"Yes. I didn't need to fight my way in," Derek said.

"And you struggled on the Path?" Maya asked. Derek sighed.

"Yes. But we won't speak of it. Not until after."

"I understand." Maya stepped forward again, taking in a deep breath.

Pass through the gates. It should be easy.

Maya ran ahead, jogging down the path and onto the tiled square before the gates. The four guards stepped forward, focusing on her intently.

"Maya Mills, you have not been authorized to undertake the Path," one man said. He was taller than the rest and took an extra step ahead of them.

He must be the leader.

"I'll prove my worth on the Path. It's my right."

"It's not a right. It's a privilege. One earned, not taken," the leader said. He turned to Derek.

"I remember you, Derek. I didn't expect such disrespect from even you."

"Strength is not disrespect, Lu Bao," Derek answered. He bowed.

"If you can defeat me, I'll step aside and let Maya enter unhindered," Lu Bao said, returning the bow.

"This is where I put my money where my mouth is," Derek said to Maya, jogging ahead of her and standing in the middle of the tiled area. Now an arena.

Lu Bao strode across and stood before Derek. He didn't ready himself at all, standing with his arms by his sides.

"When you are ready," Lu Bao said. Derek entered a ready stance and breathed in. He suddenly burst forward with a palm strike. Lu Bao dodged it easily, not returning any attacks. Derek glided into another attack, combining with a high kick. Lu Bao continued to dodge, moving just enough to avoid the attack.

This pattern continued, Derek attacking faster and faster, and Lu Bao dodging with minimal movement. Occasionally he would block an attack, but his arms would always return to his sides.

Derek can't lay a finger on him.

Derek retreated, gathering himself.

"Is that all?" Lu Bao said. His voice was purely factual, there was no tone.

"Not yet," Derek said. He closed his eyes and concentrated. Maya couldn't see any difference, but she could feel it. He seemed to be vibrating with energy.

What have you done, Derek?

Derek dashed forward, almost as fast as a Speedster. He landed a strike on Lu Bao's chest. Lu Bao rocked slightly with the strike, anticipating the next one and blocking it. The sound of contact rang out around the arena.

"That's more like it," Lu Bao said. He began to move finally, dodging by stepping aside, and blocking more attacks. But he seemed to adjust to Derek's new speed.

They're back to the same pattern. All that changed was Lu Bao is having to exert himself a bit more.

Derek retreated again. Maya could see signs of tiring.

He's using up all his Chakra. But Lu Bao doesn't look like he's expended any effort. This can't end well.

"I see you're still a failure," Lu Bao said. Derek hung his head. The energy dissipated from him, and he turned to walk back to Maya.

"You're not a failure," Maya said, meeting Derek halfway.

"I know that. Lu Bao is one of the masters. The true test is how far I will go before accepting that I cannot defeat him."

"I see. So, the true failure is..."

"Being unable to continue," Derek said, finishing the thought. Maya nodded.

"Well, you've passed that test. Only now, we need to figure out a way past. And I don't think we can just ask nicely," Maya said, observing the rest.

I think I've got an idea.

34

THE LAUGHING BUDDHA

Maya stepped past Derek and continued to the center of the arena. She stood before Lu Bao, looking him up and down.

"Why do you stand in our way?" she asked.

"We are guarding the Path. To protect its significance for those that are worthy," Lu Bao said.

"You don't determine who is worthy, that's the task of the Path itself. By preventing me from taking part, you're assuming the role of the Path yourself."

"Your logic is incorrect." Lu Bao shifted his stance slightly.

"No, not this time. If you say I am not worthy, yet I succeed on the Path and unlock the Command Chakra, it shows that your judgment is wrong. You cannot ever again prejudge someone as unworthy. So, it's better for you to keep me away, to prevent us from discovering your flaws of reasoning." Maya spoke without emotion, hoping the strength of her argument would move him. Lu Bao regarded her strangely.

He seems to be considering my words. Maybe there's a chance here.

"So, you're saying, that if I wish to verify my judgment of

your worthiness, I must let you fail on the Path itself. By not allowing you to even attempt it, I am implying that you might succeed otherwise."

"Yes, that's correct. Thank you for your vote of confidence in me." Maya smiled at him.

"And you're intent on this course of action?"

"Nothing can stop me from this. I'll just find another way." Maya stared at Lu Bao, defiantly. Letting the strength of her will add weight to the words. He slowly nodded.

"So be it. Test yourself. I will not take satisfaction at your failure, but I will feel vindicated in my judgment of you." Lu Bao stepped aside, and waved Maya on.

"C'mon Derek. Same argument works for you too," Maya said, beckoning for Derek to join her. The three remaining guards pushed the giant doors open and waited by the side.

"Wish me luck," Maya said as she stepped through the gate.

"I don't believe in luck," Lu Bao said. Maya couldn't help grinning.

Here we are. We're on our way.

Maya continued on a stone path, Derek falling in beside her.

"I'm impressed. You handled that well," Derek said.

"The academic in me came out. I wasn't sure it would work," Maya said with a chuckle.

"Really? You were so serious!" Derek said.

"It was a long shot. But the way he tested you, just twigged something for me. I'm glad it worked. Much easier than trying to sneak or break our way in."

"Easy for you maybe," Derek said. He wiped a bead of sweat from his brow.

"What was it you did back there? When you became so... energized?" Maya asked.

"I opened all my Chakras and infused my body. They call it Flowering."

"Right. I saw that term in a book. Flowering? Really?" Maya said, giving Derek a skeptical look while scrunching up her face.

"Of course. I realize it's a little strange, but like I said, this is not just a fighting Bloodline. Although it is known as one. They also say that once you have the sight, that when someone is Flowering, you'll see bursts of Chakra radiating out of them like they are blooming," Derek said, sounding a little embarrassed. Maya nodded along.

"I can imagine it. Hopefully, we'll both see that soon." Maya gave him a hopeful smile and continue pressing ahead. The path started straight but began to wind around the terrain. The edges of the path had the occasional lantern, but the glow was just enough to light the path. Outside the path looked like grass and trees, but they appeared as just murky outlines. Maya could begin to make out shapes in the distance.

"The first challenge would be easiest, right?" Maya said, trying to be casual.

"Of course. Each challenge increases in difficulty."

"And you completed this one," Maya added. She glanced over at Derek, and he nodded.

"Any tips?"

"Sorry, no. Divulging any details of the test would make me ineligible. I hope you understand." Derek paused and gave her a short bow; however, she noticed a wry smile on his face.

"You're up to something, aren't you?" Maya said. Derek shrugged.

"I absolutely cannot say anything about the upcoming trial. Except that it will be at the first landmark we approach." Derek focused his attention directly ahead and Maya took the hint.

He can't say anything, but he does want to help. I wonder what's going on.

Maya spent the time in her own thoughts, remembering the trials she had already completed to get here. It was a good way to distract herself from what was ahead. And the creepy silence that surrounded them.

After a short walk she could finally see what was ahead. A large, paved courtyard with a few buildings at the rear. The main one was topped by a giant golden Buddha. He was sitting comfortably with a giant smile. Regarding her curiously.

"I think we're here," Maya said. "Is that thing alive?"

"No, it's not," Derek said with a chuckle. He kept advancing and Maya matched his pace.

"There's nobody here," Maya said.

"It would seem that way," Derek said. He started to slow as he reached the middle of the courtyard. Maya stopped beside him.

"Can you at least explain how to start it?" Maya said. Derek held his finger up, suggesting she be quiet. After a moment, he gestured toward the Buddha. Maya sighed and nodded. She took a few steps ahead peering into the darkness and trying to figure out what was going to happen. Suddenly there was a flash, and she drew in a deep breath.

Maya looked around. It was daylight. The courtyard looked the same, but the Buddha was missing.

Something's not right.

She looked around, checking for enemies. There was nobody around. But she heard a rhythmic thumping sound. Thump. Thump. Thump. Whirling around, she noticed something in the distance. Something large was heading toward her. Blinding rays of light forced her to look away. As the light moved, she opened her eyes and looked up again. A giant golden smiling Buddha settled onto the building, sitting on top.

Just like the statue. But it's alive?

Maya gulped, taking a step back. The golden Buddha stared at her, the smile creeping across its face. It looked like it was about to speak, but instead of words a torrent of air burst out of the Buddha's mouth.

Stand your ground.

Maya thought back to the meditation she had practiced for the first Chakra. Stability and resilience. Connection to the earth. She planted herself firmly, not letting herself be blown away. The wind began to howl, the speed ramping up.

This is way worse than the wind tunnel. I can't hear a thing.

Maya's feet began to shift, but she held her ground.

This is the easiest challenge. It's not even real, you can do this.

Maya calmed herself, and let the wind wrap around her. She was stable, she would not be moved. The Buddha started to laugh. But it wasn't just sound. A torrent of water started to spill out from its mouth.

Hang on here.

Within moments her feet were submerged in water. The wind was not letting up. The running water was loosening her footing. Scenarios started to play in her head. Getting swept away by the water and wind. Or becoming drowned.

Relax. Be with the elements. Let them flow around you.

Maya closed her eyes. There was no benefit to watching the show around her. She had to focus on herself, activating her Chakras and being present. The water and wind raged around her. Fear crept in, but she embraced it.

I'm alive. I can deal with this. It's just a stone in my shoe, and I can keep moving forward. Wait, moving forward.

Maya opened her eyes. The Buddha's face was barely visible in the storm. But she smiled back. And she took a step. The water was up to her waist now and rising. But she ignored it. Forward was all she needed to do. She took another step, working her way through the elements. Step by step, she could make it. Something else was building up.

Maya soon saw what it was. A giant wave, rising to a great height before surging toward her. She was going to be completely smashed by it.

Remember the water trial.

Maya continued, acknowledging the fear inside, but giving it time and focus.

It's ok to be scared. But you must move on.

The giant wave towered above her, poised to strike. Maya forced down the last of the fear and dove forward into it. As the wave connected it suddenly disappeared. Maya landed on the courtyard with a smack. She looked around, confused. It was night again.

Maya slowly picked herself up. She was still wet.

How?

Maya noticed Derek standing next to her. He was also drenched.

"Did we pass?" Maya said. Derek grinned at her.

"Yes, we did. You did well for your first time." Derek winked at her.

"You're not as clever as I thought. That was..." Maya said but Derek interrupted her by touching her shoulder.

"Not here. Let's move on," he said. Maya nodded and they turned toward the golden Buddha. It was still perched up on the building, but Maya couldn't forget how it had moved. It almost looked like it was laughing at them.

"Where do we go?" Maya said.

"Go straight and through the building," Derek said. He started walking immediately and Maya fell in beside him. They crossed the courtyard quickly, entering the building ahead. However it was originally furnished was unknown, the interior was filled with black cloth and fairy lights. It was almost as if they were walking amongst the stars.

I can't see where I'm going. If there's any traps here, we can't avoid them.

Trying to appear confident, Maya walked alongside Derek. Their path seemed to curve lightly, and slope down. Eventually, they reached a heavy wooden door. Derek stopped before it.

"You do the honors," he said. Maya stepped forward and

leaned into the door. It wasn't as heavy as she expected, and beyond it was the cool night air. She walked through the door, finding another path beyond it.

"We're done then?" Maya said.

"We're done. That was the first challenge. There will be a place up ahead to rest and dry off," Derek said.

"It was all in my head, wasn't it? But how'd I get wet?" Maya said. Derek chuckled.

"It's all part of the ceremony, but you'll never find out exactly how they do it. Just accept that you passed."

"Can't argue with that," Maya said. She looked ahead and noticed what seemed to be another temple building. Only this one had light streaming out.

"That's our stop. It's a place to rest. Built in the style of the other temples." Derek increased his pace, and Maya was all too happy to do the same.

If there's food and a fire I don't even care if there's a bed.

The building had a wide entrance with gas heaters out front. Inside was a large open fire, and wooden beds lining the edges of the circular room. Next to the fire, Maya spotted a black pot.

"Come warm yourself by the fire and we can talk," Derek said. He picked a spot and knelt. Maya sat next to him, enjoying the intensity of the fire.

"Is it safe here?" she asked. Derek nodded; his attention still focused on the fire.

"Yes, we will not be observed. The rituals are followed, and we are left to recover on our own. Tomorrow will be a harder test."

"Fine by me. I can see how you were inspired to create my Chakra tests," Maya said, finally getting the words out that had been bottled up since she observed the Buddha.

"Inspired is the right word. I think I still get kudos for building them so well, and so quickly," Derek said with a grin.

"Oh, I'm not annoyed. I'm incredibly lucky. I just hope that the next test is close to something I've already done."

"I'd like to reassure you..." Derek said.

"But you can't say," Maya said, finishing his sentence.

"You're learning," Derek said with a laugh. He lifted the lid on the black pot and smelled the contents.

35

THE DISTANT TEMPLE

Maya suddenly noticed her surroundings. She was walking purposefully through a dimly lit warehouse.

Why am I here? Is this another test?

She tried to spot details that would help explain her location. The walls were rough brick, the ceiling very high. There were rows and rows of metal shelves with no identifying marks. Yet she was striding through the place in a hurry.

What's here?

Maya let herself draw back and just follow along. She seemed to know where she was going, and why. She rounded a corner and increased her speed. At the end of the row, she stopped suddenly, searching the shelves.

Something near the bottom caught her eye, and she squatted down to take a closer look. There was an ancient box tucked behind a standard cardboard filing box. She carefully retrieved the ancient box, marveling at the impossibly old wood. It was gnarled and dark. The touch of it sending shivers down her spine.

Why am I afraid of it? I think he must have left it here.

Maya reached out tentatively, searching for a latch or a way to open it. She found a simple metal catch on the other side. It was a geometric shape.

"Seven sides," she whispered as she traced her fingers over it. This was what she had come to find.

I can't take the box, they'll know. I'll have to open it.

Maya held the latch tightly and was about to throw it open when her eyes suddenly opened.

Derek was crouched over her, shaking her.

"Maya, wake up. Wake up," Derek said. Maya blinked and saw the concern in his face.

"Where am I?" Maya said lazily, looking around. She saw a row of empty cots.

The rest stop.

"You were thrashing in your sleep. Are you alright?"

"I was asleep. I was dreaming?" Maya said, staring out into the distance.

"Yes. What was happening?" Derek kept watching her closely. Maya slowly sat up, looking at the remainder of the fire. Only a few glowing embers were left.

"I was searching for something in a warehouse. A box. I think the Master Sage had left it there. But I was afraid of it."

"An odd dream then," Derek said. He stepped back and stretched. Maya could see the tension leaving his body.

"It wasn't an ordinary dream. At first I thought I was in some sort of test."

"No, the masters don't do that. You'll know when you're in a trial." Derek wandered over to the front door, looking outside. "We should head out. Unless you are still hungry." Derek grinned back at her, and Maya shuddered. She looked back over at the pot by the fire.

"Oh, no, I had my fill last night." Maya stood carefully and took a moment to assess herself.

You're fine. Get moving. It was just a dream.

She nodded at Derek.

"Let's make a start," she said. Derek stepped outside and she joined him. There was a light drizzle and a lot of mist in the air.

"Not exactly great hiking weather," Maya said.

"We're not even hiking yet." Derek stared up into the fog. "The next trial is much further up. In there."

"Are we going to fight in a cloud?" Maya said with a laugh.

"Quite possibly." Derek started off at a walk, and Maya rushed after him.

"This is where I start questioning you about the next trial," Maya said after a few moments.

"I know. But you already know my answer."

"Give me something vague. Something one of the masters would say." Maya watched Derek and he looked like he was considering it. But he kept walking.

Just wait. He'll give you something.

Maya kept quiet as they walked. They followed the path of a river, and the road was relatively easy. After a while Maya had completely forgotten about her attempt to get Derek talking, and instead was focusing entirely on their steps.

"Our first stop is the old bridge. It's about eight or nine kilometers away."

"OK. Will that save us some time?" Maya said.

I'll take any information he's willing to share.

"No, it's been destroyed. We'll take the winding hiking trail."

"Of course. Is that the nine thousand steps?"

"No, it's only about six and a half," Derek said with a chuckle.

"Path of the Hopeful, they call it. I can see why."

"And then we reach the other side of that bridge."

"You know what, I'm going to stop you there. Let's just walk," Maya said.

"Fine by me. Oh, and we won't be making tourist stops," Derek said. Maya pretended to check her pockets.

"Lucky you for I didn't bring my camera."

"You're going to want to take snaps at the top," Derek said with a laugh.

"Yeah, I'll take a Chakra mastery selfie with you." Maya couldn't control her laughter at that one. Derek just shook his head and kept walking.

The ancient bridge was destroyed, as Derek had promised. Maya's heart sank as she looked ahead to where it originally led. More rubble, but significantly further up the mountain. Derek was true to his word about the lack of sightseeing. They had neglected to visit either the waterfall or another ancient pavilion on the way. Maya took one last wistful glance behind her and pushed ahead to the hiking path.

I know we're on a mission and a timeline, but this just isn't fair. I'll have to come back here someday to do a proper tour.

Maya sighed and kept walking. Her focus was on the path ahead. But also, the challenge she had to face next.

"You've got to give me something. About this next challenge," she blurted out. Derek nodded and kept walking, methodically.

"I'm sure when you went to do this, you had a little guidance," Maya added.

"I don't want to make a mistake. Of course, I'll help, how I can." Derek spoke quietly but didn't turn to face her. He kept looking into the distance. A few minutes passed and they rounded a corner, coming to a flat section.

"Nice place for a break," Derek said. He paused and looked down at the way they had come. Maya followed along, looking back as well. She instantly drew in a breath.

"That's quite a way. I didn't realize we were so high," she said.

"It's the reason why we need to pause sometimes. We're so caught up in the journey we are on, we forget about how far we've come." Derek smiled and turned to her.

"True. It's easy to get caught up in it all." Maya smiled back and waited.

Is he going to say something else?

"I can feel your anticipation," Derek said with a laugh. "I feel like I'm not ready to be a teacher yet, but we don't really have the luxury of waiting." Derek paused for a moment, and Maya waited.

"I can explain this much. As you've already figured out, the first challenge represented the first two Chakras. The second challenge will test you on the next two."

"That's good. What else?" Maya said, not bothering to disguise the eagerness in her voice.

"Saying more would give things away. I can only recommend that you consider the trials you already faced, and the lessons you learned attaining those Chakras." Derek gave her a wry smile and started off again.

"You sure sound like a teacher," Maya grumbled as she took off after him.

He's right though. I should think about how I was tested, and how I could use that in the next challenge.

Maya continued her ascent, not asking any more questions. Instead, she reflected on the previous trials. The path stopped climbing in height, instead they were traversing deeper into the mountain range. She could see some higher peaks in the distance, but they weren't where she was heading.

"I guess the next stop is somewhere in the middle here?" Maya said, gesturing at the expanse ahead of them.

"Yes, it's a little too far to go in one trek, and we need to stop for the next test," Derek said. "In fact, you can probably start to see where we are heading."

Maya stopped and peered into the distance. She could start to picture the outline of something. But it wasn't clear.

"I see something," she said finally. "But I can't really make out what it is."

"I suppose we should keep going then." Derek winked at her, and they kept walking. From that point on Maya kept her gaze on the structure she had seen. No matter how close they reached, it always seemed a little bit fuzzy. After a while, she stopped. Derek noticed her stop and turned back.

"Something wrong?" he said with a grin.

He's finding this too funny.

"This is a trick, isn't it?" Maya said.

"What makes you say that?" Derek said. His eyes were smiling even though his face was otherwise expressionless.

"You can see it properly. Can't you?"

"Yes."

"Great. Amazing." Maya turned from Derek and stared at the foggy shape.

The temple is there, but I can't see it properly. Why?

Maya stared harder, noticing that her eyes were glancing across it and not focusing properly.

This is weird. Focus.

She remembered the staring contest she had with one of the instructors. The heat and intensity of his gaze.

Use that Fire now. Don't let them get away with this nonsense.

Maya stoked her anger, but in a controlled way. Not a boundless fury, but a focused anger. She could feel the Fire rising, her Chakra activating. The surge of it tingled, but she ignored those feelings. She concentrated her focus through her eyes, staring at the shape of the temple.

This time she didn't let her eyes wander. She treated it like a challenge of wills. The temple itself was trying to distract her away, stop her from seeing. But she wouldn't be stopped. Couldn't be stopped.

She could feel the resistance. Like a pressure in front of her eyes. And then it popped. It was over. The temple zoomed into view. She could see every stone brick, the gentle slope of the roof, and the large imposing pillars showing the entrance.

"I see now," Maya said. Derek stood next to her and looked on as well.

"It's a fine temple, isn't it?" he said.

"We're pretty close now. Would I have smacked into it?" Maya said, keeping her full attention on the temple.

"No, you'd be doing laps around it until you figured it out," Derek said. Silence hung in the air. Maya burst out laughing.

"Well done keeping a straight face. Does everyone struggle with this?"

"Yes. Part of the test is figuring out that there's a test. After you." Derek gestured ahead.

"Here goes." Maya started off toward the temple, wondering what other tricks were in store for her.

36

THE NEXT TRIAL

Maya strode through the main gateway, following the path through the ancient courtyard. Tufts of grass poked up here and there, and the surrounding stones were uneven.

I wonder how old this is.

There was nothing of interest in the courtyard, and the temple loomed above her, even larger than she had realized before. The entrance had looked tiny from a distance but was cavernous and seemed ready to swallow her up. Inside the temple was so dark that she couldn't see anything at all.

As she closed in on the temple, she noticed a sound. Or rather the lack of a sound. Turning, she noticed Derek had stopped on the path.

"I must wait here," he said, bowing to her.

"Don't you have to do this as well?" she said, confused.

"I will, but after you. This must be done one at a time."

"I see." Maya sighed. "Good luck."

"To you as well. See you on the other side," Derek said with a smile. Maya waved and turned back to the entrance. Staring in the darkness sent a shiver down her spine.

It'll be fine. You've faced worse before.

As she passed through the threshold, she felt a prolonged chill. Goosebumps ran up her arms. After almost stumbling, she realized that the ground was sloping down. And becoming stairs.

Don't fall. Breathe.

Maya steadied herself and kept going. The sensation of being swallowed up intensified as she descended further into pitch darkness. Her footsteps and her breathing were the only sounds she could hear. It was like the world was swallowing all other sounds. Into a void of nothing.

Easy now. It's just a test. You're great at tests.

Maya kept moving forward. She was still descending, but at least the steps were even. It was easy to fall into a rhythm. Provided you pretended that you weren't walking down practically invisible steps in a pit of endless darkness.

Suddenly the stairs ended, and Maya almost tumbled over. She caught herself and paused, letting the shock pass.

Progress. This is good.

She stepped forward and didn't fall down any holes. Reassured, she took more steps, reaching out with her arms to sense if there was anything else ahead.

Just emptiness. And a floor.

Spurring herself on, Maya tried increasing her speed slowly. Every few steps of safety, she kept going a little faster until she had resumed a normal walking pace.

Maybe this is just an endurance challenge. I can do this.

On her next step the ground wasn't there. Maya tumbled down and lay on the cold stones.

Nice one. Had to be walking faster, didn't you?

She picked herself up and checked behind her. It was just one large step.

Designed to make you fall. So pleasant.

Maya took a deep breath and stepped forward again. The ground was there. But she also heard something.

A song? Can't quite make it out.

Maya turned until the faint song was clearer. She walked in that direction. Soon she had forgotten all about the tricky step, instead wholly focused on the song. It was tantalizingly out of reach. No matter how far she walked, it was just that bit further.

I'm going nowhere. It's another trick.

Maya stopped walking and listened again. She spun around slowly, trying to orient herself better. The sound was clearly coming from a specific direction. One that she was heading in.

I need to seek this out and start from there. It's my only clue.

Maya pushed the doubt to the back of her mind and forced herself to forget about the previous stumbles. The harder she pushed herself ahead toward the sound, the closer she became.

This is working.

Maya stumbled over another hidden step but kept her stride. Not only was the sound clearer, but she saw a light in the distance.

Bingo.

Maya started to jog ahead, the scant light helping guide her. She knew that any source of light would help her see better and would help with the enclosing darkness. Jogging soon eased into sprinting, anything to get to the next stage of the trial. A wave of force knocked the wind out of her, Maya dropped to her knees.

Not force, emotion.

Maya looked around, confused.

That was a wave of despair. How could I be affected like that? By someone else's pain?

Maya looked up and saw the light in the distance. She forced herself to her feet and stepped closer. She could begin to make out the shape. It looked like a person. Well, the outline of a person. Burning.

It can't be a real person burning out there. But it's something.

Maya took another step and was almost bowled over again. The wave was stronger.

Despair and loneliness. Pain. It's unbearable.

Maya felt a rush of emotions wash over her. The feelings from that strange figure mixed in with pity and sadness. And a desire to help. Maya turned away from the figure, to investigate the darkness beyond. She felt an obvious shift.

It's relief. If I turn away from her pain, I feel better. That's twisted.

Maya turned back, not shrugging back from the dark feelings. If anything, they seemed heightened. Like she was being punished for looking away.

This is madness. They can't turn someone's pain into a test. I won't let them get away with this.

Maya felt the flame rise in her. Anger and resolve mixing. But she paused, tempering the feelings. Channeling them inside, rather than letting them overtake her. She felt the Chakras open, a sense of resolve, peace, and passion burning within.

I've got this.

Maya strode forward, not shying away from the wave of feelings. As she approached, the feelings of despair and dark gloom were joined with something else. Intense heat. She wasn't just uncomfortable with the oppressive feelings surging out at her, but now the rising heat. She was sweating, each step getting harder and harder.

The air was difficult to breathe. Now that she was closer, she could see the details of the figure before her. It was a woman, made of fire. Not on fire but burning all the same.

Like an elemental. Is this a vision? Or a real person?

But the answer didn't matter. Maya felt the concern either way.

I have to help her. Screw the test, this isn't right.

Maya connected with the pain of the figure. This close, the knot of feelings revealed even more. Regret, guilt, despair, mixed with a dark foreboding. The sense that things could not get better and were destined to get worse. Maya forced a smile, despite it all.

"There's always hope," she said. The figure turned suddenly, focusing her attention on Maya. This close, the heat was unbearable. Maya thought that her clothes were burning away. But she couldn't look and check. Her gaze was fixed on the woman. The woman of flame, wearing Maya's face. This last detail was enough to disrupt her concentration, and Maya tumbled to the ground.

Getting up was impossible. Her muscles ached and felt watery and loose. A blanket of dark feelings was shoving her down, grinding her into the stony floor beneath her.

You can't fail now. Get up. Get. Up.

Maya closed her eyes and took a deep, agonizing breath. Slowly, she began to rise. So subtle was the movement that it was almost nothing. But with every second she gained a little more momentum and a little more strength. By sheer force of will she dragged herself up, and then straightened, staring the woman of fire in the face.

"I'm here to help," Maya said. She walked forward again, embracing the fire, the heat. The pain on the woman's face made her own heart ache. But it wasn't the ache of heartbreak. Or loss. Or loneliness. It was the ache of connection, of empathy. She felt the pain of the woman before her, recognizing many of the feelings inside.

"I'm here now," Maya said, reaching forward and pulling the flames into a hug. For a single perfect moment, she felt total connection with the strange woman. And then a raging inferno as a pillar of fire surrounded them both.

Maya slowly opened her eyes. She was lying on stone, the evening sky above her. A cool breeze slowly brushed past her face.

That's a refreshing change.

The memories of her recent encounter all rushed together at once. For an instant she was back there. But the moment passed, and she remembered that she had triumphed. It was over. Turning her head slightly, she saw Derek sitting next to her, staring into the distance.

"Congratulations," he said, turning to face her.

How is he so composed?

"You make this look easy. How long have you been sitting there?" Maya said. Derek gave her a wry smile.

"Do you want the truth?"

"No."

"You took so long in there, that I finished the trial, had a quick nap, and composed some haiku."

"Not bad. I might have bought that. You do look quite rested," Maya said with a chuckle.

"In truth, I awoke not that long before you. I suspect they don't want the mysteries of the test to be revealed, so I was kept asleep too." Derek stretched out a little, before lying down next to her.

"Two down, one to go," Maya said. She looked over at Derek, and the smile was gone.

"This is where it gets real, huh?"

"Yes. I know what I'm up against. What we're up against. In some ways it's worse."

"It's definitely not worse." Maya sat up, giving her body a moment to adjust.

Everything feels fine. Not burnt.

Maya stood up, stretching her muscles.

"My usual approach is often to sit and dwell on things. On this occasion, I don't think it's wise. How far to the next trial?"

"Are you sure? You just passed the last one," Derek said, sitting up.

"We're both rested, we can take it. Or at least we can get closer." Maya peered into the distance. She heard Derek pushing himself up and standing next to her.

"Well, if we keep up a steady pace, we should arrive around dawn. It would look pretty spectacular," Derek said, musing.

"Arriving at an ancient temple, high in the mountains, at the break of dawn. Before attempting an unbelievable test of enlightenment and awakening. Sounds perfect."

"When you put it like that, there's no other option, is there?" Derek started off and Maya walked alongside him.

"I'm not even going to ask my next question. Since you know what it is," Maya said. Derek shook his head.

"No, I can't tell you what the trial is. Or why I failed. But I can tell you that it follows the same pattern of testing you on the next two Chakras." Derek moved onto a new path, this one lined with tiny lamps at regular intervals.

"But I haven't opened the sixth Chakra. The command one."

"You're not supposed to do it by yourself. You need to do it up there."

"I feel like that's a lot of pressure. The last one was very hard to achieve," Maya said. Derek stopped and turned to face her.

"This is the way. Besides, most of your breakthroughs have been in the middle of a trial. Remember?"

"You're right. You've prepared me well. I just hope you've done yourself the same favor. Can't have the student surpassing the teacher, after all." Maya grinned, but quickly stopped when she noticed Derek's expression.

"Sorry, I was trying to lighten the mood but that didn't really work. I know you'll pass. Faster than me, no doubt."

"I hope that by the time we arrive, I share your optimism." Derek set off again and Maya quickly sped up to match his pace.

37

ENDLESS STRUGGLE

Maya darted up the steps, the winding path becoming second nature now. Derek was not waiting for her, setting a cracking pace. It took all of Maya's skill and concentration to keep up and not tumble down the side of the mountain.

"I don't think these stairs...are...designed for this...kind of speed," Maya grunted.

"Trust me," Derek said. He increased his speed even more.

Why are we pushing ourselves so hard right before a critical trial?

Maya could sense they were starting to reach the top. She pushed herself extra hard, almost stumbling on a broken stone step. She pivoted and kept going, using the momentum, and maintaining her balance. Derek had stopped just past the stairs, and Maya quickly came to a halt. She looked up and felt her mouth gape open.

Before them were two temples, perched on the top of two narrow mountains. They were built from stone, one with a red roof and the other a golden one. Each temple was connected by a stone bridge that extended over a giant drop. Behind the temples the sun was rising, a golden orange aura blanketing everything.

"This was worth it," Maya said, trying to take it all in.

I can't believe such a place even exists. How?

"I hoped it might be. I never saw it like this last time," Derek said. Neither of them moved from the spot, enjoying the moment. Maya took in a deep breath.

"The air is much thinner," she said. Derek nodded.

"We're very high up now. Our next trial is in the temple ahead." Derek pointed to the stone temple in front of them with the red roof.

"This one represents the present moment." Derek paused, then pointed at the other temple.

"That one represents the unrealized future."

"And the bridge?" Maya asked.

"Your path, of course." Derek gave her a smile. He started to walk along the stone footpath. Maya followed him, noticing the off tuft of grass poking through. She felt a strange mix of sensations. Being alone in a massive space, but also being perched somewhere where she could fall at any moment.

Derek seemed to have no such hesitation, walking forward with confidence. The entrance to the temple was a giant wooden door with red trim. Derek stopped in front of it. Once Maya joined him, he turned to face her.

"You must knock three times, and then enter. Once you do so, your preparation for the trial will begin. We will not see each other until it is concluded."

"This is it, then?" Maya asked.

"Yes." Derek stepped forward and pulled Maya into a hug. At first, she was surprised, but then leaned into it.

He's a good man.

Derek released the hug and bowed before Maya.

"You have earned your place here. Now show them why." Derek grinned.

"You too! See you on the other side." Maya smiled back and returned the bow. Derek nodded and turned to the door. He knocked three times, and it opened slowly. Maya couldn't see inside, but as soon as Derek entered the doors closed again.

Here we are. It's your turn next. You can do this. Whatever it is. Just don't back down. Believe in yourself. Anders is counting on you.

Maya took in a deep breath and knocked three times on the door. As before, it opened slowly, only darkness within. Maya stepped through immediately and was blanketed in bright light.

She stepped into a different space altogether. Maya looked around, bewildered.

How is this possible?

She was standing in her backyard. The one from her childhood home. The sun was shining with a few clouds in the distance. The rickety fence to the side looked the same with the newer back fence and opposite side made from a different type of wood altogether. There was that lone tree in the corner with dried leaves strewn all over the ground below. Behind it was the raised lawn at the back, built high on top of a shelf of rock.

All of it was there. But also, something else. An unnatural stillness.

It's like a picture. It's not alive.

Maya bent down to feel the grass. It felt normal but didn't move to the touch. She stood back up and studied the sky. The clouds weren't moving, not even a little.

Am I stuck in a memory? Or a place?

Maya walked around the yard, studying everything in closer detail. It all stacked up.

A moment frozen in time. But what moment?

Maya whirled around, looking back toward the house. The back courtyard was empty, the tiles and table empty and undisturbed. She wandered toward it, coming around to the back door. She peered through the glass panels in the door into the kitchen. Her mum was cooking, well, frozen in the act of cooking. Glancing at the pots she recognized the meal.

This is before I graduated. I had argued with my dad and stormed outside. What were we arguing about?

Maya looked at the ground, deep in thought. It felt so long ago, which it technically was. But in terms of her memories, it wasn't that far back.

Why is it so hard to grasp?

Suddenly the memory jumped to her. Maya started back to the yard and started pacing around the grass.

We were discussing my future. My dad insisted I do my Masters. This is where I decided to agree with him. Even though it's not what I wanted.

Maya paused the pacing, letting out a sigh. With the memories coming back, she also felt the emotions as well. The anger, frustration, and sadness.

Why couldn't he understand me? We're so alike in so many ways. It doesn't matter now; I need to leave this.

Maya strode down the side passage of the house, not wanting to walk past her parents.

I can't have that conversation again. It's too painful.

She reached the side gate and tugged on the wrought iron frame. It didn't budge.

This is never locked.

Maya checked the latch, and it was unlocked. She shrugged and tugged the gate again. Harder this time. It didn't move.

What? Doesn't matter, this isn't real.

Maya focused for a moment, and then struck the gate with her palm. She visualized it flying off its hinges and clattering to the ground. Only it didn't move at all, and her hand ached. She looked at her hand, puzzled.

Where's my power?

Maya looked inside herself, focusing on her breathing and exercises to activate her Chakras. Nothing happened.

Forget that this is some sort of dream. Just leave another way.

Maya walked back, heading to the other side passage. This one led to the garage but was still worth investigating. The path was exactly as she remembered with all the odd furniture and equipment that was due to be put out at the next major clean-up. She stepped into the garage and saw the car there. She let her hand trail over the black surface and peered inside.

Exactly the same.

Maya turned her attention to the garage door button. It was covered in dust, but she pressed it all the same. The red button didn't move at all.

I can't move this thing by hand. This is getting annoying.

Maya wheeled around and took off at speed. She back-tracked around the house and arrived at the back door again.

Fine, I'll confront my past and show how I've grown or changed.

She turned the door handle, but it didn't move. Frowning, Maya tried again. It didn't budge.

What's going on here?

Maya walked back to the grass and stopped to think.

Nothing moves or changes, but I can move about this space. It must just be a function of how this space works. I'll climb over the fence, nothing to operate there.

Maya slowly approached the fence, looking for a good place to climb. She gravitated to the tree and circled it looking for the right branch to use. Instead, she noticed the pile of old bricks stacked neatly behind.

This'll do.

Maya stepped onto the bricks and steadied herself, before putting her hands onto the fence. It seemed to hold fine, so she thrust herself forward to get her legs onto the fence. Her leg overshot the fence slightly and banged into something solid. The shock of it knocked Maya back and she landed unceremoniously on her bottom.

Hang on.

Maya scrambled back up to her feet and climbed onto the bricks again. This time she used her hands to explore past the fence. She pushed up against something solid. Like a wall.

Invisible wall. Just great.

Maya swore under her breath and checked each of the fences around the yard. Each one behaved the same. Past the fence was a solid invisible wall that extended as high as she could reach. She found a small pebble on the ground and threw it over the fence. It bounced back at her.

I'm officially trapped now. Great trial. Really loving it.

Maya found a bigger rock to sit down on to review her situation.

There's no explanation. Just barriers. How do I leave this space? What am I supposed to do?

Maya closed her eyes and started thinking. Letting her mind wander. She considered all the trials she had done before, and how the obstacles had been right before her. It was always clear what to do, or what to overcome. This was different.

The memory must be a clue, or at least relevant. If I'm being honest, this moment was a complete failure. I didn't stand up to my father and tell him what I really wanted. I suppressed myself to make him happy. I've changed, haven't I?

Maya stood slowly and let her eyes open. She took in the sight once last time, the yard she had grown up in. She looked over at the back door, thinking about what was about to happen inside. There was one thing different, between now and then. Not something she had quite mastered, but that was the point after all.

Mastery over oneself. And the world around. I understand now.

Maya walked confidently over to the side gate, the one that was immovable. She stared at it and gathered her resolve.

"Open," she commanded, throwing the strength of her will at it. She could feel the gate trying to move, but something was resisting it. She took a deep breath and tried again.

OPEN.

This time she wasn't pitting her will against any other. She was issuing the command with the certainty that it would be carried out. The gate swung slowly open. Maya stepped toward it, a smile on her face.

Before she could revel in the triumph, she was blanketed in a field of white.

38

ANOTHER WAY

Maya was momentarily disoriented but found her bearings quickly. She was standing in an arena. There were familiar elements she noticed. The same surface that she had fought on in the LifeDeath Academy tournament. But the outside of the arena looked like the coliseum with its many tiered stone levels and arches.

Instead of a sky, pitch black blanketed the space above. Not a star to be seen.

What's next?

Maya took a few cautious steps ahead, not seeing any goal or opponent here. She paused for a moment, closing her eyes, and trying to feel her Chakras. She could feel the sixth one now, but it wasn't like the others.

It's like I've found it but haven't opened it properly.

Maya opened her eyes and noticed another before her. A woman. Herself. But the eyes looked harder, and there was a desperate intensity in them.

"Hello," Maya said. The other Maya nodded.

"I'm not here to have a chat," the other said.

"Are you me?" Maya said. The other Maya just stared at her.

"I'm Shadow. A blend of what you are, and what you might become." Shadow glanced down, and suddenly burst ahead. Maya reflexively raised a hand and was knocked back, almost tripping over.

"Next one won't be so light," Shadow said. She smiled and her right hand was encased in darkness.

I can't let that hit me.

Maya watched out for the attack, readying her Chakra. While she was waiting, she tried to prepare her body for faster speed and reactions. She almost missed the start of the attack, narrowly dodging the cursed strike, and blocking the punch from Shadow's other hand.

But the time taken to block had cost her. Shadow landed another quick hit, the black hand marking Maya's left arm. She stumbled back, the pain washing over her. Her arm began to seize up instantly.

"I don't think that's going to work for much longer," Shadow said with a wicked grin. Maya stared at the arm in shock.

C'mon, resist. Heal up. You can counter the curse.

But her body didn't have the strength in LifeDeath, not right now. Within moments the arm was blackened and immobile. Maya looked up in horror.

"You think that's bad?" Shadow laughed. And suddenly she appeared behind Maya, knocking her down with a regular strike. Maya fell to her knees, pain blossoming through her back.

"How did you..." Maya said, trying to catch her breath.

"If you survive this, you'll access great power. And with each bloodline you'll get more." Shadow was pacing around. Maya watched cautiously while she steadied her breathing.

I must find a way to fight back.

"But what will you become? Will you do his bidding? Or

will you be a fugitive, running your whole life?" Shadow almost spat out the words, a rising anger coming through her voice. It sounded so harsh; Maya couldn't believe it. She'd never heard her own voice like that.

"You'll have to harden up. Because you're too weak."

"And you're strong?" Maya said. Her words caused Shadow to pause, so she kept going. "Just because you have power, doesn't mean you have strength. Beating me up proves nothing."

"I'm but a fraction of what the Master Sage is. Do you think you could survive even a second of his full power and attention?" Shadow said. She resumed her pacing around. Maya sensed something and rolled away. The ground beneath her exploded with force, and a giant crack appeared where she had just been crouched.

Maya remembered the ball of energy she had used in the LifeDeath tournament and began to focus her Chakra.

You've learned so much more, you can do it better this time.

Shadow stopped her motion, and concentrated. Her other hand was now blanketed in darkness.

"Kid gloves are totally off now. Whatever you're preparing, it better be good." Shadow started circling Maya, every few steps leaning forward like she was going to strike. Each time Maya flinched, Shadow laughed.

"I know where you're weak. I know your true intentions. What you'll admit to nobody else." Shadow paused for effect. "You're just going along with it all. You can't stop and think, or you'll realize how futile the struggle is." Shadow surged forward, but Maya was ready. She dashed back, keeping her mobile arm in a defensive pose but continuing to gather her Chakra.

"I bring a healthy dose of reality." Shadow shimmered and vanished. Maya turned and thrust all her Chakra out in a blaze of blue light. The size and intensity of the ball shocked her. Shadow appeared in front of Maya attacking with both hands. Her face was a picture of total focus, and she completely ignored the Chakra ball. It impacted against her chest, and she shrugged it off, quickly pivoting. Shadow landed two neat strikes, taking out Maya's legs.

Maya crumpled to the floor. She forced herself up on her knees, then her legs stopped responding as they turned black.

The curse.

"One working arm, that's all you have left," Shadow said softly. She approached and leaned in closer.

"That's all I need," Maya said with a smile. She kept grinning. Shadow looked at her with contempt.

"Empty words. You've got nothing," Shadow hissed back at Maya.

"You know, a wise person once told me something. And you're giving me a real opportunity to prove him right," Maya said. Shadow was inches from her now, staring into Maya's eyes.

Such anger, and resentment. Are these feelings in me?

"Go on, then," Shadow said.

"The Chakra bloodline is not about fighting," Maya said. She quickly used her good arm to pull Shadow in closer and embraced her in a tight hug.

"Your mind games won't work," Shadow said, struggling to pull away. But Maya hugged her tighter.

"I don't need to fight you," Maya whispered. "You're part of me. Come back."

Maya closed her eyes. She felt a shift in her consciousness. She wasn't fighting against Shadow, she was acknowledging and incorporating her. Because Maya was the one in control. Shadow only had power at Maya's whim.

A blossoming warmth overtook Maya. She opened her eyes and quickly shut them again, seeing only bright light. Too bright. With her eyes closed, she saw bright lights and patterns.

Remnants of the over-exposure to light. She opened her eyes again, hoping to blink them away.

Instead, she saw something else. A scene played out before her. She could see herself, somewhere down below. Concentrating in a featureless room. The scene suddenly changed.

Maya was now watching herself walk through a vault. It was made of brick with rows and rows of shelves. It had high ceilings and felt important. Like someone's life's work was contained within. As she tried to look more closely the vision suddenly went dark.

Maya felt the cold stone for the first time. She awoke to pitch black. Her senses started to return, and she recognized where she was.

It's the temple. The one with the trial. I passed?

Maya sat up and looked within herself. There was the sixth Chakra, opened and flowing. But she noticed something else too. Her LifeDeath power. It was also flowing through her, a separate channel running alongside her Chakra.

"I actually did it," Maya whispered. Her body felt so strange. She stood and focused on her surroundings. There was a glimmer of light in the distance, so she headed off toward it. With each step she grew more confident, surer. As she reached it, she held out her hand and lightly shoved the stone wall, knowing it would open.

Maya stepped into a world of oranges, yellows, and reds. The blazing sunrise surrounded the mountaintop so completely that she took in a breath.

I'm in the sunrise.

She took a step forward, looking ahead. A man stood on the bridge, blocking her way. Lu Bao.

"If you think you've passed, you're mistaken," he said carefully.

"I've opened the Chakra, and I've regained access to my

power. It's over," Maya said. Lu Bao readied himself, easing into a combat pose with his arms raised.

"The revelation must be secured and unshakable. I will show you how far you've yet to travel," Lu Bao said, tensing to strike.

39

DOWN THE MOUNTAIN

Maya studied Lu Bao, watching his movements. Now that she had opened her sixth Chakra, her vision was enhanced. It took extra focusing, but she adapted quickly.

I can't believe this. It's like I never saw properly before.

Lu Bao was cycling Chakra through his body. Maya could now visualize his Chakra points.

They seem wider and more open than mine. And the seventh one. It looks like he has touched it.

"Are you just now seeing the difference between us? Once you try and land a blow, you'll feel the difference too," Lu Bao said. He seemed to inject this set of words with a bit of extra venom. Maya started to react, but something stopped her.

He seems off somehow. He's not trying to attack; he's just standing ready.

Maya watched his movements more closely. He seemed to be going back and forth over the same spot, not moving around at all. He effectively blocked the bridge with only a small space between him and the edge on either side.

Focusing more on his footwork, Maya spotted something else odd.

Is his Chakra bleeding into the ground? I've never heard of that before.

"Why do you hesitate? Is it fear? Do you want to turn back now?" Lu Bao said. Maya detected something else in his voice. *Is he nervous? Why would he be nervous?*

Maya focused on her own body. She watched the Chakra moving around her own channels. It didn't seem like she had more power, not obviously. And her LifeDeath power was something else, moving and vibrating differently.

"I'm readying myself," Maya said, buying time. She took a step forward and saw Lu Bao tense up. She turned her gaze to his feet again, watching their movement. With more concentration she looked past them, into the structure itself. The stones he was standing on, and next to.

What is it? What's he doing?

Maya peered closer, no longer caring how she looked while doing it. Her intuition told her something was here. Something important.

"Is that all you can do? Look? I knew you were out of your league. It is good that you finally noticed," Lu Bao said. Maya tuned out to his voice. She could see it for what it was. Just baiting her.

"That might have worked before," she said in a distracted voice. "But now..." Maya completely blocked out everything else. The entirety of her will and attention was now on the thread of Chakra she couldn't identify. The one that seemed off.

Relax. Let the Chakra guide you.

Maya let her tension release. Her vision flared, the colors going brighter still. The thread of Chakra she was trying to see became a thick cord running the length of the bridge. She noticed another on the other side of the bridge. Lu Bao was not stepping on either one. Quite deliberately.

Why have Chakra running through the bridge? I didn't even

know that was possible. Although it does explain all the strange tests they have performed before. Tests.

Maya refocused her attention back on Lu Bao. Then she laughed.

"I see now. You know, they should have sent someone else to administer this test. Someone with more subtlety," Maya said.

"I don't know what you're talking about," Lu Bao said. He shifted his stance slightly and Maya knew.

"The Chakra bloodline is not about fighting. Even though it can appear that way. I don't need to fight you to cross this bridge," Maya said. Lu Bao's face tightened, and he said nothing.

"Are you going to move?" Maya said. Lu Bao stared at her, hostility in his eyes. Begging for a fight. Maya sighed. She relaxed into herself and drew up her will.

"MOVE," she commanded, gesturing to the side with her right hand. The Chakra in the bridge running along the left-hand side flared up, pushing Lu Bao aside. At the same time, the Chakra on the right-hand side flared too, somehow pulling him in and holding him there.

"Thank you," Maya said, walking ahead.

"This isn't over," Lu Bao said as Maya passed him.

"I'm sure there's a fat lady singing somewhere," Maya said and kept walking. The end of the bridge was overshadowed by a large doorway. However, there was no door. Just darkness. Maya stepped into it without hesitation.

Blinding light surrounded Maya. She struggled to see. As her eyes adjusted, she saw a shape coming closer. It had the outline of a man. He seemed to be the source of the light.

"Who are you?" Maya said. A hint of nervousness tinged her voice, she couldn't stop it.

"A memory, from another time. I have a message for those that would steer the future." The man paused right in front of Maya. She couldn't make out any details, except that he seemed to be wearing a robe.

"What..." Maya started but the man talked over her.

It's just a recording.

"I am the Master Sage. Like you, I have studied in Atlantis and mastered the Chakra bloodline. Chakra being my first bloodline, I have pushed it further than the rest. To heights that I hope you will also reach. My pursuit of the Crown Chakra has given me an insight I wish to share with you." The man paused.

He sounds different to the Master Sage I know. Was there another?

"Bloodline powers are surging and expanding at a dangerous rate. If left unchecked, they will lead to the destruction of our world. Continue your mastery of Chakra, and you will see it as I do." The man paused again.

"I cannot stand by and let this happen. I have devised a way to halt this process, but should I fail I am passing this mission on to you. Brothers and sisters of the Chakra clan, you have the wisdom and clarity to see the right path and succeed where I have stumbled. I humbly beg for your assistance." The man bowed, before fading into the light.

Maya blinked and found herself in a large circular stone courtyard. Light streamed in from the arches lining the walls. Six elders in hooded robes stood around the perimeter of the room. But Maya only really saw the man standing in the middle. Derek smiled back at her, his presence truly relaxed.

"I hope I didn't keep you waiting too long," Maya said. Derek rushed over and enveloped her in a giant hug.

"I knew you'd make it. That you'd succeed where I failed."

"It was the bridge, wasn't it?" she said. Derek withdrew and nodded gently.

"I knew instantly what I had done wrong. Which is why they didn't want me to retry. They thought I didn't deserve it."

"If you knew, why were you so nervous?"

"I thought that maybe I wasn't strong enough to even reach the bridge again," Derek answered. He seemed almost embarrassed by the answer.

"We're both here now. They can't take it away from us," Maya said. There was a flash behind her, and she turned to see Lu Bao enter the courtyard.

"You think you're so clever. We'll never support you," Lu Bao said, a dark expression on his face.

"I don't need your support. I just need you to stay out of my way," Maya said. Lu Bao dashed forward but Maya saw his movement. From the initial flash of Chakra to the entire motion she saw.

He's not that fast.

Maya caught Lu Bao's arm with her right hand.

"Is this what you really want?" she said. Lu Bao glared at her.

"You don't possess true power, whatever you may believe," he said.

"Oh, I agree with you on that. But I can hold my own. Can you?" Maya started gathering her LifeDeath power in the hand that held Lu Bao. He burst back with an explosion of power, standing back at the edge of the courtyard.

"Do not deign to compare yourself with me. With the elders." Lu Bao started cycling his Chakra. A nearby elder shook his head and Lu Bao settled back into a relaxed stance.

"Lu Bao, you've let your passion get the better of you today. Fall back," the elder said. Lu Bao nodded and turned and left without a word. He stepped back into the dark entrance he had arrived by and disappeared.

"Nicely done. I can see your LifeDeath power has returned as well," Derek said.

"It has," Maya said. She turned to the elder who had addressed Lu Bao. "Excuse me, elder, but could you direct me to the fastest way to get back down?"

The elder nodded and pointed to the far end of the room. There was another doorway. But this one looked like a normal one.

"Shall we?" Maya said.

"Of course. Anders is waiting," Derek said. The two of them walked briskly through the courtyard. They stepped through the doorway and entered a covered hallway lit by torches. Maya relaxed, letting the tension out of her shoulders.

"I'm glad that's behind us. But I can't fully relax until we get back to Anders."

"I know. But once we're past the restricted area it should be quick." Derek took the lead, opening a door, and holding it open for Maya. Beyond it was a stairway heading down.

"I've made the return journey before," Derek said, and Maya nodded.

Not going to start that conversation again. It's best left alone now.

They rushed down the stairs and through the darkened passage. There were torches sparsely placed along the walls to provide minimal light.

"They're not exactly being generous with the torches," Maya commented.

"This passage is designed for elders, and ones that have just opened their sixth Chakra. Sight shouldn't be an issue," Derek said. Maya laughed.

"Of course, that makes a lot of sense. Sorry."

"No need to apologize. Let's just pick up the pace." Derek started into a jog and Maya matched him, her speed increasing with each step.

"Just one thing," Maya said. "Did you see some sort of vision with a man..."

"Yes. I've heard talk of a message, but now I've seen it too. Let's talk about it later."

"Sure." Maya pushed the thoughts aside for now and focused on speed.

Anders is the priority now.

Derek made a few phone calls while Maya drove. She focused on the road ahead and not on the conversations he was having. Within an hour he put the phone down and smiled.

"We have transportation. I pulled a few strings and they're going to meet us soon."

"Is that wise?" Maya said.

"Don't worry, I have it covered. Oh, I think you'll be hearing them soon." Derek pointed to the distance. Maya glanced up and didn't see anything. But she heard something.

"A helicopter?"

"That's right. I think there's a field nearby. You should pull over there."

"Happy to." Maya sped up and noticed a dirt track leading away from the road. She turned the vehicle and with a few bumps they were driving over the wild grass. Maya saw the helicopter now and quickly stopped the car. She switched off the engine and watched. The helicopter rotors began to slow until the helicopter was completely still.

Maya opened the door and closed it quickly, running toward the helicopter. Within moments Derek was by her side. The main helicopter doors opened as she approached. Maya pulled herself up and inside. There was a single stretcher inside with Anders lying there asleep. A woman crouched next to him, checking on his vitals.

"I figured that when you were ready, it was better to bring him to you," Derek said from behind.

Maya couldn't talk, she was taking in the view of Anders. She could see his body clearly now. Unlike the Chakra lines or even her own LifeDeath lines, he had something else. Lifelines.

"They're blocked by the poison. I can see it choking him to death," Maya said. Her eyes drifted over to his bad leg. It was a different problem. But one she could now see.

"I'll try and negate the poison now. Did you have any tips?"

"No, but the usual cure is to overcome it with Chakra. But you can't project your Chakra. Maybe you can do something else with your LifeDeath power."

"I'm sure I can." Maya placed her hand on Anders' chest. She took a deep breath and focused her power. She reached out and used her power to heal Anders like she had practiced back at the academy. He seemed to relax a little, and his breathing sounded easier. But the darkness of the poison didn't move.

"How about..." Maya said, trying something else. She kept the stream of her power flowing into him, but this time tried to mix the Chakra and LifeDeath together. It didn't work.

This has to work. Find a way.

Maya turned her attention to the two sources of power, watching them interact in her body as she tried to combine them. The Chakra was more fluid and ethereal, and the Life-Death was more oozing.

"Maybe if their speeds match..." Maya muttered to herself. She tried focusing on her Chakra and slowing it down. Matching it to the speed and rhythm of the LifeDeath. Making them beat together as one. They resisted, forcing apart. But she relaxed and settled into it. There was a way for them to work together, not just coexist. It didn't work. Until they suddenly clicked into unity.

It worked?

Her shock almost lost her the victory, but she held onto the new mix and pushed it into Anders. She could see the new power working through his body. And when it encountered the darkness of the poison there was momentary resistance, until the poison disappeared.

She watched with extreme concentration, keeping her attention on both Anders and the mix of powers she was using. It was a slow process, but the conclusion was inevitable. If she could keep it up.

Maya had no concept of time. All she could do was will the power forward and keep the two sources in sync. But she was tiring. She wasn't fresh, and she'd literally walked up and down a mountain.

You can't fail him. Hold on.

Suddenly it was over. Maya took a few seconds to acknowledge what she had done, and then collapsed.

40

KEEPING A PROMISE

Maya awoke in her own bed. Gentle sunlight drifted in through the window. She blinked and then sat up, next to her, Anders sat up and stretched. He was reclining in a chair dragged in from the main room of her suite.

"Are you OK?" Maya asked. Anders smiled at her.

"I was going to ask you that," he said. Maya stared into his face.

He's really OK.

"Well, I'd normally say something like 'sure', or 'I feel ok so probably', but now I can be a little more definitive." Maya looked at herself, relaxing into her Chakra vision. Her Chakras all looked clear, and her powers were flowing through her normally. Not mixed, as she had forced them before.

"What's the definitive answer?"

"Fine. That's the technical term for it." Maya turned her attention to Anders. "Stand up, will you?" He stood up slowly, still favoring one leg.

"You're mostly fine, but there's still that leg."

"It's fine, don't worry about that," Anders said, looking concerned.

"Oh, I'm not leaving this. Sit on the edge of the bed," she said, gesturing to the spot. Anders hobbled over and eased himself down. Maya took a deep breath and swung herself over to the side of the bed. Standing up was easy.

Phew. Wasn't so sure about that.

Maya walked around the bed and dragged the chair Anders had been using over. She sat and held his bad leg in her hands. She examined it with her enhanced vision, seeing the injury again.

"This looks a lot simpler than fixing your whole body," she said.

"This can wait, you just woke up," Anders said. He looked like he was going to keep talking until Maya silenced him with a look. She focused back on the leg.

"It should be easier this time. Just relax." Maya started by trying to heal his leg. It didn't have any obvious effect.

"It's good to see that those LifeDeath healers weren't lying to you. Now let's see here." Maya focused inwards, remembering how she had blended her powers together. She slowed everything down, finding the same synchronization she had previously used. It came a little easier.

Less resistance this time. I think I should practice this more.

Maya pushed the combined power into Anders' leg. However, this time she had to wield it more carefully. Rather than pushing it through his whole system, she used it to cut away the injury from within. It took a few attempts. But after refining her technique it finally cleared. As soon as that happened, the injury broke apart and was absorbed by her power.

Maya slowly withdrew the mixed power and let it separate again. She felt the strain in her body pass through like a wave. But she didn't faint. Taking a moment and a deep breath, she pushed LifeDeath back to complete the healing. She repaired the bones, ligaments, and muscles.

"I think that's it," Maya said, leaning back into the chair and resting. She suddenly felt a bit weaker. Anders looked at her with concern.

"Oh no, I'm fine. Test it out."

"As you wish. I hope you're not pulling my leg." Anders stood and put weight on his formerly bad leg. It seemed fine. Next, he started walking around the room.

"You're still limping, but the leg is fine. Run on the spot," Maya said. Anders didn't respond but began running on the spot. Slowly at first, but then faster and faster. Suddenly he stopped, then ran over to her.

"You did it. I can't believe it. Thank you. Thank you." Anders reached down and pulled her into a big hug.

"It was my pleasure. I made you a promise, and I intended on keeping it."

"I don't know how I can ever thank you enough. Seriously." Anders sat on the bed opposite her.

"Let's start with breakfast. As it turns out, healing people makes you really hungry." Maya laughed and Anders joined in.

"Breakfast it is," he said, reaching out with his hand, and helping her up.

Maya looked across the table at her friends. Derek and Anders watched her expectantly. Kora was intently reading something on her tablet.

"You're probably all wondering what we do next," Maya said slowly.

"Not me," Kora said.

"I'm still working it out. It's a bit of a crossroads. I have my power back, and I can defend myself. That's...comforting."

Derek cleared his throat loudly and then began to speak.

"My apologies, I don't want to be the one to say this. But you can't defend yourself from him yet. He put you in a glass jar, remember?"

"What?" Anders blurted out.

"I'll fill you in on a few things," Maya said sheepishly. She turned back to Derek. "You're right, while I feel more capable, I still can't stand up to him. But at least he can't be everywhere at once."

"But he's also creating new MultiBlood henchmen," Kora added without looking up.

"Care to explain?" Maya said, focusing all her attention on Kora.

"That sample you got back from the warehouse. They're trialing adding LifeDeath to people who are Speedsters." Kora spun her tablet around and showed them the screen. It was a chart showing two bloodlines plotted against time. One line was stable, but the other was increasing steadily.

"He's given himself the seventh bloodline, now he's figuring out how to do the others," Maya said slowly, thinking it through.

"I'm trying to understand how this fits in with what we heard at the temple. From the original Master Sage," Derek said. "He was opposed to the strengthening of bloodlines. Our Master Sage seems to be quite the opposite."

"He's all about control, isn't he? He doesn't just want power, he wants to control who else has it," Maya mused. She got up and started pacing around the room.

"You're just going to have to catch me up on all this later." Anders sighed.

"I promise." Maya closed her eyes for a moment, thinking back to her experience at the temple.

"What was your vision, Derek? When you achieved the sixth Chakra?"

"I was in a Chakra school. I was leading students," Derek said with a smile. Maya ran over and hugged him immediately.

"I'm so happy for you. That's where you need to be," Maya said, her voice tinged with sadness. She stepped back and withdrew into herself again.

"What about you?" Derek asked softly.

"I was in an underground space, looking for something that the Master Sage had hidden."

"Your fate is not to shy away from the world. For now, at least. They say that the insights you learn from Chakra mastery are about your next step. Not your last."

"That's reassuring." Maya paused and refocused inwards, feeling the two powers within her. A shiver went down her spine.

Two powers feels crazy. What will all seven feel like? Will I still be human?

"Your next step will probably involve Speedsters since they're the ones that are being experimented on. If you describe the location you saw in your vision, I can cross reference it with known locations," Kora said. Maya quickly swiveled to look at her.

"That's a great idea. What about that device you were working on for the seventh bloodline? Did you get anywhere with it?" Maya asked. Kora grinned.

"I was wondering when you were going to ask. I have something to test out." Kora rose quickly and left the room.

"She's pretty much a wizard," Anders said with a chuckle.

"Pretty much? I think she passed wizard rank a while ago. Maybe there's an eight bloodline."

"Don't even joke about that," Derek said. Maya smiled at him.

I may not have my family. But somehow, I have them.

Valerie's eyes snapped open. She was lying on the floor in a dark room. She tried to sit up, but an overwhelming pressure was on her.

Where am I? What is this?

"What's going on?" Valerie demanded from the room. Harsh lights snapped on and she was temporarily blinded. As her eyes adjusted, she saw a man standing in what looked like a control room behind a glass window.

"Valerie, I've been told you want to get stronger. Stronger than Maya," the man said.

"And you are?"

"My name is Elias. I've been tasked with ensuring that you accelerate your LifeDeath training."

"Fine. Why can't I move?" Valerie tried again to sit up but could barely move.

"You're in what's referred to as a Degeneration Field. It's trying to break you down at the cellular level. Your LifeDeath power is resisting it."

"You call this training?"

"Maya napped through this level of resistance and sat up without effort," Elias said with a chuckle. Even at this distance Valerie could recognize the smirk on his face.

You can't let her win.

Valerie strained her muscles. Nothing happened.

Don't let them hold you back.

She drew on her strength again and this time didn't strain. She just started moving very slowly. Inch by inch hauling herself up until she was in a seated position.

"Wonderful. Let's begin," Elias said, adjusting the dials. Valerie felt the force upon her increasing.

If she did this, so can I.

Valerie gritted her teeth and kept her focus.

THE STORY CONTINUES

HASTENED

BOOK THREE OF THE BLOODSTORM

Unseen foes, unmatched speed: Maya's high-stakes heist.

LET'S CONTINUE THE JOURNEY TOGETHER

Hey there, fellow adventure-seeker!

Want to stay in the loop and hear about my bookish escapades before anyone else? Just pop your email into my newsletter. You'll get all the fun updates, behind-the-scenes peeks, and even some exclusive goodies.

Plus, my website is always there for a quick fix of story magic. Let's have some fun on this wild ride of words together!

www.vaughanwsmith.com

ABOUT THE AUTHOR

My name is Vaughan, and I believe that writing should transport you to a fantastic place, and bring you back feeling better than when you left.

I live in Sydney, Australia and I'm constantly devouring new books, TV shows, and movies. My favourite genres are Fantasy, Mystery and Thrillers, and Science Fiction.

Milton Keynes UK
Ingram Content Group UK Ltd.
UKHW041843010923
427938UK00010B/131/J

9 781922 569028